TREACHEROUS TWINS: JUSTICE

NATISHA RAYNOR

CONTENTS

JUSTICE

I stood on the side of the brick building that housed a local convenience store with one foot propped against the wall. With a chuckle, I pulled from the blunt I was holding onto as a brown Lincoln cruised by with the windows rolled down.

I'll always come back to you. I'll always come back to you.

The nostalgia I felt every time I heard that old school classic by The Isley Brothers put me in a sentimental zone every single time. Each time I heard the song no matter where I was, the first time I ever heard it played in my head like a movie.

I was on the bottom bunk of the bed in the room that I'd been assigned when I got to the group home, I was forced to live in. When the woman that adopted me and my brother as babies died there wasn't any family around that would or could take us in. Immediately my brother, Loyal, was taken in by a family that didn't want the both of us. It took cruel ass people to separate twins. We had no other blood family that we knew of. All Loyal and I really had were each other. For thirteen years we were inseparable and all it took was the word of one selfish ass person to rip us apart.

1

If the Johnson's didn't want both of us, they shouldn't have taken either of us. Loyal and I grew up with our adopted mother, Janice. It was just the three of us until Loyal and I turned twelve, then Janice got custody of her niece, Tonya, because Tonya's mother went to prison.

Life with Janice was cool up until she died three days after me and Loyal's thirteenth birthday. Loyal and I ended up in foster care, and Tonya, who was seventeen, was able to get a place in the projects because she was pregnant and not far away from her eighteenth birthday. It crushed my soul when a family took him and said fuck me, but there wasn't anything I could do about it. I was flat on my back with one arm behind my head, while the staff working night shift was playing music like she was at the club or some shit. The sounds of the Isley Brothers floated down the hallway and into my bedroom. There was always supposed to be two staff in the house at all times, but the second employee snuck out like she normally did after midnight to go do whatever it was that she did. There were eight boys in the four-bedroom house and there was never supposed to be less than two staff in the home at all times. Just the week before, a fifteen-year-old kid stabbed one of the other residents of the group home who was only thirteen. Mya was bold as hell to sneak away from work. Since the stabbing incident, the state had been snooping around the home and popping up unannounced.

My cell phone vibrated underneath my pillow, and I lifted my head and pulled it out.

TWIN:

Come outside.

My eyes narrowed as I stared at the message. Come outside? I got up and walked over to the window. Using two fingers, I separated the slats in the blinds and stared out into the darkness. Directly across the street from the group home parked underneath a streetlight was a white Camry. The headlights were shining brightly.

"I know he didn't," I mumbled underneath my breath. My twin would never steer me wrong, so if he told me to come outside then outside was obviously where I needed to be.

I didn't give a damn about anything that I had in the closets or dresser drawers. To hell with all that shit. All I needed was the pair of worn sneakers that I stuffed my feet into before exiting the room and making my way towards the living room with a pounding heart. Since the music was playing, Lakia wouldn't hear me creeping down the hallway, but if I opened the front door, the alarm would sound. I inhaled a deep breath and prepared myself to run my ass off. I didn't know what tricks Loyal had up his sleeve, but I was riding with my brother right or wrong. I held my breath as I unlocked the dead bolt lock first then the regular one. As soon as I pulled the door open, the alarm blared, and I took off running down the long driveway. I could hear the engine running in the Camry, and I couldn't even be for sure that Loyal was in that particular vehicle waiting for me, but I didn't care.

I ran as fast as I could towards the waiting car. "Hey! Get back in here!" Lakia's frantic voice pierced through the night air as I yanked on the door handle and jumped inside the car.

I barely had the door closed before Loyal mashed the gas making the car jerk forward. "Nigga, whose car is this?" I asked incredulously as Loyal hit a sharp left turn damn near giving me whip lash.

"My foster mother's," he stared straight ahead with a devilish grin. "I hit Tonya up on Facebook messenger. She said we can stay with her until we get our own place. I told her that we shouldn't have to be there longer than two months tops."

My jaw slacked. "Nigga, are you crazy? How in the hell can we get our own place at thirteen?"

3

"We gon' get this money," Loyal looked over at me with furrowed brows. "You trying to stay in that fuck ass group home until you're eighteen? Migo told us a minute ago that he'd put us on. All we have to do is hustle and save our money then get a fiend to get us a crib in their name. We won't have shit else to do but make money. We can't go back to school. Social workers will probably be there first thing in the morning waiting to snatch us up."

I sat back and stared out of the window all while ignoring my brother driving reckless as hell. We'd never been given any lessons, so I could only assume he taught himself how to drive, and he needed a lot more practice. Still, he managed to get us near our destination without killing us. We ditched the car about a mile from Tonya's crib and walked the rest of the way. The only reason social workers would go hard looking for us would be because we ran away, and we would make the group home staff, the Johnsons, and the system look bad if they didn't find us. I didn't know the first thing about being on my own or selling drugs, but as long as I had my twin, I was good. We were going to figure that shit out together. I would have rather gone into any difficult situation with Loyal by my side rather than facing obstacles alone.

And figure it out was what we did. We started out stealing clothes and items from various stores that we could sell. Our best customers were single parents and dope boys because we used to steal fly shit from the mall and sell the items for half the price. That was the fastest way for us to have money to put food in our bellies and to save up, so we would be able to purchase coke from a dealer by the name of Migo. We were young but even at our young ages, we didn't want to go to him asking for handouts. When we should have been playing football or basketball and spending summers at the pool and the Boy's and Girl's Club, Loyal and I had no choice but to hustle like grown ass men.

We had to learn how to shoot and fight, so we wouldn't be prey.

Once we started hustling, there were definitely some older people that thought they could punk us, and we had to show them that was far from the truth. After we beat enough niggas that were twice our age, we began to get a lot of respect in the hood. Neither one of us wanted to be dumb, so as soon as we turned sixteen, Loyal and I enrolled to get our GED's. By that time, we had been living on our own for three years in a low-income apartment in the hood that a fiend by the name of Lillian got for us. There was one time after we'd been there for a year that she tried to pop her shit and say if we didn't give her free drugs, she was going to have us put out. After I got somebody to beat her ass, she didn't try that shit again. There were times that we looked out for her but at the end of the day, we had rent and bills to pay. We had already compensated her for doing us a favor, and she wasn't about to be smoking off of us for free for the rest of her life.

Being in survival mode at such a young age and becoming stuck there could traumatize a person. Loyal and I had barely gotten through puberty before we had to start being responsible for our own laundry, feeding ourselves, and getting all of the basic necessities of life that we needed. All Janice ever told us about our mother was that she had us when she was very young, and she wasn't ready to take care of one baby let alone two. It would have been easy to blame our mother for the fact that we had it rough, but we didn't know anything about her. Maybe she was just like us. Maybe life had dealt her an unfortunate hand, and she was out fending for herself just like us. If that was the case, giving us to someone that could take care of us wasn't the worst thing in the world. Janice raised me and Loyal. Shit, we didn't even know we were adopted until she had a talk with us when we were seven. She knew as we got older, we'd have certain questions, that she didn't want to have to lie about. For instance, she had no birth stories. She couldn't tell us how long she was in labor or show us any photos of her being pregnant. She couldn't tell us who or where our father was.

Janice was the only mother we knew for thirteen years, and we loved her. She wasn't rich, but she provided a decent life for us. A life that we realized we took for granted when we didn't have it anymore. All of the love and nurturing that Janice provided us with for thirteen years was damn near wiped away after spending the years we did in survival and hustle mode. Not having any family aside from Tonya to take us in when Janice died made me and Loyal feel some type of way. Where were our grandparents? Where was our father? We didn't have aunts and uncles? Nobody that cared? Having to constantly look over our shoulders while we were out on the block, constantly running away from authority figures, and having the weight of the world on our shoulders, hardened me and my brother a lot.

I didn't have a lot of patience, and I didn't like being bothered. I was the epitome of an introvert, and my temper could be bad as hell at times. Loyal could draw his ass off. Actually, we could both draw, but he was a lot better than me. When he turned eighteen, he started doing tattoos. At the age of twenty-one, he got his bartending license, and when he wasn't doing tattoos, he worked a few nights a week at a sports bar. Me on the other hand, I got my money from selling coke and robbing niggas. I sold drugs mostly, but I wasn't above robbing a nigga. Shit, it was a dog eat dog world. I made no apologies for the way I had to adapt to a life that I didn't ask for.

The sounds of The Isley Brothers faded away as the car drove past, and I chuckled once again. My brother damn sure came back for me. He pulled a bold move, but that was Loyal. He wasn't going to leave me in that group home. That's just how we rocked. We may not have had any family that gave a damn about us, but as long as we had each other, we would forever be okay. Which was the reason that I always felt guilty when Loyal pointed out that we'd be separated if I ever got caught up in my shit and went to prison. Because he got out of the streets, he wanted the same for me, but I wasn't interested. I liked making fast money. Tattoos were how Loyal made the bulk of his income. He worked when he wanted, and he actually enjoyed doing tattoos. There was nothing that I enjoyed doing that I could make money from, and I wasn't punching nobody's clock. I had a problem with authority. Wasn't nobody telling me what to do.

The sun began to set, and I glanced down at the Patek that adorned my wrist. I wasn't a broke nigga, but I wasn't paying five figures for a watch when I could take somebody else's. I had traveled a few cities over a few weeks back and hit a dealer by the name of Sco. Sco wasn't just a drug dealer. He was also an informant, and he had come to Diamond Cove, North Carolina a few times to get work from local hustlers and set them up. So, I went to Wilson, North Carolina where he lived and ran up in his house. I got three ounces of coke, a pound of weed, $18,000, and a Patek off him.

"You leaving man?" An addict by the name of Dennis called out as I started walking towards my blue Volkswagen.

I looked over my shoulder with a scowl on my face. "Yeah. I been out here for four hours. If you haven't hustled up any bread by now, then you're just shit out of luck." He had been begging since I got on the block for me to front him some crack and after I told him no once, I started ignoring his ass each time he asked after that.

"I got $40 man."

I tossed an icy glare his way. It was possible that he'd hustled up $40, but it was also possible that he had the money the entire time but wanted to save it so I could front him crack to get high with now, and he would save the money for later. I'd seen it all when it came to drug addicts trying to finesse. I had something to do, so I pulled the product from my pocket and slapped it into his ashy palm. Dennis passed me the folded up bills, and I got inside my car. I couldn't drive my vehicle to the destination I had in mind, so I was going to park it at my house and jump in the black Honda Accord that I only used for certain things. Like when I went to rob niggas. There was a flashy hustler by the name of Rico that had been bragging and flaussin' for way too long. He wanted the world to know what he had, so I was going to relieve him of some of it. It was only right. If he kept taunting niggas with the shit, he deserved whatever he got.

I had been studying Rico's every move for two weeks. He might not have been broke, but he didn't have it like he claimed he did. For starters, he re-upped on coke weekly. If he could afford to buy a bunch of weight all at once, he wouldn't need to re-up as often as he did. His second mistake was having a routine. I should have never been able to learn his schedule after only observing him for two weeks. Rico re-upped every Thursday around seven PM. He would then go back to his house and bag up product. On Friday, he would start out early in the morning selling the product that he purchased.

I drove to the neighborhood that he lived in and parked one street over from the one his house was on. Inside the car, I put a ski mask over my face and gloves on my hands. With my gun tucked in hand, I exited the car and walked swiftly with my head down and my hands stuffed inside the pocket of my hoodie. Rico didn't live in the suburbs, but the area wasn't too hood either. It was more like middle class. Thankfully, there weren't many streetlights, so if anyone was out on their porch or looking out of a window, they wouldn't be able to see that I had a ski mask over my face. I found Rico's house, walked around to the side of it, and waited. I was outside listening to crickets chirp for fifteen minutes before I heard a car pulling up into the driveway.

I waited until I heard his car door close before I crept to the edge of the house. The moment Rico's foot hit the first step leading up to his porch, I moved with the speed of light. Before he could reach the top of the steps, I had my gun pressed into his back. Rico froze, and I spoke in a low tone between clenched teeth.

"Pass me that bag." There was a black duffel bag secured at Rico's side, and I knew it contained the drugs that he'd just purchased.

He hesitated for one second too long, and I hit him in the back of the head with the butt of my gun making him stumble forward. I snatched him back by his shirt and hit him in the head two more times before his body crumpled. As Rico lay out on the porch, I snatched the duffel bag strap off his shoulder and picked the keys up that had fallen from his hand. I took it upon myself to enter Rico's house, and my eyes darted around the living room. A lamp had been left on in the corner, but the rest of the house was dark. Moving swiftly, I made my way down the hallway and felt along the wall for a light switch. I peeked into each door until I located what appeared to be the master bedroom. I snatched open dresser drawers, lifted the mattress, and rummaged through shoe boxes. Nigga had more than fifty shoe boxes, and I had to look in about twenty of them to find the one filled with cash. Hastily, I unzipped the duffel bag and stuffed the shoe box inside before rushing from the house.

I stepped over Rico's body. He was still sprawled out on the porch snoring loudly. I made my way down the street and back towards my car with my newfound treasure in hand.

LAUREN

I tried my best to focus on what the leasing agent was saying as she gave me a tour of the one-bedroom apartment that I was viewing. I had eyes to see the features in the apartment, so the extras that she was going on and on about such as the vaulted ceilings and the extra-large kitchen pantry were irrelevant to me anyway. Every word that left her mouth sounded like gibberish because my mind was already going crazy with its' own wild thoughts. There was a nagging voice telling me that I was wasting my time. Trying to run away from my problems while remaining in the same city as my problems was insane. Wise had reach. A lot of reach. There was no need for me to run because if he didn't want to let me go, then he wasn't going to let me go. Even if he continued to be a thorn in my side, I could only hope and pray that if I got my own place and moved out of the apartment that he'd been paying for since I was sixteen, maybe that would help some. As long as he paid the rent and utilities, Wise would continue to feel as if he owned me.

Wise wasn't my man. We didn't have a typical relationship. I wasn't even sure what kind of relationship we had. I couldn't call him my captor because I wasn't really being held against my will. Or was I? Shit, how would I know when I'd never tried to leave?

"What do you think?" The blonde-haired leasing agent turned towards me with a broad smile on her face.

"I really like it. It's $100 to apply?"

"Yes. That will cover the background and credit check along with the application fee. If there's nothing on your credit or background, we typically get the results back in less than twenty-four hours. If you apply now, I should have an answer for you by tomorrow afternoon."

"Sounds good." I gave her a smile of my own. My lips were so dry, smiling was literally painful.

My lip gloss was in the car, so I just licked my lips nervously and followed the agent out of the apartment. Since Wise paid the bills at the apartment, I had been saving all of my money for the past seven months. I hadn't been getting my hair or nails done. I only had lash extensions because I put them on myself. My curly hair was dyed honey blonde, and I had a cherry red patch on the left side. The color combination was fire, and I either wore my curls hanging or pulled up into a messy bun. I hadn't purchased any clothes or anything that wasn't considered a necessity. I'd even been picking up extra shifts at the club that I worked in. I hadn't been on my own financially for the past six years, but that shit came with a price.

It took less than twenty minutes for me to complete the rental application. I walked out to my mint green Jeep Cherokee, and my stomach was rumbling, but I wasn't hungry. I was nervous. My phone rang, and a chill ran down my spine when I saw Wise's name on the screen. I looked around nervously before getting inside my Jeep. Wise had no reason to have anybody watching me, but my paranoia came from knowing that I had just done something that he probably wouldn't approve of.

"Hello?" I tried to keep my tone even.

"Where are you at?"

"Out running errands. What's up?" The thing I hated about Wise was that even all these years later, he felt like I was supposed to be available to him at the drop of a dime, and I was getting tired of that shit. My debt to him had more than been paid. If we were being completely honest, I never really owed the nigga shit.

"I need you to run this broad by the abortion clinic. They won't do the abortion if she doesn't have someone to drive her home, and I'm not going up in that muhfucka with her. I'll text you her address. She has to be there in an hour and a half. That should be enough time for you to wrap up whatever it is you're doing."

I simply narrowed my eyes. I didn't have to speak because Wise ended the call. He wasn't ever going to give me a chance to protest his orders. The older I got and the longer I knew that man the more my disdain for him grew. I'd gone through so many different emotions in the time that I knew Wise. Every year, I felt something different for him. I met Wise when I was sixteen, and he was thirty-four. I had actually attempted to steal some dope that one of his workers left in a stash spot near the projects, and Wise caught my ass. He asked me how old I was, and I told him. I also had to nervously tell him my situation because all I'd ever heard about fine ass Wise was how ruthless he was, and I didn't want him to kill me.

I told him that I was on my own because my mother was physically and mentally abusive. I'd seen people treat their dogs better than my mother treated me. My father was a deadbeat, and my grandparents lived two hours away. I ran away from home and stayed with my best friend for a few nights, but her mother kept trying to convince me to go home, so I left. An older guy by the name of Mike had been trying to talk to me. He was damn near thirty and ugly as fuck, but I was in survival mode. I kept trying to hype myself up to sleep with him because that was the only way he'd get me a hotel room, but I couldn't go through with it. I would rather steal his money than fuck him for it, and that's what I tried to do. Until Wise caught me. I didn't even get to keep the shit, but he claimed that I owed him because had I been anyone else, he would have killed me.

I thought he was going to try and sleep with me, but he actually put me up in an apartment and made me start trafficking dope for him. I was young, dumb, and he'd told me more than once that I better be glad he didn't kill me. Because of those things, I never thought twice about transporting enough dope to get me double digit numbers in prison had I gotten caught. Foolishly, I began to view Wise as my savior. I went from not having to worry about where I was going to sleep every night and what I was going to eat to living in a nicely furnished apartment in a nice area not too far from the beach, and the kitchen was stocked with food. I felt like an adult and the best part was, I didn't have anyone sharing my space that acted as if they hated me and treated me like dirt. So, if all I had to do was move some dope to keep a roof over my head, I did so with a smile on my face and felt like a bad bitch from a rap video while I did it.

I trafficked dope for Wise at least twice a week. Then he started leaving large amounts of cocaine and guns in the apartment that I lived in. He never paid me specifically for any of the tasks that I completed for him but once a month, he gave me money for clothes, shoes, personal hygiene items, etc. In my young naïve mind, I had it made. I was afraid that the wrong person would find out that I was involved somehow with the notorious Wise Jacobs, so I kept my mouth shut about where I lived. I continued to go to school every day and the kicker was, my mom never came looking for me not even once.

Wise came by the apartment to check on me almost daily. He also began to incorporate other small jobs into my daily routine such as going to his trap houses and cooking dope, cutting it, bagging it up, even making some sales for him when he was busy. I felt like the Bonnie to Wise's Clyde even though at that point, he'd never tried to sleep with me. It was hard for me to view him as a fatherly figure because I was a hormonal young woman, and he wasn't my father. Every time I was around him, I'd take in Wise's 6'4 stature, his rich dark skin, his jet-black hair that had enough waves to make a person seasick, and his muscular physique. Wise always always smelled amazing. He smelled clean and like money, and the man was a walking fashion ad. He didn't wear his pants sagging off his ass nor did he wear tacky designer clothes with the logos plastered all over them.

There were plenty of times that I had no clue who the designer was of the shirt or pants that Wise wore, but everything he donned looked like it cost an arm and a leg. He looked like money. The man walked rich. He talked rich. Wise was everything to me. The way people in the city uttered his name with either the utmost respect or genuine fear. Wise didn't look at me in that way, but he had a few workers that did, and I got attention from boys at school and pretty much anywhere I went. At 5'4, 135 pounds, skin the color of melted caramel, and honey-colored eyes, there was no shortage of men wanting to talk to me. Even at my young age, Wise had set the bar high, and I was either going to talk to a boss or no one at all.

Shortly after I turned seventeen, Wise must have sensed that I was conversing with guys and hanging out with friends a lot because he sat me down and had a talk with me. He made it clear that I was never to have any guys at the apartment or in my car when I had product. He told me that if any of his work came up missing, then I would too. It was then that it really hit me. That man wasn't thinking about me for real. I was his drug mule. I was his bottom bitch. The one that committed illegal activities for him and was part of the reason he made as much money as he did, while he broke me off crumbs. Still, there was a sense of appreciation there because regardless of how it came about, Wise was still the reason that I wasn't homeless.

One time, Wise had to go out of town, and he sent his girlfriend to pick up some money from me. I was in awe when I laid eyes on her. She was drop dead gorgeous. Her dark skin made her look exotic damn near. She was flyer than any female rapper or hood princess that I'd ever seen. Jewel was draped in diamonds and designer labels. Her long silky weave hung to the small of her back, and she was literally perfect from head to toe. Not a single hair was out of place. Her clothes looked as if she'd just popped the tags off them. The purse draped across her shoulder cost more than six months' worth of the rent where I lived. Jewel was nice. When I opened the door for her, she wore a warm smile. The way she entered my apartment with her head held high, and the sincere politeness in her tone made me aware that she didn't deem me a threat at all. I mean, technically, I wasn't, but she didn't know that for sure. I was probably nothing more in Jewel's eyes than Wise's flunky. He had plenty of male flunkies, so maybe a female one wasn't any different.

When Jewel left, I felt some kind of way. No, I'd never been romantically involved with Wise, but like a lovesick puppy, anytime he came around, I had stars in my eyes. I actually felt special when he handed me $1,000 to get things for myself when the shoes that Jewel wore cost more than $1,000. Even if he was paying me to transport his drugs, I would have made more than $1,000. Wise was using the fuck out of me, and I was letting him.

Yes, he gave me a place to live, but so what? One day I boldly looked inside the duffel bag that Wise had placed in the old ass Camry that I was driving, and there were fifteen bricks of cocaine inside. Had I gotten caught that shit could have gotten me at least twenty years in prison.

The haze that I was blinded by slowly started to lift. My crush on Wise began to dissipate and as I got older, I started thinking of ways to distance myself from him because I didn't want to go to prison for him and his drug empire. Wise's name fit him to a T because there was nothing slow or dumb about that man. Every time I had a shift in my mood or began to think certain things, it was almost as if he was clairvoyant and could hear my thoughts. When I turned eighteen, Wise pulled some strings to get me a job as a bartender at a local club. I wasn't even old enough to drink alcohol, so I wasn't supposed to be serving it, but he knew the owner. At that point, I didn't have to traffic drugs in my vehicle anymore, but I made some transactions for him here and there at the club. I liked that better than riding around with a large amount of drugs, and I was making money in the process. Since Wise paid the bills at the house, I began to spend the money I made from work on any and everything that I wanted.

I also started dating, and I was in a good place. One night, I went to the club with my friends, and when I got home, Wise was at the apartment waiting for me. He was the same suave Wise that he always was, but I could tell by his red rimmed eyes that he was under the influence of something himself. For the first time ever, Wise made a move on me. We had sex, and it was mind blowing, but I didn't expect anything less. Wise excelled in everything that he did. The man was a boss in every sense of the word. He was handsome owned a fleet of luxury cars, he had the power to go along with the respect and the money, women threw themselves at his feet. That man was everything, and he had been inside my walls.

After we had sex, that sick schoolgirl crush that I had on him once before began to resurface. I started once again ogling Wise with stars in my eyes meanwhile, he'd used dick to fuck with my head. He stoked my silly ass right back into a trance, and then he reminded me every chance he got, that I wasn't shit to him. Of course, he didn't say the words, but he started sending Jewel by the house more to pick up money. He would bring her in the club some nights, and then I saw her getting out of a cherry red BMW with a round belly. She was pregnant. He asked me to take ten bricks of cocaine to Charlotte, North Carolina and when I said no, he choked me and told me I didn't have a choice. The nigga basically said he wished I would tell him no when he'd done more for me than my own mother. He also made it a point to tell me once every few weeks that until he decided he was done with me, I would pay off my debt to him for as long as he saw fit.

Wise had seen a desperate teenager trying to rob his worker because I needed a place to lay my head and food to put in my belly, and he used that against me for years. At the age of twenty-two, I was still under Wise's thumb, but that shit was about to end. We'd only had sex that one time. He'd tried a few other times, but I turned him down. Wise was a lot of things but thankfully, a rapist wasn't one of them. When I didn't want to have sex with him, he eyed me with a deep anger, but he didn't force me to sleep with him. The more I sat and thought about it, Wise never saved me. He preyed upon me and as I got older, I became more and more repulsed by him. It was now or never as far as getting away from him. I just had to pray that the consequences wouldn't be too dire.

I had been touring apartments for the past two hours, and I was starving, so I stopped to get food before heading to pick up whoever it was that Wise was sending to get an abortion. I didn't know much about Wise's personal life. I had no clue where he lived. I wasn't even sure if he and Jewel were still together, but the streets said they shared a four-year-old daughter named Imani. I had seen him with a few other women over the years. All of them gorgeous but none of them Jewel. It made sense though because men didn't keep what they loved close to their bullshit. There was no way Wise would have the mother of his child around anything that could put her freedom or her life at stake. He clearly didn't care if I got caught and thrown under the jail. During my transition of seeing Wise as a savior to seeing him as a predator, my eyes were open to a lot.

I kissed my teeth when I pulled up at the address that Wise had texted to me. I had no clue who I was picking up, so I would either have to just blow the horn or get out of the car. I had work later, and I wanted to be at home sleeping rather than being Wise's errand girl for the day. I jumped out of my jeep and walked towards the door. Before I could reach it, the door opened, and a pretty brown-skinned girl stepped outside. I could tell instantly that she was black and Asian.

"Lauren?" she asked skeptically.

"That's me. Wise sent me."

"Okay. Give me one second."

The woman didn't appear to be over the age of twenty. The large brick house that she lived in was gorgeous on the outside, and the front yard had the greenest grass I'd ever seen. There was a black Lexus parked in the driveway, and I found myself wondering about this person. I hoped she was at least eighteen. Wise didn't sleep with me until I was of age, but that didn't mean the same held true for everyone else. I got back inside my Jeep and waited for her to come back. She emerged from the house a minute later with a Louis Vuitton purse hanging sideways across her body. The girl was dressed in black leggings and a black sports bra. She was petite with a handful of ass and small breasts. Her silky black hair was up in a messy bun, and she wore two Van Cleef bracelets.

"$10,000 on her wrist," I mumbled while wondering if the bracelets were courtesy of Wise or maybe her parents. She definitely looked like she could pass for a spoiled rich kid.

"Hi," she smiled nervously as she got in the car.

"Hey." I smiled back because I had no reason to make her feel uncomfortable. It wasn't her fault that Wise was a piece of shit. She appeared unsure and scared, and I wasn't going to add to her discomfort.

I drove towards the abortion clinic. Aside from the music playing, the car ride was silent for the first ten minutes.

"How do you know Wise?" she finally asked, prompting me to chuckle.

"It's a long story. I've known him for years. Our relationship is pretty much business although he's the only one that really benefits from the business," I stated dryly.

"Oh okay. It wasn't until after I found out that I was pregnant that he told me I couldn't have the baby because he had enough kids and because he has a girlfriend. I wish he would have volunteered that information when we met," she murmured.

My interest was piqued. "How many kids does he have?" I glanced over at her quickly before directing my attention back to the road in front of me.

"He said he has six."

My eyes widened. "Woah. I never knew that."

"Yeah," she sighed. "I'm only twenty, and I'm in my second year of college. I met Wise at a restaurant when one of my friends was having a birthday dinner. He was having a business meeting, and he stopped me on my way back from the bathroom. Though he was very handsome, I could tell off the bat that he was too old for me. Wise was very persistent. He ended up paying for everyone at the table, and the tab was like $700. When my friends went over to thank him, he told them he'd give $1,000 to whichever one of them gave him my number." The girl paused to chuckle. "Needless to say, he got what he wanted and five months later, we're here."

"Wow. What's your name?"

"Morgan."

I gave a curt nod. I wasn't sure what to say. Her story made Wise sound exactly like the predator that he was. I had only been around Jewel a handful of times. I didn't know much about her, but nothing gave me the impression that she was a weak or naïve person. Wise had the good sense to wife a smart woman while he preyed on the young dumb ones. Typical man. I could tell that Morgan was extremely nervous, so I just let her vent. She clearly needed someone to talk to.

"Is this what you want to do?" I looked over at her again.

"Yes. I'm not ready for a child. College is hard enough; I can't imagine having to go to school and take care of a child. Not to mention, my parents would literally kill me. If they cut me off, I'd just be assed out because Wise made it clear that he doesn't want the child. He gave me $5,000 to get rid of it."

"Wow, wow, wow." I chuckled.

I could understand why Morgan didn't tell her parents about the abortion, but I wondered why she didn't have friends that could have gone with her and supported her. Like the one that gave Wise her friend's number for $1,000. I really had better things to do than to accompany a stranger to the abortion clinic, but once I met her and heard her story, I wanted to offer her support. Wise was a low-down dirty piece of shit. I had never been to an abortion clinic before, so it tripped me out seeing the people out front holding signs and protesting. It really looked like a scene from a television show. I shook my head as I pulled into a parking space.

"You gonna be okay walking through that?" None of those people knew anybody's story. It was easy to sit back and judge but thinking about how my mother used to treat me, there were really some women that didn't deserve kids. They would torture and abuse their kids and sometimes end up killing them. Personally, I'd rather a woman get an abortion than have a child and mistreat him or her and maybe even end their life. I'd heard horror stories that brought tears to my eyes.

"Yeah, I'll be fine. I'm just ready to get this over with. Coming with me may not have been your choice but thank you."

"You're welcome."

Morgan and I got out of the Jeep and speed walked towards the entrance. I didn't care about the hecklers. I wasn't pregnant, so they weren't hurting my feelings. We ignored them and when we reached the door, I held it open for Morgan. I waited while she checked in and assured the nurse that I'd be in the area, and she could call me when it was time to pick Morgan up. There was a shopping center across the street, and I was going to kill time by looking for some home décor. I didn't even know if I'd been approved for the apartment, but I was going to have faith.

I had just pulled the seatbelt across my body when my phone rang. "Grrrrrrrrrrrr!" I gritted my teeth and growled loudly when I saw Wise's name on my phone screen. I was sick of his ass. "Hello?" I didn't even try to mask my agitation.

I could tell that Wise was taken aback by my tone because there was a brief moment of silence, and there was hardly ever a moment when Wise was rendered speechless. "You might want to check that tone. You're acting like I'm getting on your nerves. But that's too bad. I have something else that I need you to do."

JUSTICE

My eyes slid down Giselle's frame as I trekked through the club doors. Giselle was a bottle girl, and she was thicker than peanut butter. I used to have sex with her on a regular basis while her nigga was in prison. When he came home, she started being stingy with the pussy. I didn't beg for shit, but I would still look. I could tell when her and that nigga were into it because she'd start flirting with me, but I wasn't getting in the middle of their domestic situations.

"What's going on, Justice?" Giselle licked her lips as she watched me just as intensely as I was watching her. I hadn't been with her in about five months, and it looked like she'd gotten thicker.

"What up with you?" I asked a rhetorical question and kept walking. I wasn't sticking around for the answer. I went straight to the bar.

There were two bouncers and one bottle girl that had all hit me up about buying some coke. I had $200 waiting on me in the club, so I decided after I got my money to sit down and have a few drinks. If I sat there long enough, I knew I could make more than that.

"Let me get henny and coke," I ordered after the bartender greeted me. I had seen her once from a distance but up close, shorty was bad.

Thick honey blonde curls framed her face, and the left side had a patch of fire engine red curls. I'd never seen that color combination before, but it was dope as hell. My orbs zeroed in on her ass as she sauntered off to make my drink, and my dick jumped at the sight of her plump ass. She wore black shorts that hugged her ample backside. They were so short they could have passed for panties. There was a huge colorful tattoo on her right thigh, and I bet she looked sexy as hell with all of her clothes off.

"What's your name?" I asked as she came back and placed my drink in front of me.

"Lauren. What about you?"

"Justice."

"Nice to meet you, Justice," she smiled and walked off.

I took the opportunity to stare at her body again. I had a few minutes to decide if I was going to crack on her or leave her be. I was at the club more for business than pleasure, so I wasn't going to stay long. I started off sipping my drink but as the crowd grew thicker, I downed it with one gulp. I decided to order one more drink. Someone said something to Lauren, and she smiled wide showing off a slight gap between her two front teeth. Yeah, she was bad and since I didn't have plans to have sex with Giselle again, I wouldn't feel bad about getting at her co-worker.

Lauren set my second drink in front of me, but before I could ask for her number, her co-worker came over to her and started talking. I picked the cup up and had my lips on the plastic rim when my brows furrowed. I lowered the drink and peered down into it. There was a slight white foam in the liquid, and I narrowed my eyes because the first drink wasn't like that. The coke was carbonated, but I'd never had a henny and coke look like that. My eyes narrowed as a few different thoughts flashed through my mind. The more I stared at the drink, the angrier I became. I stood up and waited for Lauren to pay me some attention. I had already paid for my drinks.

"Let me holla at you over here," I jerked my head to the left.

"Um, okay." Lauren stepped from behind the car, and I walked off to the corner between the bar and the bathrooms.

"Drink this shit," I ordered while extending the cup towards her.

Lauren drew back and frowned. "Excuse me?"

"Drink this shit," I repeated through clenched teeth. "Because if you don't, I'm gon' blow yo' muhfuckin' brains out, and I put that on yo' mama." I lifted my shirt, so she could see that I had my gun tucked in the waistband of my jeans.

"What is wrong with you?" Lauren was trying her best to sound pissed off, but I could see the fear in her eyes and practically smell it oozing off of her.

"I'm not a fan of repeating myself. Drink this shit," I shoved the drink towards her. The cup was touching her lip, and she jumped back.

"I'm at work."

"You put something in my muhfuckin' drink," I invaded her personal space.

I had never put my hands on a woman, but as soon as I found out why Lauren's ass tried to drug me, she was as good as dead for even having the gall to play with me like that.

"Wise wants me to bring you to him."

I laughed in her face like a maniac. "Wise wants *you* to bring me to *him*? You and what muhfuckin' army?"

"The drink was supposed to make you more relaxed. I get off

in thirty minutes. 1 was supposed to get you in my car. He wants to see you."

"Fuck he want to see me for?" I spat as I looked her up and down.

"That's something you have to ask him."

I narrowed my eyes as I studied Lauren. She was pretty as shit but too bad, I might kill the fuck out of her. "I just might let you live long enough to take me to the nigga since you're his errand girl and shit. And I'm not waiting thirty fuckin' minutes for you to get off."

The fear had disappeared from Lauren's eyes, and she kissed her teeth. "I'm not too worried about you killing me. You might want to hope that Wise doesn't kill you." Lauren turned to walk away, and it took every ounce of restraint that I possessed to keep from yanking her ass back. Fuck did Wise want to see me for?

I jumped off the porch early, so of course I'd heard of the infamous Wise. He was a king pin. One of Diamond Cove's biggest players. He had half the city on lock. I'd seen him in passing but never talked to the nigga or bought dope from him. When I was coming up, he only sold major weight and by the time I could afford to cop weight, he had people moving his work for him. As far as I knew, Wise no longer got his hands dirty. He had plenty of people on payroll for that. Word on the street was he had a police officer moving dope for him. I was stumped and had no clue why he wanted to see me. I was never scared, but I was very intrigued, and I wondered if I should let Loyal know what was up. I had that thang on me, but I knew I would be outnumbered like a muhfucka. Wise had niggas on payroll that would wipe his ass if he wanted them to. I was sure that his flunkies would be at his side and wouldn't hesitate to take me out if that was what Wise wanted.

I was so lost in my thoughts that I didn't even know how long it took for Lauren to get back to me. But when she approached me, she had a cross-body bag draped across the front of her body and car keys in hand.

"Where are we going?" I asked. "I'm not riding with you. I'm driving my own shit."

I gritted my back teeth together as Lauren rolled her eyes. Shorty was pissing me off. She rattled off an address to me, and I texted it to Loyal. I wasn't going into the situation with Wise without letting my people know where I was at.

"I'm parked out back in a Jeep. Mint green," she stated dryly.

"I'll pull around. I'll be in a Volkswagen. Don't try no stupid shit."

"Look," Lauren snaked her neck at me. "I get that you're upset and all, but I did what Wise told me to do. Take it up with him when you see him, but all that acting like you run me isn't going to fly."

I licked my lips and flicked the tip of my nose as I stepped towards her. "You got a fuckin' death wish?" I asked her with a scowl. "Because patience is one thing I don't possess. You got me fucked up, and I'm trying real hard not to get ignorant with you. Just from the shit you pulled with the drink, you should be missing some teeth right now."

"Boy fuck you." Lauren pivoted and walked off, and I hated that my eyes went to her plump ass.

Shorty had a mouth on her, and I was real close to forgetting that she was a female. I didn't give a damn what Wise told her to do. The fact remained that she chose to listen to him, and she attempted to drug me was a choice. She wasn't getting a pass for that. I texted my brother as I walked out to my car and before I could start the engine he was calling my phone.

"Yo." I reached for the half smoked blunt that was in my ashtray.

"What you mean Wisc sent for you? What business you got with Wise?"

"I don't have no business with that nigga. I don't know him, and he doesn't know me. And the fact that he told this bitch to drug me has me rubbed the wrong way. I'm not approaching him on no friendly shit, so if I end up shooting it out with his minions, I hope I take him with me if they kill me."

"Man," Loyal drawled, and I could literally see him shaking his head. "This shit is crazy. You might make it there before me, but I'm about to finish up what I'm doing right now."

"Bro, if you're tattooing don't stop in the middle of your job for me. I just wanted you to know where I was going. Get your money."

"Fuck all that. I'm done anyway but even if I wasn't, I don't care nothing about that. I'll be leaving here in about ten minutes. Please hold tight and don't lose your cool."

"I got you," I lied because that was a promise that I couldn't make.

Loyal was the mature, quiet, laid back one. I was the temperamental live wire that didn't take any shit. My brother didn't have a pussy bone in his body. He could still shoot, and he could for sure still fight, but he wasn't on that type of time. He got money the legal way, and he stayed out the way. I never wanted my brother to get caught up in any of my mess and get sucked into any trouble. I drove around to the back of the club and spotted the brake lights of the Jeep that Lauren was driving. I pulled up behind her, and she took off.

"Bitch," I mumbled.

My phone rang, and I glanced at the dashboard to see who was calling. I sucked my teeth when I saw Carmen's name. I had been dealing with Carmen off and on for two years, and she was five months pregnant with my daughter. For the past few weeks, she'd been emotional as hell, and I wasn't in the mood for it. She cried over the smallest thing, and I didn't have the patience for all that. Especially when she cried over dumb shit like me going to the store to get her Sherbert and them being out. I knew she couldn't help it but got damn. She wasn't my girl, and the child wasn't planned. I was going to step up to the plate and be a father, but I didn't sign up for the extra stuff. I told her she could quit her job, and I started paying all of her bills even though we weren't together, and she still found reasons to cry and complain.

Feverishly, I hit the blunt back-to-back in an effort to calm my nerves. According to my GPS I was ten miles away from the destination. It was dark out, but I paid attention to my surroundings. I wanted to remember exactly what area I was going to. Finally, Lauren's Jeep turned into an apartment complex. There were at least ten buildings in the complex, and each building had three floors. An apartment wasn't an ideal place for a shootout, so maybe Wise wasn't on any dumb shit. I was still taking my gun inside, however.

Lauren parked, and there was no room beside her, so I drove a few parking spaces down and pulled in. I exited my car and walked towards where she was parked. Asking her who was inside was on the tip of my tongue, but I knew if she gave me a smart response, it would further piss me off. I followed Lauren to the building that we'd parked in front of and up the stairs to the second floor. With her keys in hand, Lauren walked up to one of the doors and put the key in the lock. I was on high alert as I stepped over the threshold and followed her into the apartment. I immediately saw Wise sitting on a black leather couch. He didn't look threatening. He was staring at me as hard as I was looking at him, but his facial muscles were relaxed. The nigga was clad in dark denim jeans, a grey Polo zip up hoodie, and grey and white sneakers. I peeped the

Rolex on his wrist and the diamond encrusted Cuban link around his neck.

"Justice. Come in and have a seat."

Lauren walked towards a room that I assumed was the bedroom and closed the door. My eyes darted around the space, and it appeared that Wise was alone. If he wanted to meet with me on a cordial tip, he could have come at me like a man rather than trying to have a female drug me, so he was already on my bad side. But since he didn't look like he was interested in turning up, I sat across from him.

"Why am I here? Better yet, why did you try to have me drugged?" I looked Wise in the eyes as I spoke and didn't even blink. I wanted him to know that no matter how powerful he was in the city of Diamond Cove, I wasn't afraid of him. I wasn't a yes man, and I wasn't going to kiss his ass.

"I think you may have something that belongs to me." Wise leaned forward and picked a blunt up off the coffee table. He stared at me while he reached in his pocket for a lighter. I frowned at his words, but I didn't speak. "You know a cat by the name of Rico? He was robbed recently."

"Fuck that gotta do with me?" I looked Wise directly in his eyes while I played dumb.

"You may think that you're under the radar when it comes to this robbing shit, but it's my job to know damn near everything. And I know that you sell drugs, but you also pull off capers. And not many are as successful as you. But still, the shit with Rico has your name on it."

My upper lip curled. "If you risked shorty's life asking her to drug me just so she could bring me here, and I what? Confess to some shit you *think* I did; you just wasted your muhfuckin' time and mine."

"I may not know for certain that it was you, but my gut tells me that it was. And if you were anybody else, the conversation would already be over, and you'd be laid out on the floor leaking. But that's not the reason I brought you here. I'm your father."

I stared at Wise for all of five seconds before a loud chortle left my throat. "My what?" He had thrown me for a loop with that one. I stared into his face with a different purpose than before. I scanned every inch of his face looking for similarities between him, me, and my brother. The almond-shaped eyes. The sharp nose. The silky hair.

"I'm your father. Is your mother's name Simone Trent?"

I didn't reply. It wasn't often that I was stuck but I was in that moment. I was twenty-four years old and had never known the first thing about where I came from. If my father was indeed a cold-blooded savage like Wise, it would sure as hell be fitting.

"I don't know what her name is. I was raised by a woman named Janice. My brother and I were adopted."

Wise bobbed his head as he ran one finger across his bottom lip. "I heard a minute ago about the young ass twins that were out in the streets doing their thing. I was a little intrigued, but it was more because I respected the hustle than anything else. Even the first time I caught a glimpse of you, I did a double take because you look like me, but the person that birthed my kids had triplets not twins. So, I thought no way were you mine. But over the years, the shit plagued me. What if one of the babies died or some shit only leaving two kids? So, I did some digging."

All I could do was stare at Wise while he spoke. I had no clue why he wanted me to come see him, but I never in a million years would have guessed it was because he thought he was my father.

"I managed to locate Simone. It was like pulling teeth to get information out of her ass, but she finally told me that she gave birth to three boys. Truce, Loyal, and Justice. She was in no position at the age of fifteen to raise triplets. Her parents were disappointed that she got pregnant at such a young age, but they couldn't let her abort three babies. Even though raising them would have put a strain on them, they were determined to do it. Simone didn't want anything to do with triplets, so she found a woman that wanted to adopt two of the babies. As much as she wanted kids, three was a bit too much for her, so Simone pretty much sold you and Loyal to her for $3,000, and she was forced to keep Truce."

My face crumpled. This had to be some kind of joke. Shit, I mean it was possible but still. Nah. My father was muhfuckin' Wise?! One of the biggest hustlers in the city, and me and my twin had spent years selling dope, stealing, and finessing our way through life, when the entire time, our father had money? I was agitated as fuck. I needed to hear the entire story before I told Wise to suck my dick. Maybe what I went through wasn't his fault. Triplets? I needed to sit down, and I was already sitting down. My phone vibrated in my pocket, and I was sure it was Loyal, but I couldn't even move to retrieve my phone from my pocket.

"When Simone got pregnant, she was fifteen, and I was seventeen. I had just started hustling. I didn't have money like that. We were never in a relationship. I was young and immature, and I didn't want a kid. She didn't either. When she told me she was pregnant with triplets, I didn't believe her. No way was she pregnant with three muhfuckin' babies, but she was. Simone assured me that she was giving all three kids up for adoption, and that I wouldn't ever see the kids. Honestly, at the time, it was what it was. I couldn't afford one baby let alone three, so I let her do her thing. I never even knew that her parents kept Truce and raised him."

I thought about Carmen, and how I felt when she first told me she was pregnant. I was a grown ass man, and I wasn't broke, but I was still hesitant to become a father. Having a child was about more than taking care of him or her financially. Actually being active in the child's life and raising them was a full-time job that never ended. It would require me to change the way I moved and the way I thought. As a grown ass man, I wasn't quite sure about that at first, so could I really be mad that a fifteen and a seventeen-year-old weren't ready for the responsibility of three kids at once?

I ran my hand down my face as my phone began to vibrate once again. I pulled the device out and swiped my finger across the screen. I already knew it was Loyal. "Yo bruh you good?" I could hear the urgency in my brother's tone. "I've been sitting in the parking lot for five minutes. I see your car. Which apartment are you in?"

"Building 500 apartment 506." I ended the call because there wasn't shit else to say. He was about to find out what was up just like I had.

"Who was that?" Wise inquired.

"Loyal."

"I know this is a lot for you to process. I hate that it took me all this time to get adamant about tracking Simone down. Finding you all has been on my mind for years now. I was thinking that maybe some rich ass family adopted the three of you, and you were all happy and healthy on some TV sitcom type shit, and I'd be a fuck nigga for coming in and disrupting that."

I snorted. "TV sitcom is a stretch, but I don't have any complaints about the woman that raised us. Jancie didn't mistreat us. She wasn't the most affectionate person in the world, but we were boys, so that shit don't matter for real. She kept us clothed, fed, and she made sure we did good in school. Me and my brother played sports, and life was cool. Until she died, and the bitch ass foster mother that took Loyal in didn't want me. We were separated for a bit. I was in a group home until we linked back up, and we been out here thuggin' it ever since."

Wise inhaled deeply through his nostrils before staring up at the ceiling. What he heard bothered him. There was a knock at the door, and I wasted no time standing up to answer it. The moment I opened the door, Loyal's eyes swept over my frame to make sure I was good. When his gaze landed back on my face, his brows furrowed. "What's up?"

Looking at Loyal was like looking into a mirror. He was me, and I was him. Even when my hair was braided to the back and his was in single plaits, we were identical in every other way aside from clothes. We even had some of the same habits like biting our nails and eating all of our food separately. If there was chicken, rice, and peas on our plates, we would eat all of the peas, then all of the rice, and the chicken last. Weird shit.

"I hope you got some weed in your system for this shit," I mumbled while stepping back so Loyal could enter what I assumed was Lauren's apartment.

Loyal walked in with a creased forehead. Looking around in confusion, his eyes went from Wise to me.

"Wise says he's our father."

"What?" Loyal chuckled. When he saw that I was serious, he drew back. "Fuck you mean Wise says he's our father."

"There's no plainer way to say it," Wise interjected. He ran the same story down to Loyal that he'd just told me.

"And you're saying we have another brother," Loyal said slowly when Wise was done talking. "The nigga I saw at the bar." He turned to face me.

Loyal had sworn on Janice's grave that he saw a guy in a bar that looked just like us. It wasn't that far-fetched to me that he could've been a cousin or an uncle, but Loyal swore he had to be a sibling. That was a possibility also, but to know that he was our triplet? That shit was wild. Even I thought Loyal was being a bit dramatic when Loyal declared that the guy was the spitting image of us.

"We can take a blood test if that will make you feel better, but I don't need one. I know what I know."

"Respectfully," I flicked the tip of my nose. "What is knowing going to do? Because as you can see my brother and I are grown men. We're kind of past the needing a daddy stage."

"You're never too old to need family. I can't come into your life and step into the role of father right off the bat, but you have a father. You have other siblings. You have grandparents. You're not interested in knowing them? You're not interested in letting go of that bullshit robbing and really get this muhfuckin' money," Wise's eyes bore into mine.

"Robbing wasn't bullshit when it was putting clothes on my back, food in my belly, and a roof over my head," I stated with conviction. "I wouldn't have needed to rob if I had parents that cared."

"I gotta go over that entire spiel again? I'm not expecting you to run towards me with open arms and open hearts. You can be upset. You can feel some type of way. But I want to get to know all of my sons. It's never too late to make amends."

"This shit is crazy," Loyal mumbled. He dropped his head and shook it.

"You have three sisters. Winter is nineteen, Fatima is sixteen, and Imani is four."

"Their mothers kept them, huh?" I chuckled.

"Yeah, they did," Wise answered with a hint of agitation in his tone. Fatima was born when I was twenty-two. That's a lot different from seventeen. Her mother was twenty-one. That's a lot different than fifteen." Wise stood up. "It's getting late. You two have a lot to process, but I'd like to hear from you soon. Can I have your numbers?"

Loyal and I remained silent. At the end of the day, I could be pissed with Wise. I could be stubborn as shit and say I didn't want anything to do with him or my siblings. But it would be stupid not to know the family that I had out there. In his defense, he was thinking that my mother put us up for adoption. Plus, I never wanted to try and holla at any of my siblings. I knew their names but still...

Loyal gave Wise his number, and I gave him mine. In return, Wise gave us his number, but I didn't plan on using it anytime soon.

LAUREN

When I glanced down at the watch on my wrist and saw that it was four minutes past the end of my shift, I was elated. I had been irritated since I woke up that morning, and I wasn't even sure why. A big part of it was probably nerves. I'd been approved for the apartment that I applied for. The next part was paying the deposit and moving in. I knew Wise wouldn't be happy about it, but I was tired of being underneath his thumb. The question was whether he'd let me go, or if he'd try and make me suffer for leaving.

There was no way Wise should have had control of me for so long for a failed robbery attempt. He made sure that I would need him, so he gave me a place to live, and my stupid ass got comfortable. I should have attempted to leave long ago. But a stupid crush had me blinded for a bit along with his subtle threats. I finally had the guts to call his bluff, and my nerves were shot. After saying goodbye to my co-workers, I grabbed my things from my employee locker and walked out to my Jeep.

"What up?"

My head lifted super-fast at the deep voice that cut through the quietness of the night. I kissed my teeth as I laid eyes on Justice. "What do you want?" I asked in an icy tone. I had eavesdropped the night before and heard all about how Wise was his father, and Justice was a triplet. I almost felt sorry for him, but I remembered how much of an asshole he was.

"I told you last night that you had to see me for attempting to drug me."

I frowned. Not because I didn't believe that Justice would kill me. I just wasn't in the fuckin' mood. The way life had been going maybe he should have put me out of my misery. "Nigga," I closed my eyes and sucked in a sharp breath. "Either do what the fuck you're going to do or leave me alone. My feet hurt," I snapped. "I already told you that Wise told me to do it. You damn sure didn't get at him last night, but you took the time to come looking for me. You should be thanking me." As soon as the words left my mouth, I regretted them. I didn't want him to know that I'd been listening last night.

"Thank you?" Justice looked me up and down. "I'm not thanking you for shit."

I parted my lips to speak, but the words got tangled in my throat. My chest tightened as my eyes widened. "Justice get down," I urged him in a harsh whisper before ducking myself.

I jumped each time a loud pop pierced the air. My chest heaved up and down, and my heart was beating like a drum as four shots rang out before an eerie silence loomed in the air. Lifting my head, I groaned inwardly as I saw Justice sprawled out on the ground. "Fuck," I fought back tears.

My eyes darted around the darkness checking my surroundings as I made my way over to him. Justice was on his back, so I dropped to my knees. His orbs shifted in my direction, and I breathed a sigh of relief when I saw that he was still alive.

With trembling hands, I rummaged through my purse for my cell phone. As I waited on an operator to answer, I inspected Justice's body. He had on dark clothes, so it was damn near impossible for me to discern where he'd been shot.

The call connected, and I tried to remain calm as I gave the 9-1-1 dispatcher the address of the club. Even in the dark, I could see Justice gritting his teeth together. His body was trembling, and I wasn't sure if he was cold, in pain, or in shock. Tears spilled over my eyelids as I grabbed his hand. "Please hurry," I begged. "He has on dark clothes. I don't know how many times he's been shot or where." I didn't even wait for her instructions. I lifted Justice's hoodie to try and locate a bullet wound, so I could put pressure on it.

I saw that he'd been shot in the right side. I pulled a head scarf from my purse and balled it up in my hands. Justice groaned as I pressed my scarf covered hand onto the wound applying pressure. "I'm sorry," I whispered.

The dispatcher asked me a few more questions and assured me that help was on the way. Finally, I could hear sirens in the distance, and I breathed another sigh of relief. Justice looked over at me. "Tell my brother I love him."

My heart sank. "No. I'm not. You're going to tell him yourself. Your mean ass isn't fucking dying on me. Not after all the times you threatened to kill me. You better not die." My chest felt as if it was caving in. Right before his body dropped, my only thought had been that Justice got on my damn nerves.

Now, here I was afraid that I was going to have to watch him take his last breath. "This shit hurts," he was shaking harder, and his eyes were glassy.

The ambulance raced into the parking lot, and I waved them over. Justice couldn't die. I didn't know him from a can of paint, but he couldn't die. Maybe it was dumb of me to want him to live after all the times he'd threatened me, but I didn't really take him serious. From what I heard while eavesdropping, I knew that Justice and his brother had a hard life after their mother died. I could relate to their story all too well, and it made me sympathize with both of them. If that was the reason why Justice was such a hard ass, I couldn't even blame him. I'd been told more than once by more than one man, that I was difficult, didn't know how to let a man lead, and that I was mean. A person that didn't grow up constantly in survival mode would never understand me, and I didn't even have the desire to make anyone try. Childhood trauma was the main reason that I was such a loner.

Reluctantly, I let Justice's hand go, so the EMT's could do their job. I wanted to make sure he was okay, but I wasn't sure if I should go to the hospital with him. I didn't even know Justice. The police came, and I answered some questions.

"Where are you taking him?" I asked the paramedics as they put the gurney onto the ambulance.

"Diamond Cove Memorial."

"Can I go?" I asked the officers that were standing in front of me. I had told them everything I knew. I didn't see the guy's face because he had a mask on. He wore a black jacket and black jeans. I was too busy ducking to pay attention to anything else. I knew the club had security cameras outside, but I couldn't be for sure that the shooting was caught on camera.

"Yes. If we need you, we'll be in touch." One of the officers responded to me.

I hadn't been sure if I should go to the hospital with Justice but the moment I saw them loading him into the ambulance, I had the sudden urge to jump in my car. I just didn't want him to be alone. The only person that I knew of to call was Wise, and I didn't want to talk to his ass for one and for two, I didn't even know if Justice would want him there. I bit my bottom lip as I drove. How in the hell could I get in touch with his brother?

I just had to pray that Justice would remain conscious, and that he would reach out to whoever it was that he wanted there. When I arrived at the hospital, I rushed towards the registration desk. I didn't even know Justice's last name.

"Hi, a gunshot victim should have been brought in maybe minutes ago. Black male. His name is Justice."

"Are you related to the victim?"

"I'm his girlfriend," I lied. If she asked me for his last name or any other important information, I was screwed. Time seemed to slow down, and I could feel my heartbeat in my throat. "I was with him when he got shot. I'm just worried."

"You can come back. Wait in triage room fifteen."

"Thank you."

I found the correct room, but Justice wasn't there. I wasn't sure if he had to get surgery or what. It was just a waiting game. I had been so ready to get off work. I was tired, and my feet hurt, but it looked like I wouldn't be seeing my place for a while. I didn't want to have boxes in the apartment, so each time I packed a box, I took it out to my car immediately or put it in the closet. All of the furniture and the décor in the apartment belonged to Wise, and I wasn't taking any of it. It could have been a bachelor pad or something before he moved me in but whatever it had been, it could go back to being that. I no longer desired to live under Wise's roof. I rested my head against the wall and closed my eyes. Just as I started to doze off, I heard a gurney being pushed into the room. My eyes flew open, and I sat straight up. Justice's eyes were open, but they were glassy and heavy. It looked as if he was fighting to keep them open. His clothes had been removed, and he had on a hospital gown. He looked over at me, but he didn't say anything. The nurses moved around the room hooking up various monitors, asking him questions, hooking him up to an IV, etc. It took about fifteen minutes for them to leave the room.

"I wasn't sure if you'd be awake to call anyone. I didn't want you up here alone," I stated in a small voice.

"I appreciate that. My phone is in that bag over there. Can you get it for me?"

I stood up and walked over to the large clear bag that the nurse had placed in the corner. I pushed the clothes and shoes aside and grabbed Justice's cell phone. The screen was lit up, and he had several missed calls and text messages.

"Thank you," he grimaced as he reached for the phone.

"I'll get out of here. I just wanted to make sure you were okay."

"Thank you, Lauren." I gave him a small smile and turned to leave the room. "Aye, what's your connection to Wise?" Justice asked in a raspy voice.

"Strictly business. Take care." I gave him another small smile and left the room. What a freakin' night.

"You finally did it, huh? I'm proud of you," My best friend, Loso stated as he mounted my television on the living room wall. We became really cool when I first started bartending. He was one of the bouncers at the club, and fine as hell.

Loso was a lady's man for sure, but he was always scared to talk to me because he thought I belonged to Wise. By the time he realized that me and Wise weren't like that, I had heard too many stories about him and the many women he hooked up with, and I had no desire to deal with him, but he took the rejection well. We continued to be cool, and we had grown really close. He had even changed his whorish ways and settled down.

"Yeah, don't be too proud too soon. I don't know how he's going to take me leaving. I even told Jacob that I needed some time off for a family emergency. I know he's cool with Wise, and I don't even want Wise in my business or to come to the club looking for me. I got a job at a lounge out in Durham."

"Damn. You're really trying to get away from him. Again, I'm proud of you. And do you think he'll trip like that? You don't owe Wise shit, and he knows it. He just played on your naivety for as long as he could."

"Absolutely," I agreed somberly. "I just got tired of not even trying to get away. If he does something, then he just does something, but I wasn't about to keep going along with his fuckery. Even though I don't transport drugs for him in the car anymore, I still make sales in the club. I'm not going to prison for Wise. Fuck him."

"I know his ass is at least forty, and he's had the streets on lock since he was a teenager. He has a heap of kids and probably more money than he can spend. He should just retire before his luck runs out, and he finds himself in prison."

"I should be so lucky," I responded dryly.

"He's definitely going to get what's coming to his ass. Wise has been up to his bullshit for years. Don't even ruin your mood by thinking about that fuck nigga. You should be proud of yourself. Open that housewarming gift I bought you," Loso referred to the bottle of Don Julio that he brought me along with gift cards to Target and Ikea.

I smiled as I walked into the kitchen to open the bottle and pour some drinks. I scanned the contents of the fridge before deciding on pineapple juice as a chaser. After making our drinks, I carried two plastic cups back into the living room. Loso was done with the television and about to start on the credenza that I purchased.

"You coming to Arielle's birthday dinner next week?" he asked as I took a large sip of my drink.

"Yeah, I'm coming. Who would have ever thought I'd be attending a surprise birthday dinner that you're throwing for your girlfriend. I guess in your case the saying once a hoe always a hoe isn't true."

Loso shook his head. "You act like I was the worst nigga on the planet. I was a single man doing what single men do. It wasn't like I was lying to good women and shitting on them. I ran across some scandalous broads. The ones that lie about being pregnant to try and finesse abortion money, or the ones cheating on their niggas. When I found a good woman, I acted accordingly."

"Okay, I give you that one." I continued to sip as he took pieces out of the box to assemble. Grabbing the remote, I focused on finding something interesting to watch on TV. It felt good to have my own place and being the only one with a key. At the old apartment, Wise showed up whenever he wanted and with whoever he wanted. I could be standing in the kitchen in my bra and panties, and he'd come in with no warning and have three niggas with him.

"What are you getting Arielle for her birthday?" I inquired.

"What do all women want? Purses." Loso shook his head. "Got me spending racks on a damn bag."

I giggled. "I have one designer bag. I mean they're cool and all, but it's not something I have to have," I shrugged passively. "I'm not the type to want a man to shower me with gifts because he feels guilty for all the bullshit he puts me through. And most of these men with designer bag money will take you through unnecessary shit."

"I won't dispute you on that. I know there are some cruddy ass niggas out here, but I'm one of the exceptions to the rule. I won't say I don't get tempted because I damn sure do. But for the most part, I don't think about cheating on Arielle because she makes me happy, and I haven't found in other women what I've found in her."

"Awwww," I stuck out my bottom lip. "That's so sweet. Maybe, I'll find that one day. I won't hold my breath that it'll be any time soon. I've never seen a healthy relationship up close and personal. My mother couldn't keep a man to save her life. I think that's why she treated me like shit. They hurt her and well you know how the saying goes. Hurt people hurt people." I downed my drink and stood to go to the kitchen for a refill.

"Your mother is just a hateful ass bitch," Loso extended his cup towards me, so I could give him a refill as well.

"You ain't never lied."

I had just finished pouring our drinks when I heard my phone ringing from the living room. I walked as fast as I could with the drinks in my hand to retrieve my phone from the couch. My cousin, Sade was calling. Sade's mom and my mom were first cousins. My mom didn't act like a complete bitch to me around other people, so no one but me and whatever man my mom was screwing at the time, knew how bad the verbal abuse could get. Sade's mom did know however, that my mom was a mean bitch, and she let me spend the weekend with Sade at least twice a month. Of course, she couldn't take me in without my mom's permission and two, she had five kids of her own, so there wasn't a lot of room in her home for another mouth to feed.

"Hey, boo," I answered the call.

"Hey. You busy?"

I passed Loso his cup. "No. What's up?" With one leg tucked underneath my bottom, I sat down on the couch.

I knew when Sade expelled a breath that something heavy was coming. Or some bullshit. Probably some heavy bullshit. Deciding that I would more than likely need to be tipsy for the conversation, I took a big gulp of my drink.

"This man, Niles came to my mom's house today. He asked for your phone number, but of course, we wouldn't give it to him without your permission. Instead, we told him to give us his number. He says he's your father, Lauren."

My brows furrowed as I jerked my head back slightly. "My father. Okay, my father's name is James."

"I can't tell you if he's your father or not, but you and him really do favor. And his story was convincing as hell. He said that when your mother got pregnant, he wanted to be in your life, but he didn't want to be with her. She told him that you and her were a package deal, and a few weeks later, she started dealing with James. He claims that James isn't your father. He said once she started dealing with James, he felt that she probably was a hoe, and the baby might not be his. But once you were born, someone showed him a picture of you, and he contacted her and asked for a blood test. She said no."

My eyes narrowed because that sounded just like that vindictive bitch.

"He went on to say that he reached out to her several more times over the years, and she told him no each time. One day, he just showed up at her house when you were seventeen, and you weren't even living there. He said he's been looking for you, but he left the state two years ago. He just got back last month, and he tracked my mom's address down."

My mom and James broke up when I was five, and that's when she really started being evil towards me. When her and James broke up, he said fuck me, but I honestly thought it was because he wasn't shit. But after hearing what Sade had to say, he probably said fuck me because he knew I wasn't his. All I could do was shake my head. My mother was one bitch that didn't need the privilege of procreating.

"I wouldn't even know what to say to him if I did reach out to him. This is crazy as hell. Just give him my number, and I'll hear him out if he contacts me."

"Gotcha. How are you doing though? I know you just moved into a new place."

Sade and I caught up for a bit and by the time we were done talking, I was tipsy. When I ended the call, I just stared at the floor for a few minutes trying to process everything that she told me on the phone.

"What's good? Why you looking like that?" Loso asked.

I lifted my head and peered into his face. "Some bullshit."

TRUCE

"Pops?" I asked with a frown.

"Yeah. I just found out about him a few days ago myself, but his name is Wise, and he feels strongly that we're his kids. We meaning me, you, and my twin brother Justice. I saw you a few weeks back at Louies."

I looked over my shoulder at my grandfather, and he looked as if he'd seen a ghost. One of the names on the birth certificates that I found was Loyal. And the other was Justice. The man looked just like me. He for sure couldn't be lying. I turned back to face the spitting image of me that was standing at my grandfather's door.

"My brother, shit I guess our brother, Justice was shot. He's in the hospital, and Wise wants you to come up there."

Hearing that Loyal had just recently found out about Wise himself made me feel better. I wasn't the only one in the dark and if I wanted answers, I may as well go with him because I damn sure wouldn't get them from Simone. "Let me get my keys."

"You can ride with me. That way, I can fill you in on the way to the hospital."

"Alright. I'll be back Gramps." My grandfather still looked like he was going to pass out at any moment, but he wasn't the only one.

I followed Loyal out to a white Audi. Inside the car, he didn't waste any time getting started on the information that he'd recently found out. "Wise felt that my brother robbed one of his workers, and he had someone bring my brother to him. Kind of the same way I'm bringing you to him. Before that, he speculated that we were his kids, but he was stumped because he knew that Simone had triplets and not twins, so he didn't know why there were only two of us. Your mom named Simone?"

I kissed my teeth. "If you want to call her a mom. Yeah, her name is Simone."

"Wise finally caught up with her, and she admitted that there were three of us. The woman that she gave me and Justice to didn't want three babies. So, we were raised together by her until she died when we were thirteen. We went into foster care, and I was immediately taken in by a family that didn't want two kids. Seems that we keep getting split up because people don't want multiple kids," Loyal chuckled. "Justice went to a group home until I stole my foster mother's car and went and got him. We ran away and started hustling, and we been out here on our own ever since."

"Damn." Compared to what they went through, my life was a walk in the park.

"The woman that adopted us didn't know anything about our father, and all she told us about Simone was that she was young when she had us. We never even knew her name. Damn sure didn't know that she gave us up for $3,000 until Wise told us. So, Simone isn't in your life?"

Just hearing her name left a bad taste in my mouth, and it made my face contort. "Hell no. My grandparents raised me. Even when she was in the house with us, she didn't deal with me for real. She treated me like I was her annoying little brother or some shit. I never even looked at her as a mother figure. It was my grandmother that was affectionate and hugged and kissed me, bathed me, cooked for me, all that. As soon as Simone turned eighteen, she left the house with some nigga and never looked back. Fuck that bitch."

"Even with her being the way she was, it still seems like you grew up around love, and that's what's up. Janice was good people, and Justice and I had it good until she died. Life after that was a straight jungle for us. Every day we had to wake up in survival mode, and we weren't even in high school yet."

"I'm sorry to hear that. I always used to wonder if I had siblings on my dad's side because of course, I knew my mom, and I'd never seen her pregnant again. Until now. She's having a little girl in two months."

"Got damn. It seems like all we have is sisters. If Wise truly is our father, he has three other daughters. I think he said Imani is four, Fatima is sixteen, and Winter is nineteen."

"Wow." I was thrown for a loop. This was the craziest thing I'd ever gone through in my life. "How is this Wise character?"

Loyal's shoulders lifted into a shrug. "He's aight, I guess. I mean, if the nigga was only seventeen without a pot to piss in, and he got a fifteen-year-old pregnant with triplets, I can't blame him for not wanting her to keep the kids. I do believe that he thought we'd all been adopted and were somewhere happy and being taken care of. I see so much of Justice in that man it's scary. I really think he's our father. As far as Simone, I can't even have too much respect for her. If Janice didn't want all three of the babies, she shouldn't have given her two."

I looked over at Loyal and stared at him. He turned his head in my direction with raised brows. "What?"

"We have our hair the exact same way," I shook my head in awe. Two thick French braids. "This shit is crazy."

Loyal chuckled. "Tell me about it. My head has been spinning ever since Wise contacted us. I don't know man," Loyal stared straight ahead. "I can't say I wanted you to be out there thuggin' it with us because for a short time shit was rough. Rougher than any kids should have to experience. You were raised with love. But at the same time, it's just fucked up that it wasn't the three of us navigating this shit together. We were in the womb three deep. Loyal and I are best fuckin' friends, and I'd lay anybody down for him. Nobody should have denied us the chance to have that with you."

I bobbed my head. "I never in life would have imagined that I was a part of a trio. I guess I can't even blame my grandfather for not telling me. That would have just left me with more questions that Simone wouldn't have given me answers to."

We arrived at the hospital, and Loyal parked the car. "Justice can be a live wire," Loyal spoke as we walked towards the building. "Sometimes, he can be cranky as shit and ill tempered. I almost know him better than he knows himself, so I know when to give him space. If he acts like an asshole when you meet him, don't take it personal."

Again, I just nodded. We were three grown ass men all with our own different personalities and I'm sure trauma from our childhood. I didn't expect it to be an instant kumbaya moment with hugs and laughs. I didn't even know how I was going to feel when I met Wise. As we rode on the elevator, my stomach felt as if it was doing somersaults. My nerves were getting the best of me. Why though? I wasn't a kid. If Justice was receptive of me, I'd be receptive of him. If it was fuck me, it was fuck him and Wise?

Wise I really didn't know. I had spent all my life wondering about my father, and I was about to meet him face to face. I needed to smoke. Bad.

Walking down the corridor of the hospital felt like walking the green mile but finally, we reached Justice's room. The door was closed, and Loyal used his knuckles to tap on the door three times before he pushed it open. I walked in behind him, and the first person my gaze landed on was Wise. I knew it was him. Old ass gangsta nigga, but he wasn't even really old. Honestly, he didn't look a day over thirty. He looked like he was smooth as hell and could sell water to a whale. He was dressed down in camo print cargo shorts, a khaki tee, and white, brown, and black sneakers. Wise was iced out and probably had close to a million dollars' worth of jewelry adorning his body.

"Truce," he stated when I walked into the room. He said my name slowly and stared as if he was in awe. "Got damn. I have three fuckin' sons."

"Damn."

I looked over at Justice, and he was studying me with awe all over his face too. If it wasn't for the age difference, it would have been easy for one to assume that we were quadruplets. I was willing to bet every dollar that I had that Wise was our father. I didn't even need to see the results of a paternity test. I didn't even know what to say. Loyal sat down while I remained standing and leaned against the wall with my hands in my pockets.

"Did Loyal run everything down to you, or do you need me to fill you in?"

"He pretty much told me what it is, I guess. You and Simone were young. You thought she gave us all up for adoption. That's pretty much it, right?"

"Long story short, yeah. I had no clue that Simone kept you. I thought the three of you were together."

I scoffed at his comment. "Simone didn't keep me. Her parents did. She's never even so much as given me a hug. Simone was in the house with me, but she didn't fuck with me. She looked right through me."

"I won't even sit here and try to make excuses for her. What I will say is while I know she wasn't ready at her age to take on triplets and giving you up would have probably been the best thing, we can't say how it affected her mentally. Maybe looking at you was a reminder that she had two other kids out there."

I snorted. "Yeah, that may have been the case, but I'll never have empathy or sympathy for that broad. I'm good on Simone." He should have been pleading his own case rather than trying to get me to see things from Simone's point of view, 'cus fuck her.

"If that's how you feel I can't do anything but respect it. Like I told Loyal and Justice, I know this is a lot for you to process. If you have to take some time to let it sink in, that's what it is. But I want you to meet your sisters. I want you to meet my parents and my siblings. My brother Chicago is a year older than me, and my sister, Trinity is two years younger than me. Also, I've put a hundred niggas on. There's no way I'm not putting my sons on. You can get all the weight you can sell."

I shook my head. "Respectfully, I'm not in the dope game. I sell a little weed but that's only to save money until my business really takes off. I do carpentry work, and landscaping. I get enough jobs to get by. I also purchased a house that I'm renovating to sell."

Wise's brows lifted, and I could tell he was impressed. "I'm not mad that that. I have a few properties myself. Give me an amount. I'll invest in your business. Whatever you need I got you."

I was stuck and didn't really know how to respond when Loyal spoke up. "Yeah, I don't do that hustling shit either. I'm a tattoo artist."

Wise peered at Loyal. "You have your own shop?"

"Nah. I work in somebody else's."

"Not anymore. I'll have my realtor show you some buildings tomorrow."

Loyal chuckled. "I appreciate that and al——"

"Listen," Wise cut him off. "If y'all are anything like me you're stubborn as hell. I already expect it. You're grown men and have made it thus far without a father or handouts. You built your shit from the ground up with blood, sweat, and tears, and I respect the hell out of that. Nobody blinks an eye when white people set their kids up with generational wealth. Fuck all that I'm too good for handouts bullshit. I dropped the ball twenty-four years ago, but I've hustled my ass off, and I'm rich as fuck. If you don't want to look at it as a handout, look at it as a businessman trying to invest in your business. I just want to see y'all win."

I wasn't looking for handouts. But he was right about one thing. I knew I could get it out the mud and make something out of nothing, but what was so bad about having help? That's what parents were for right? To help us make it in life. I had a child on the way myself, and I never wanted him or her to ever struggle. I didn't care if he or she was fifty. If my child needed me I'd be there with no hesitation. I wasn't selling drugs other than weed, but if Wise wanted to invest in my business or pay me to work on his properties, I wasn't going to say no.

"I'll take a look at your properties later in the week if you have time," I spoke up, and a broad grin crossed Wise's face.

"That's what's up. My realtor will be contacting you too, Loyal." He said it in a way that let me know he wasn't taking no for an answer. His attention shifted towards Justice. "What about you?"

"All I know how to do is sell dope," he admitted in a slurred tone. He was probably high as hell off pain medication.

Wise's eyes lit up while Loyal's body stiffened. If I had to guess, I'd say that he didn't like the fact that Justice was in the streets. Wise and I exchanged numbers, and he left the room. There was a bit of awkward silence for a moment until Justice looked over at me.

"You can sit down. We don't bite around this muhfucka," he chuckled.

I walked over to the chair. I had not one but two brothers. I had missed twenty-four years with them. Simone truly wasn't shit.

"I'm Justice. A hot head that hates a lot of talking, and I don't have patience. I have a kid on the way by a crazy bitch, and I stay out the way and get my money. Nice to meet you."

I grinned at his introduction and description of himself. I agreed with Loyal that he had a lot of Wise in him. "I guess you already know my name and birthday. Shit, I don't do much. I sell a lil' weed mostly do carpentry and landscape work. I have a kid on the way too. Just found out today, so it'll be another eight months or so."

Justice and I looked over at Loyal, and he shook his head. "You niggas are corny. Hi, I'm Loyal," he stated in a fake chipper tone. "I love doing tattoos and fucking bad bitches. If I'm not at the shop, tattooing, or laid up, I'm home out the streets and out the way. I'm around people all day, so when I go home at night, I want quiet and peace."

I bobbed my head. I was still trying to process the fact that I had brothers when the door opened, and a short bad ass female walked in. Worry was etched all over her pretty dark-skinned face. My gaze shifted, and I saw that she had a small baby bump. She must be the baby mama. She stood about 5'3 with a big ass and childbearing hips. Dressed in white leggings and a fitted white tee that hugged her bump, her many Cartier and other bracelets jingled as she rushed towards the bed. Her long, small braids hung past her ass and almost to her ankles.

"Why didn't you call me?" She asked as she reached Justice's bed. "Nobody called me," she whipped around with a menacing glare that I was sure was meant to be directed at Loyal, but as her eyes ping ponged between our faces her jaw slacked. "What the fuck?" Her mouth was hanging open in shock. "Loyal?" she continued to stare.

"Right here, shawty," he spoke up. "This is our brother, Truce. We're triplets. It's a long story and shit. But um, we've had a lot going on. My bad for not reaching out."

"Nice to meet you," she stated slowly as she took me in. She stared briefly before turning back towards Justice. "I'm family. I'm the mother of your child. I should have been the first one up here."

"I'm not in the mood to talk about shoulda, woulda, coulda's, Carmen," Justice spoke with warning in his tone. "I'm sore as fuck. I was shot twice. Don't come in here getting on my nerves, or you can go right back out. I didn't call anyone but my brother."

I couldn't see the look on her face, but she remained silent. I felt kind of awkward like maybe I should give them some privacy. Either Loyal was feeling the same, or he read my mind because he looked over at me. "You ready to be out?"

"Yeah." I stood up, and Carmen turned around to look at me again. Shorty was stumped. I nodded my head at Justice. "Feel better soon. Maybe once you're out of here, we can all link up."

"Fa sho'."

Loyal walked over to the bed and extended his fist for Justice to bump with his. "Call me if you need anything."

"You already know."

I almost felt out of the loop because they already shared a bond. The three of us might have shared the same womb, but I was an outsider. Simone truly wasn't shit. However, I guess the phrase better late than never was true when it came to meeting my brothers. Loyal and I walked towards the elevator in silence. I wasn't sure of what to say, and maybe he wasn't either. By the time we made it to his car, a thought had entered my mind.

"Maybe if you have time, you can come in and meet my grandfather. I guess it's only right since you almost gave him a heart attack," I chuckled. "He's great people. Our grandmother died when I was ten, but up until the day she died, they both gave me the love and support that Simone never cared to."

"I'm cool with that. Like I told you before, you had it good. Life would have been a hell of a lot different if the streets didn't have a hand in raising me and Justice. Neither one of us turned out bad, but the streets have a hold on Justice that he's not quite ready to let go of."

"We all look just alike, but it's going to be hard being around the two of you and feeling like I belong," I admitted wondering if I sounded like a sucka.

"I think we can both attest to the fact that being family doesn't mean shit. I've had strangers treat me better than blood. So, nah, just because you're our brother doesn't mean we're going to have our guard down and go all in because for all we know you could be grimy as hell. But once we see that you're solid, we have all the time in the world to catch up. If the three of us were in the womb together, then you're far from an outsider. For twenty-four years it was only me and Justice. It'll take some getting used to, but I think we'll be good."

We were all born two to four minutes apart, so in my eyes, it didn't matter who was older or younger. When Loyal pulled up at my grandfather's house, I saw Orlando's car in the driveway. I looked over at Shalaine's house and it dawned on me that I hadn't talked to her in a few hours. She was skeptical about being pregnant, and it probably looked like I had gone MIA, but once I broke it down to her, she'd understand.

Inside the house, I found my grandfather sitting on the couch looking more stressed than when I left. Orlando had already seen Loyal once before at the bar, but his jaw still dropped when he saw us side by side. "I told you!" He exclaimed in awe.

"This is our cousin, Orlando. He was with me at the bar that day, and he told me I should say something to you. He swore then that you were my twin. This," I nodded my head in my grandfather's direction. "Is our grandfather, Alvin."

"Nice to meet you. I'm Loyal."

My grandfather shook his head. "I'm surprised I haven't dropped dead from a heart attack. I never in life thought I'd see you or your brother again." My grandfather's eyes became moist with tears. "When Simone came home from the hospital that day, and she only had Truce, my heart was broken. Your grandmother cried for hours. Simone carried you and gave birth to you, but we just didn't feel that she had the right to do what she did when we were more than willing to help her. Three babies would have been a lot, but we were willing to try. As bad as I hated that you all were separated, I was at least glad that she kept one of you."

"I definitely told Truce how lucky he was. Justice and I were lucky for thirteen years, but then our mother died, and we went into the system. That didn't last long before we ran away, and we've been on our own since the age of thirteen."

"I'm so sorry," my grandfather's voice cracked. I hadn't seen him cry since my grandmother died.

"It's not your fault."

Loyal sat down, and he talked with my grandfather for almost an hour before he left. We exchanged numbers, and me and Orlando sat on the porch and smoked a blunt. I had two damn brothers.

Shalaine was laying on her side stroking my beard. Hours had passed. The kids were asleep, and I had spilled my guts to her about everything that had transpired.

"The fact that you are a triplet is dope as hell. And scary. Lord, I hope there's not three babies up in my uterus," she giggled. "God please don't do me like that."

"What if you have three girls?"

"Please, Truce. I promise I'd never stop crying. I wonder if you all are fraternal or if two of you were identical and one fraternal. Two babies can share a sac for sure, but I'm not sure if three babies can share one sac. I'll have to google that."

"It would be hard to tell by looking because we all look identical. That's a question that only trifling ass Simone knows the answer to."

"This is really weird. I'm happy for you, but I'm sure you don't know how to feel. How do you feel about Wise?"

"He seems aight. I don't know him from a can of paint. His intentions could be genuine and pure, or he could be on some good bullshit. You know how in the movies, the long-lost parent reaches out because they need a kidney or some shit."

Shalaine sniggered. "Let's hope that's not the case. One thing that I've admired about you from the day we met is the fact that you aren't afraid to get your hands dirty. You work hard. I know you're not the type to sit around and wait for or even expect anyone to do anything for you, but don't block your blessings. Remember what you told me? You deserve good things. Don't be all prideful and shit and turn down his help. My parents still look out for me, and I'll be looking out for Tevin and Janay as long as I have breath in my body. Don't be stubborn."

"You don't know me for real," I joked because she'd pulled my entire card.

"Oh, I know you very well."

I inhaled a deep breath. "I will definitely work on his properties if he needs me to, and I'll charge him the same thing I charge everyone else. As far as him wanting to invest, if he does, I'll get a new truck and some extra equipment, so Hendrix can help me out. Shit, maybe I could stand to hire two people. That way, they can do the bulk of the work, and I won't miss out on so much of the weed money."

"See? Now wasn't that easy?" Shalaine lifted her head and peered down at me.

"Not really. And nothing is written in stone. He only has one time to say something to piss me off or rub me the wrong way, and he can take his money and get the fuck on," I declared, and Shalaine groaned.

"Positive thoughts, Truce. You remember all those motivational speeches you used to give me?"

"Different scenario."

"Not really."

"I hear you. When are you going to call and make a doctor's appointment?"

"I'll call in the morning. Hopefully they'll have something on one of my days off. I never know when I'm going to have a flare up that's severe, and I don't want to miss unnecessary time especially when I just started."

"That's understandable. Just let me know the date and the time, and I'll be there."

"You don't think this all happened too fast?"

"Shit, you know how many people get pregnant from one-night stands? We haven't known each other a super long time, but it is what it is."

Shalaine didn't respond, and I knew she was overthinking. I laid flat on my back and pulled her on top of me. "Whatever thoughts are going through that big ass head of yours stop."

"Nigga," Shalaine kissed her teeth. "I know you aren't talking about anybody's head."

"I am. Give me a kiss."

Shalaine pecked my lips, and that led to us having sex. She was out like a light and asleep in my arms, but sleep was the furthest thing from my mind. I had a baby on the way, and I had two brothers and three sisters. Damn.

JUSTICE

"You talked to Lauren since the night you were shot?" Wise asked me. I had been in the hospital for three days, and I had just learned that I'd be discharged the next day. Wise, Carmen, Loyal, and Truce came to see me every day. I hadn't heard from Lauren, but I'd thought about her more than once or twice.

"Nah. I don't have her number or anything. Why?" When I asked her about her relationship with Wise, she stated that it was just business.

"Her ass took her things and left the apartment. She's not answering the phone for me either. She must want me to put my foot in her ass." Even if Wise's forehead wasn't puckered, I would still be able to tell that he was pissed by his venom laced tone.

"That your chick or something?" I questioned.

Wise snorted. "Hell no. I caught her young ass trying to steal some dope from me when she was sixteen. She said she only did it because she needed a place to stay. I put her up in an apartment, bought her clothes and shoes, kept her fed, and gave her a car to drive. In return, she had to move dope for me, cook it, bag it, and do whatever else I told her to do."

"Like drug niggas," I offered.

"Something like that. I fucked her before, but that wasn't my purpose for keeping her around. I have more women than I know what to do with, and her young ass wasn't even one of my top three. I told her ass though that I would decide when I was done with her. She wants to be slick and try to sneak off. I should break her fuckin' jaw."

"How old is she?"

"Twenty-two."

"If she tried to steal your dope at sixteen, that was six years ago. How long do you think she's supposed to pay off her debt?"

Wise frowned. "For as long as I say. It turned into more than her trying to steal from me when I put her up in a nice crib and clothed and fed her for six years."

"That sounds crazy as hell to me," I shrugged. "Shorty was a kid, and she was out in the streets trying to survive. Of course, she wasn't going to turn down a place to live if it was offered to her. Making her do what you tell her for six years is a little excessive seeing as how she didn't even get away with the dope."

"You want to fuck her?" Wise asked matter of factly.

I chuckled. "I wanted to kill her ass, but that's not what I went to the club to do. I honestly wasn't even sure what I was going to do. Shorty has a fly ass mouth. But before I could do or say anything, a nigga popped me, and she pretty much saved my life. Let the girl go if you not on her like that."

I saw a flicker in Wise's eyes that I couldn't quite read. I knew he wasn't the type that liked to be challenged or told what to do. I was just giving him my honest opinion. Maybe I did want to fuck her because I was lowkey disappointed when he said he had sex with her. I didn't know Wise like that, but in case he was my father, I didn't want to run up in a chick behind him.

"Your hospital bill has been taken care of." Wise changed the subject. "Take all the time you need to get well. I don't know what your clientele is looking like but when you're ready go get back to it, I can give you twenty bricks."

My brows lifted. I wasn't jumping for joy because Wise was handing out money and granting wishes like a genie, but I'd be a muhfuckin' fool to turn down twenty free bricks. Especially when I needed to chill out with the robbing. I didn't even know who shot me, but Wise said he was looking into it. I was used to taking care of myself and putting in my own work. I didn't need Wise and his shooters coming in trying to take over and save the day. Whoever tried to kill me, I wanted to look that man in the eyes and let it sink in that he failed right before I took his life.

Before I could respond, there was a knock on the door. "Come in."

I didn't recognize the skinny young girl that entered my hospital room. She had skin the color of cinnamon and light brown doe shaped eyes. Her long natural lashes were thick, and she had drawn on or filled in her eyebrows, but aside from gloss that was the only make-up that she wore. A Gucci headband pushed her hair back from her face. Shorty didn't even look like she was old enough to drink, but she donned a Rolex on her wrist.

"Hi, daddy," she smiled, and Wise wrapped one arm around her waist.

I studied her. She was fly as hell in denim jeans, a white crop top, Gucci sneakers, and two Cuban link chains around her neck. Diamonds glistened in her ears, and draped across her body was a Fendi bag. Shorty had grown up a spoiled, privileged, rich kid, while me and Loyal had to fight grown men and keep them from robbing us for our dope. Must be nice.

"Hi, I'm Winter," she smiled at me showing me her brace covered teeth. "Dad always told me I had triplet brothers, but I never thought I'd meet you."

"Word?" I was surprised that he'd talked about us with his other kids.

"Yeap, especially when he was trying to find y'all. I just think he got tired of having all girls, and he wanted to go find his sons," she rolled her eyes making me chuckle.

I already had a quick temper and a bad attitude. The last thing I needed was three sisters to be protective over, but I had them.

"I'm Justice. It's nice to meet you."

"My friends are already asking me to send them pictures of how you look."

"Justice doesn't want any of your young ass friends," Wise scoffed.

I really didn't, but that was weird to me that he said that when he admitted to having sex with Lauren, and if Winter was nineteen, Lauren was literally old enough to be his daughter.

"I would hope he doesn't," Winter frowned. "That would be cringe."

Wise stood up. "And stop thinking I won't notice if you turn your location off for a few hours then turn it back on. Next time I try to check your location and it says not found, I'm taking the car." Wise hugged Winter again and kissed her forehead before giving me a fist bump.

I felt like a little bitch at the twinge of jealousy that shot through me. Glancing down at Winter's keys, I saw the BMW emblem on her key fob. Shorty was nineteen pushing a BMW and wearing a Rolex. She had parents that checked her location and cared about her. It's crazy how people swore God didn't have favorites, but that had to be a damn lie. What did me and Loyal do to deserve being thrown to the wolves?

Winter sat down. "I can't stay long because I have to go to class," she rolled her eyes upwards. "I'm in college. This is my second year, and I want to be a pediatric nurse."

"That's what's up. You live in the dorm?"

"No. Me and my best friend, Yogi have a condo downtown."

Figured. "You the only kid your mom has with Wise, or do you and our other sisters share a mother too?"

A smile eased across Winter's face. "Oh, you don't know the tea I see. So boom, my mom and Fatima's mom are half-sisters, but they can't stand each other. They have the same father but different mothers. My grandmother is still married to their dad, and Fatima's mom hates my mom. My mom was dealing with Wise and got pregnant by him and three years later, he got Fatima's mom pregnant. Imani's mom is a chick that he was dealing with for about six years, but I think he has a new girlfriend now. Our pops is a hoe."

"Sounds like a regular soap opera."

"And is. I can't wait to meet Truce and Loyal."

"Do you and Fatima get along?"

"Yeah. Pops isn't playing that sibling rivalry shit. He doesn't care how much our moms don't like each other. He always made sure we saw each other weekly, and he would pick us up, so we could have sleepovers at his house once a month. Anytime we get into it and stop speaking, he cuts us off financially until we make up. And for the record, like I said, he talked about his sons all the time. He didn't even know your names, but he made sure we knew we had brothers that were triplets."

I nodded. I guess that made me feel a little better. The door opened, and I turned to see who was coming into the room. The moment Carmen stepped in and saw Winter, her face contorted into a frown. Her nostrils flared, but she knew better than to straight come in on that dumb shit. Pregnant by me or not, she wasn't my girl. I damn sure wasn't trying to have kids spread all over the city by different women like Wise, but I wasn't going to be with Carmen just because she was pregnant.

"Hi. I didn't know you had company." Her tone was flat, and she was doing a bad job of hiding the fact that she felt some kind of way. I could see her studying Winter from head to toe.

"How would you know? You didn't call before you came. This is my sister, Winter," I stated dryly.

Carmen's mood shifted instantly, and a big fake ass smile covered her face. "Oh, hi! Damn, Jus, you have siblings coming all out of the woodworks. You're so pretty," she gushed over Winter. Just moments before, her ass was breathing fire like a damn dragon.

"Thank you." Winter stood up. "Well, I have to get to class. Hopefully, I can link with you and my other brothers soon." She unlocked her cell phone and passed it to me. "Put your number in."

I locked my number in, and Winter left. "Your daddy wasn't playing no games with making kids. How do you feel about having all these brothers and sisters out the blue?"

"How am I supposed to feel?" I frowned as I shifted in the bed. I had been shot in the side and the arm, and I was sore as hell and ready to get up out of the hospital bed. I wanted to be in my own home, using my own bathroom, and sleeping in my own bed.

"I don't know. Excited maybe. I want our daughter to have a lot of siblings," she threw out there, and I chuckled.

"Our daughter can have as many siblings as you're willing to push out of your vagina."

Carmen sucked her teeth and rolled her eyes. "I don't want my kids to have different fathers, either Justice."

"I won't say I'm one and done, but I'm one and done with you. I'm one and done for a minute. I'm not having any more kids by a woman that I'm not in a relationship with. It's too hard for y'all to grasp the concept that a baby doesn't change shit. Then when I'm out doing me, you want to have an attitude."

Carmen's nostrils expanded from anger, but she didn't respond verbally. I knew she didn't like what I said, but I wasn't lying, and she couldn't dispute that. Maybe Carmen really did want a child, but her wanting this baby had more to do with her wanting me than wanting to a mother. That I was sure of. Having a child by me wasn't going to trap me or make me be anywhere that I didn't want to be. After a few moments of silence, Carmen stood up.

"I'm about to go. You never miss the opportunity to tell me that we aren't shit. All I am is someone that you were fucking and you made the mistake of getting pregnant. It's been noted. I came to make sure you were good, but if it's not about the baby, we don't have shit to discuss, so see you later."

She stormed out of the room, and I chuckled. Finally, I could get some sleep.

The next day, Loyal picked me up from the hospital and took me home. The first thing I did was take a long, steaming, hot shower while he went to go pick up food. When I was done with my shower, I put lotion on and threw on some basketball shorts and a tee. After all that, I was in pain, but fuck a pain pill. I was fiending for a blunt bad as hell, so I sat on the couch and rolled one. I was halfway done with it when Loyal came back with the food. He stopped by our favorite soul food spot, and my mouth was watering for the fried chicken, macaroni and cheese, yams, collard greens, cornbread, and peach cobbler.

"You gon' be good here by yourself?" Loyal glanced down at his watch. "I have to work at the lounge tonight."

"I'm good. Aside from washing my ass, there's not much I have to be up doing. The crib is clean. I can hold off on doing laundry for another few days, and if I get hungry, I can order food."

Loyal bobbed his head as he sat down. "Wise said he has his ears to the streets to find out who shot you."

I snorted. "I have my own ear to the streets. I don't need him flexing his power. I can find out who shot me on my own and when I do, I can put in my own work."

Loyal bit into a chicken wing. "Maybe you putting in work is the reason you got hit with two bullets. You don't want to chill out yet? Selling drugs is dangerous enough, but you rob niggas on top of it. You know Janice used to say if you play with fire long enough, you'll get burned."

I kissed my teeth while I reached inside the grease-stained bag to pluck out a piece of chicken for myself. "I should have known a lecture was coming sooner or later. The man that knocked up our mother has shown his face. You can stop acting like my daddy now," I half-joked. A part of me was dead serious.

"I didn't know I had to be your father to give you some advice. Talking to you is like talking to a brick wall though, and I can save my breath, so I'll just shut the fuck up."

I looked over at my brother and watched him chew his food with a scowl on his face. "You really mad, nigga? We go over this at least three times a year. I'm good, Loyal. Whatever happens to me, I'm good. I don't want to do tattoos. A nigga can't rap. I don't want to mow lawns or pressure wash houses. And I damn sure don't want to punch a clock for another muhfucka. So, I'm just going to stack my bread and invest. I'll be out of the streets soon enough and if I don't make it out, that's just how it was meant to be."

"Say less." Loyal was still frowning, and the way he tossed his chicken bone onto his plate let me know he was pissed.

I loved my brother with every breath in my body, and I knew he felt the same about me. I wanted him to understand that being in the streets wasn't the only way to die. Maybe it was the fastest, but it damn sure wasn't the only way. I could die in a car accident. No matter how I left this world, it would hurt him regardless, so I was lost as to why he kept harping on me selling drugs. Look at how long Wise had been running shit. It was what it was, and I didn't see why he was mad if I wanted to take the chance on going to prison or something worse happening. Whenever it was my time to leave this bullshit ass world, I didn't want anyone feeling sorry for me. Especially not my brother.

"I'm about to chill on the robbing. Wise is going to give me twenty bricks. With the money I'll make from that alone, it'll put me on the right track. Now that I'm plugged in with him, I'll get serious about investing. Once I reach a certain financial goal, I'll leave the streets alone. That's the best I can do for you."

Loyal chuckled and looked over at me. "That's the best you can do for me? Nigga, you're doing it for yourself. If you get knocked or killed, it won't be me in that cell or that casket. It'll be you."

"And I'm fine with that, Loyal. Why can't you get that through your head? I'm not afraid of death, and I'm not afraid of a bid."

"I'm done talking." He picked up another piece of chicken, and I shook my head.

"I know you have my back. You're the only person in this world that I can count on and that I trust one hundred percent. I'd take a bullet for you without thinking twice. I appreciate how you old me down, Loyal. I'm just saying don't stress yourself out about me. I'm good. Regardless of whatever," I stressed.

Loyal didn't respond, and I knew it would take a little bit of time for his irritation to subside. I could agitate that man like no one else could. And he did the same for me, but we never stayed mad with one another for long. The longest Loyal and I ever went without speaking to each other was about twelve hours. No matter what, I talked to my brother every day several times a day. Neither one of us would even go to sleep unless we knew the other was good. We were halfway through our food when Loyal spoke again.

"How you feel about having all of these new siblings all of a sudden?"

"Winter and Truce seem cool so far, but it is what it is. If they start getting on my nerves and shit, I can go right back to not dealing with them and acting like they don't exist."

"Truce was in the womb with us. That's crazy as shit."

I shrugged passively. "I don't remember that shit."

"Nigga," Loyal glared at me, and I chuckled.

"Chill out bro, got damn. Truce is a lil' different from the girls because we share the same trifling ass mother and father. But I'm not dealing with a nigga if he gets on my nerves."

"You mean the way you get on mine?"

I stuck my middle finger up and dug into my macaroni and cheese.

"They're on their way over."

"Who?" my head snapped in his direction.

"Truce and our grandfather. Dude is cool as hell. I told you he cried when he saw me. He said he didn't think he'd ever see us again. He was pissed when Simone gave us away."

I wasn't really in the mood for company, but they were coming thanks to Loyal, so I had better get ready. I placed my plate on the couch and stood up to go into the kitchen. It took three shots of Don Julio for me to feel like I could be cordial through the surprise visit that Loyal had set up. I had just sat back down on the couch and grabbed my plate when the doorbell rang. I resisted the urge to kiss my teeth as Loyal got up to answer the door.

"Nigga you could have told me you invited people to my crib," I mumbled through a mouthful of food.

I heard Loyal greeting the guests. I looked up when he entered the room with Truce and our grandfather behind him. The way the old man's eyes watered when he saw me, made the ice around my heart melt. This man was my family, and he couldn't help what his daughter did. I stood up to shake his hand and was surprised when he pulled me into a hug. I'd never been hugged by another man in my life. It didn't feel bad though.

"I can't believe this," he shook his head as he let me go. "Wow. The times we would have had if all you boys would have come up together." His tone was full of regret. I was sorry that I'd never meet my grandmother, but Simone was one person I didn't care to meet. I wasn't interested in anything that she had to say.

I gave Truce dap. "Sorry it smells like weed in here. I didn't know you were coming."

Loyal peered at me, but I knew it wasn't because I threw him under the bus. Normally, I didn't apologize for shit. Especially what I did in the comfort of my own crib, but I did have some manners. Even if I rarely exhibited them.

"That's okay," my grandfather waved me off as he sat down. "All my grandsons smoke. Truce, Hendrix, and Orlando sit on my porch all the time smoking the devil's lettuce."

I snickered at the term. I had never heard anyone outside of Janice call it that. Truce and our grandfather stayed for two hours, and I actually enjoyed the company. I even agreed to go to a barbeque at his house in the next week to meet the rest of our family. He assured us that Simone wouldn't be there. I think he was just as pissed with her as me and my brothers were.

"That wasn't so bad was it, Mr. Grouch?" Loyal asked when they left.

"Nigga, get the hell out of my house, so I can pop this pill and go to sleep."

"You don't have to tell me twice to leave this raggedy muhfucka. Later loser."

I smiled as my brother left the house.

LAUREN

My eyes widened when I looked up and saw one of the triplets walking behind the bar. I wasn't sure if it was Loyal or Truce, but I knew it wasn't Justice.

"Loyal," he smirked.

"H-hi. We didn't see each other that night, but you came to my apartment. With Wise and Justice." My breath caught in my throat. Wasn't this some shit? I came to the new lounge to try and hide from Wise, and one of his sons was behind the bar like he worked there. Just my damn luck.

"Word? Yo my brother has been wondering how to get up with you. You were with him when he got shot, right?"

"Yeah, I was. How is he doing?"

"Why haven't you reached out and tried to see for yourself?"

My weight shifted from one leg to the other. "Honestly because I um," I inhaled a deep breath. "Listen, I moved out of the apartment. It's a long story, but Wise doesn't know where I am, and I'd appreciate it if he didn't know that I worked here."

Loyal shrugged. "I don't know that nigga like that to be

snitching to him. I don't have anything to do with what y'all have going on. My brother isn't on that type of time either. I'll give you his number, so you can call him."

I wasn't sure that I would actually call Justice, but I pulled my phone from the pocket of my shorts and unlocked it. After Loyal gave me the number, I shook my head. "You and that man look just alike but seem so different 'cus he has a mouth on him," I simpered.

"That's Justice, man. Our mom used to say that he could make a Christian curse."

"I can see that for sure," I laughed.

I had been thinking about Justice since the night I left him at the hospital. I had been praying that he was okay, and I wasn't sure why it made me feel good that he wanted to talk to me. Maybe he no longer wanted to kill me. Throughout the work night, I kept stealing glances at Loyal. Not because I liked *him*, but because looking at him reminded me of Justice. After the third time, I had to internally check myself.

Girl, I know you're not crushing over that smart mouth ass nigga that threatened to kill you more than once. You can't sleep with him anyway. You slept with his father.

At that revelation, my stomach churned, and bile rose in my throat. I slept with that man's father. I was disgusted. Repulsed. Fuck! I would have rather had Justice smart mouth and all over Wise any day, but what was done was already done. The fact that Justice was off limits even if I did want to sleep with him made my mood instantly turn somber. The lounge was pretty busy and since Loyal and I were the only bartenders, my shift flew by. We didn't have a lot of time to talk, but he was cool people. Much more laid back and nicer than his brother. We made the perfect team because the fine ass niggas flirted with me, and all the thirsty women flirted with him. At the end of my shift after we split the tips, my take was $1,153. We ran that shit up! The most I ever made in one night at the club was $904, and that was a holiday weekend when the club was super packed.

Inside my Jeep, I bit the inside of my cheek as I contemplated whether or not I should hit Justice up. The text would really only be to see how he was doing because since I screwed his father, he and I couldn't ever cross that line, and I hated that for me. I wasn't even sure why that was on the table anyway because I damn sure hadn't forgotten how rude and ignorant Justice could be. Of course, he didn't talk shit in the hospital after I saved his life, but for all I knew, he was back on that same old bullshit.

I texted him quickly before I could change my mind and placed my phone in my lap. About five minutes after I texted him, my phone vibrated in my lap, and my breath caught in my throat. The fact that my heart rate increased was insane to me. Prior to him getting shot, I detested Justice. Now my heart was beating all funny because I thought he texted my phone. While I waited at a red light, I picked my phone up, and my eyes narrowed when I saw that it was actually Loso that had texted me. I kissed my teeth and was about to toss my phone in the passenger seat when it rang. It was Justice.

I cleared my throat and answered the phone. "Hello?" I had told him in the message that his brother gave me the number, so we would already have that out of the way.

"Damn you haven't checked to make sure a nigga wasn't dead or nothing. How you save my life then ghost me?" I giggled, and the rhythm of my heart returned to normal. He wasn't on bullshit, so I didn't have to be on bullshit.

"There's been a lot going on for one and for two, I didn't really know how to get in touch with you."

"You knew what hospital I was at."

"True," my voice trailed off. "But just because I saved your life

75

doesn't mean you wanted to keep seeing my face. Especially when you threatened to kill me quite a few times."

"Yo' ass didn't care about that. Talking 'bout do it then. Yo' you bugged the fuck out," he chuckled making me laugh.

"You were popping shit on the wrong night. My feet were hurting, and I have enough problems. You killing me might have ended my misery." The fact that I wasn't completely joking was a little sad, but it was what it was.

"Nah, you didn't want to die. Not the way you ducked when a nigga fired off on me. That shit was crazy. And despite the times that I threatened you, you were still scared as hell when you thought I was going to die. That lets me know that you're good people. And I was probably wrong for threatening to kill you. You shouldn't have tried to drug me though."

"You're right," I sniggered. "At the time I would have rather dealt with your wrath than the wrath of the great Wise," I stated sarcastically.

"Aye, don't be talking about my daddy."

"Man, fuck yo' daddy," I stated with a frown, and Justice laughed his ass off.

"You got me hurting over here. I got shot in the damn side, and you done made me laugh so hard, this shit hurts."

"My bad."

"Come keep me company."

His invitation shocked me. It shocked me to the point that I was speechless.

"I'm still in pain. I'm not gon' try no freaky shit. And you saved my life, so I don't want to kill you anymore. I wasn't gon' kill yo' ass anyway."

I cleared my throat. "Um, I moved and W——"

"I know Wise is looking for you. That doesn't have anything to do with me. Wise doesn't make me jump the way he made y'all jump. That nigga doesn't run me. I don't have to tell him shit."

I scowled. "I don't jump for that nigga."

"Yes, you do."

"Nig——"

"I don't want to argue with you, Lauren." The authority in his tone, and the way he said my name made my kitty purr.

"I'm not arguing." I hated how small my voice was like I'd let the nigga punk me. Or made me submit. They were the same thing really.

"Aight, then. So, I'll text you my address."

"Okay."

I wasn't exactly close to him since I was working in another city. When Justice sent me his address and I put it in the GPS, I saw that I was twenty-two minutes away from him which wasn't bad. I couldn't believe I was about to go to Justice's house. Despite what he said about not trying to get freaky, I still had to wonder if he would still try something once I was actually there. What if he was lying about forgiving me, and I was walking into a trap? I was overthinking way too much and really doing the most. I didn't know Justice or Loyal from a can of paint, but I hoped they were being truthful when they said they wouldn't tell Wise my business. I could vouch for the fact that they'd just learned he was their father, but that didn't necessarily mean that they'd be more loyal to me than to him.

The closer I got to Justice's place, my nerves began to get the best of me. I kept one hand on the wheel as I used the other hand to dig through my purse for a piece of gum. I also grabbed my lip gloss and after I pulled up at Justice's home, I pulled the visor down and swiped some gloss across my lips. After rubbing my lips together, I removed my perfume from my purse and sprayed some. I fluffed my curls which were pulled up in a high ponytail. That would have to do. Leaving my purse in the car, I hopped out and walked towards the door.

Before I reached it, the door opened, and my heart lurched forward. I almost expected Wise to step out with a menacing glare on his face but instead, I saw Justice. He had on blue pajama pants and was shirtless. I tried really hard to ignore the print that was visible in his pants. My gaze shifted to the bandage on his side and then I looked up into his face.

"Hi," I gave him a small smile.

"Do I need to pat you down?" He cocked his head to the side, and I rolled my eyes.

"Try to drug a nigga one time, and he won't forget it. Should I be afraid to come in?" I stopped in front of him.

"Look, if we're going to be cool we have to trust each other. I can forget about you trying to drug and rape me, and you can forget about me threatening to kill you."

"Drug and rape you? Your imagination is active. You should be an author," I laughed as I stepped over the threshold.

I could only see the living room, but I was thoroughly impressed. The apartment that Wise put me in was nice and considered a luxury apartment. But Justice's home was nice as hell and decorated very stylish and lavish. I really wanted to ask him if he'd decorated himself or hired someone. Or maybe a girlfriend decorated. I was up in the man's house and didn't even know his relationship status. I had to hope that if he was in a relationship he wouldn't be foul enough to have me in his house.

"You have a really nice home."

"Thanks. When you thug it in the trenches for a few years you either get used to living that way, or you decide you're never going back to living that way. I'll spend every dime I have on rent and making my place look nice. I'm never going back to sleeping on hard ass floors and using blankets for curtains. Me and Loyal used to live savage as fuck."

My eyes roamed over the dark grey sectional, the glass topped gold coffee table and end tables, and the black and white print area rug. There was a huge television mounted over the fireplace. There was a large plant in the corner by the fireplace, and the décor ranged from candles to artwork. There was a slight aroma of weed in the hair, but the room smelled like cinnamon, and it was spotless. Justice was living like a king.

"You decorated or you hired someone? Or a female did it?"

Justice snorted. "I don't need a female to turn my shit up. I did all of this by myself. I have an eye for nice things. I told you. Living savage made me want and appreciate all the finer things in life. And things don't even have to be expensive to be nice. I can make some dollar store shit look high end for real. And that's from clothes to home décor."

"That's dope. But um, speaking of females are you single? Don't have me sitting up in your house if you have a girlfriend that might pop up." Justice didn't speak. He just stared at me, and my mouth fell open. "Justice!"

He started laughing like something was funny. "I don't have a girlfriend. I do have a baby on the way. Shorty is five months pregnant, and she's the only chick that would be bold enough to pop up. She's not fucking with me at the moment though."

I shook my head. "Men." I was second guessing my decision to come over because I really didn't want to fight a pregnant person, but if she popped up on some dumb shit and touched me, I might have to repent for my actions.

"What?" he chuckled. "I swear I'm single. She's mad because I reminded her in the hospital that a baby wasn't going to change the dynamic of our relationship. She was fine not being my girlfriend for years. As soon as she got pregnant, things changed on her end. I'm going to be there for my child one hundred percent. That doesn't mean I'm going to be in a relationship if I'm not ready."

"I know things can happen like condoms breaking but, it kills me when men say they don't want to be in a relationship, but they have unprotected sex with women. You don't know how babies are made?"

"It's not just on the man. You know how many women try to get me to hit them raw because they say they don't like the way condoms feel?"

I frowned. "Barf. That's gross. The only way a condom is coming off is if that's my man, and I have absolutely no reason to believe that he's cheating on me. I don't have time to have anybody's STD."

"So, you single?" The way Justice was gazing at me had me squeezing my thighs together to try and extinguish the fire that was suddenly burning between my legs.

"I am."

"So, what's your story? How did you end up living in Wise's spot and then running from him?"

I stopped crying long ago about the way my mother used to treat me, so it didn't bother me too much to talk about her. "My mom was a bitch. She started verbally and physically abusing me when I was young as hell like around four. I don't hardly have any good memories of her. More often than not she treated me like she hated me. All she cared about was men. If she had a man, and he was treating her good, she treated me better. If a man pissed her off or broke her heart, she took that shit out on me."

Justice leaned forward and grabbed a blunt off the coffee table.

"By the time I was sixteen, I was just tired of that shit, so I ran away although I didn't really have anywhere to go. This older guy tried to talk to me, but he wouldn't pay for a hotel room for me unless I slept with him. I didn't want to sleep with him, so I tried to take his work from the spot he stashed it in, and Wise caught me. Turns out, the guy was selling the dope for him."

"Damn." Justice grabbed the lighter that was beside him on the couch and ignited the flame.

"I had to plead my case and tell him that I was homeless, because I'd heard how ruthless he was, and I was afraid he would kill me. I guess that shit runs in the family," I cut my eye at him, and Justice choked on the weed smoke he'd just inhaled.

"You okay?" I giggled patting him on the back.

"Hell nah," he scowled. "Coughing hurts like a bitch. I think you're the one that's trying to kill me."

"Dang my bad. Anyway, he asked me how old I was, and he pretended to have sympathy for me. He let me stay in the apartment, but soon, I found out it wasn't because he was trying to help me. Even though I never even took the dope, he claimed I owed him, and he started using me to traffic his drugs. Like at that age, he had me moving enough bricks to get me life in prison if I had gotten caught. I was young and dumb and really thought that shit was cool."

"He was sleeping with you when you were sixteen?" Justice asked with a voice full of disdain.

My face burned with shame. I didn't want to talk about having sex with his father. "Um, no. He never tried anything with me until I was eighteen. We slept together once, and that was it. He tried a few times after that, but I always turned him down. The older I got the more I started to see him as the predator that he was, and it disgusted me. He took me off the street and gave me a place to live, but I had to put money in his pockets to do so. I damn sure wasn't living for free like he tried to make it seem like I was."

Justice pulled from the blunt then extended it towards me. "You smoke?"

"I eat edibles sometimes. I rarely smoke, but I will." I took the blunt that he offered me and took a deep pull. The weed was super potent, and my eyes watered as I tried to hold in my cough.

"What finally made you decide to leave?"

"I just knew it would never end. It's already been six years, and he still says shit like, I'm not going to be done with you until I'm done with you. Anything that he tells me to do, I'm supposed to do it. The last time I told him no, he choked me. I don't even know what he'll do or say if I run into him, but I had to take the chance. I'm not going to be his crash dummy for the rest of my life. What if you really did kill me for trying to drug you? He wouldn't have shed one tear."

"That's kind of foul. I'm not the nicest nigga in the world, and I did threaten to kill you, but I don't put my hands on women. If he's trying to make you do illegal shit and you don't want to, that's no reason to choke you. I just met him, and I'm still trying to feel him out, but I don't condone stuff like that."

"He wasn't the worst person in the world. Like, he wasn't as bad as my mother, but I didn't really challenge him much, so I didn't see his bad side often. For a long time, I would have rather been at his place than my mom's, so I just did what he told me to."

"You were sixteen, and he was a grown ass man. He knew better. Me and my brother had to start hustling and fending for ourselves at the age of thirteen. I know what having to grow up too fast can do to a person. I saw things and went through things that no kid should have to. That shit will traumatize you and mess with your mental. I had plenty of adults try to get over on me thinking I was dumb and didn't know any better. I don't respect that shit."

I was high as hell after just a few tokes on the blunt, so I passed it back to Justice. I wasn't trying to turn him against his father, but he asked for my story, and I told him. I sure wasn't going out of my way to try and make Wise seem like a decent person. He was what he was.

"You want to know what's crazy? The man that I thought was my father this whole time might not be. The man who says he's my father texted me and asked me if I wanted to meet for breakfast next week. Including smart ass mouths, it seems like we have a lot in common. How does it feel finding your father this late in life?"

Justice pulled from the blunt and held the smoke in his lungs for a long time before slowly expelling it. "It's aight. I've only seen twenty-four birthdays, but I've been grown for a long ass time. Or at least it felt that way. He can come around, and we can be cordial and shit, but at no point can he ever son me. Janice raised me and Loyal for thirteen years, and we raised ourselves the rest of the way. Knowing Wise is cool, but I don't need an authority figure in my life. If I could figure shit out at thirteen, I can damn sure figure it out now."

"I get that," I replied softly.

"I'm giving him a chance though. I have more respect for him than I do the woman that birthed me. They were two kids that fucked up. At least one of them is trying to get it right."

"That's how I feel about my father. He said he asked for a paternity test more than once, and my mother said no. That's the kind of vindictive bitch that she is. He also said he came looking for me but by then, I had left home. So, I can't be too upset with him. It does sound like he was trying, and my mother had me thinking another man was my father this entire time. There are really some people that shouldn't be allowed to have kids."

"Exactly. Look at us trauma bonding and shit."

I narrowed my eyes at him. "Trauma and bonding. Those are pretty big words. Were they the Sesame Street words of the day?"

"Shawty fuck you."

I giggled and then yawned.

"Thanks for keeping me company though. You over there yawning and shit. Take your rock head ass home. You good to drive?"

I stared at Justice. I was sure he thought I was staring at him because of the slick comments he'd made, but while under the influence of weed, I wanted nothing more than to ride his dick until we both came. The unholy thoughts flowing through my mind had my clit throbbing. Even with frizzy braids and facial hair that needed to be shaped up, Justice was fine as fuck. I finally stopped being a pervert and found my words.

"I'm fine to drive and kiss my ass." I stood up, and he did the same.

Justice walked me to the door and told me to let him know when I made it home. I agreed. In the car I blew out a breath before looking down at my crotch. "Calm your hot ass down. You already had his daddy, so you can't have him." I kissed my teeth with disgust. "Fuck."

TRUCE

I looked around the kitchen that Wise and I were standing in. We had been in every room of the three-bedroom, three-bathroom house. The kitchen was the last stop. The house was really nice on the outside, and the inside wasn't terrible, but the home hadn't been lived in, in four years, and it needed some work. Wise also wanted new kitchen cabinets, new bathroom cabinets, new kitchen counters, every room in the house needed to be painted, and he wanted the floors done.

"I can do all of the renovations. If I hire some help maybe three people, I can have the house done in three weeks."

Wise's brows lifted. "Three weeks?"

"Yeah. When I work, I work. I don't come and bullshit for two or three hours. I get started early before it gets too hot, and I work until five or six if I don't have other jobs lined up. If I have help, no way it should take longer than that."

"Well, this is the first property of four that I need renovated, so hire all the help you need. Here are the keys, and you can get started whenever you're ready. Here's your payment up front."

Wise took the black bookbag strap off his shoulder and extended the bag towards me. When I felt how heavy the bag was, my brows lifted. "This feels kind of heavy. Unless you're paying me in small denominations, this has to be more money than I'm charging."

"And I told you I wanted to invest in your business. I don't want to be your partner. I don't want any of the profits. I see what you're doing here, and I respect it. I never thought I'd have sons that wanted to do the right thing," he chuckled. "But I'm proud. And it's not a handout," he stressed. "You better take that money and do what you need to do so that you, nor your kids, or their kids, will ever see struggle. Get a new truck. Hell, get two new trucks. Get some new equipment. Hire some people and set some of the money aside for payroll. Handle your business."

I gave a brief nod. I went from not knowing who my father was to him handing me a bookbag filled with cash. I had a baby on the way, so I'd be a fool to turn down his help. I didn't want to get caught selling weed and leave Shalaine alone with three kids while she had health issues. Having both of her baby daddies in jail would be too much for her to handle. Cliff's bitch ass was free, and he still wasn't doing what he was supposed to be doing, but that was fine by me. I didn't want him around her anyway.

Wise and I talked more about the house, and then he told me he wanted me, Loyal, and Justice to come to his house one Sunday for dinner. I agreed, and we left the house. I didn't want to be too thirsty to count the cash, but I was dying to know how much was inside. My phone was ringing off the hook with people wanting to buy weed, and I decided before I even counted the money that once the weed I had was gone, I would only reup one more time. Even though I'd purchased the house I was renovating and started working on it, I still had a few grand saved. What Wise had given me would go a long way though. I stuffed the bookbag underneath the seat and proceeded to go make a few plays.

When I had served everyone that was waiting, I drove towards my grandfather and Shalaine's neighborhood. After I killed the truck engine, I finally unzipped the bag. My eyes widened at all the stacks of cash. Each stack had a band around it that indicated it was $5,000. I pulled stack after stack out of the bag. When I was done, my heart was racing, and my mouth was hanging open. Wise had given me $100,000.

"What the fuck?" I mumbled. That shit was insane.

I could hire some help, buy a new truck, get some new equipment, create a website, get business cards made, and still have a hell of a lot of money left over. Shit, having a father wasn't so bad after all. I got out of my grandfather's truck and went over to Shalaine's house. I had a key because she worked from home, but if she was on a call when I came over, she couldn't get up and open the door until she was done with the call. I let myself in and heard her talking to a customer on the phone. Her desk/workstation was set up in the living room.

I walked over to her and placed kisses on her face and neck while she talked in her professional voice. She muted the phone, so the caller wouldn't hear her giggle. "Truceeee."

"Okay. I'll leave you alone." I pecked her once more then went to sit on the couch.

I scrolled through social media while she took a few more calls. Finally, she took her headset off and turned her chair around, so she was facing me. "Hey. You done with the meeting you and Wise had?"

"Yeap. It's a nice house. It needs a nice amount of work, but if I hire help, I can knock it out in three weeks. He has enough houses for me to be busy for a lil' bit. And he gave me some money. To invest in my business. Some money like $100,000."

Shalaine's jaw slacked the way mine had. "Oh my God, Truce. That is amazing."

"It is. Now, I can stop selling weed."

The smile that stretched across Shalaine's face told me everything that I needed to know about her character. She jumped up, ran over to where I was sitting, and threw her arms around me. She was happier that I was going to stop selling weed than she was happier about me getting 100k. Shorty wanted *me* there. It wasn't about the money, and that's why I was determined not to leave her alone with three kids.

I rubbed her back as she hugged me. "What you eating for lunch?"

"Some leftover pasta from last night. You want me to warm you up a plate?"

"Yeah. I gotta get going in a bit. I have some yards lined up."

"Okay." She kissed me on the lips before making her way into the kitchen.

The cookout that my grandfather wanted to throw was coming up, and I was excited for him. Seeing the joy that it brought my grandfather to be in the same room with me and my brothers damn near made me teary eyed. Simone hadn't just robbed me of being raised with my brothers. She robbed them of being raised with family and people that would love them. My grandfather told her about Loyal coming for me, and he said she cried and asked why none of us had reached out to her. That broad couldn't be serious. Simone could take a long walk off a short cliff, and I would give zero fucks.

Shalaine and I ate lunch together, and I kissed her goodbye before going to put up the money that Wise gave me and finish up my work for the day. I didn't have a lot of jobs lined up for the next day, so I was going to look at trucks. It didn't have to be brand new, but it was definitely going to be nice and reliable. I was also going to hire Hendrix to help me. I didn't want to hire too many people that I knew because I didn't have time for them to be half working and BS'ing because we were cool. I needed people that wanted to work for real and make money. It was time to turn shit up a notch.

A few days later, me, Loyal, and Justice sat in my grandfather's backyard smoking a blunt. I had gotten the grill started and was waiting for the coals to get hot enough to start putting the food on. Loyal and Justice came a little early, and people hadn't started arriving yet. I swore since Loyal and Justice came around, my grandfather had been having energy out of nowhere. He had even driven his truck to the grocery store to pick up a few things. I offered to go for him, but he wanted to go himself. I heard rocks and dirt crunching underneath someone's feet, and I looked up and saw Shalaine walking towards us with a smile on her face. Tevin and Janay were close behind her. Shalaine was happy because her mother was coming back to visit for a few days. Her flight was supposed to land later in the evening.

Shalaine had my manhood jumping at the sight of her dressed in jeans that had rips in the thighs and flared out at the bottom. The jeans weren't skintight, but Shalaine's curves were still very visible. She had only been pregnant for two seconds, and my baby was thickening her up already. She was rocking a simple white tube top and on her head was a white scarf. She had it back just enough so that her slicked back edges were visible, and large gold hoops hung from her ears. Shalaine was bad. Bad as hell.

"Hi," she sang as she approached us with a large bowl in her hand. "I'm done with the pasta salad, and I'm about to peel the eggs and get started on the deviled eggs."

I stood up and took the bowl from her. I almost kissed her, but I had to remember that she had the kids with her. We still hadn't told them about the baby or that we were in a relationship. "Thank you," I eyed her discreetly. Shalaine smiled bashfully.

"What?!" Janay screeched. "Why do y'all look just alike?" The way her mouth was hanging open as her head whipped back and forth made all of us laugh.

"Y'all are twins?" Tevin asked in just as much awe as Janay.

"We're triplets," I answered him. "Twins are two. Triplets are three. This is my brother, Justice, and this is my brother Loyal."

I was only able to tell them apart because Loyal had his hair in braids going straight back, and Justice had the Pop Smoke braids. I was also starting to learn their mannerisms. Justice flicked the tip of his nose a lot and was always scowling. Loyal bobbed his head a lot like there was a beat that only he could hear. He was definitely the friendlier of the two. Justice wasn't mean though. I could tell he just didn't fuck with a lot of people. Lowkey, I was a mixture of them both.

"Your mama had three babies in her stomach at the same time?" Tevin asked with wide eyes and once again, we all laughed.

"Yes, she did," Shalaine answered. "Baby, you've never seen triplets before?"

"No!"

Shalaine giggled. "I'm going to go get started on the eggs. Come on."

"Can we jump on the trampoline?" Janay looked up at me with those bright eyes that I couldn't say no to. Her father was a sucka, because if she was mine, I'd be there every day.

"Of course you can lil' homie."

Janay and Tevin ran for the trampoline, and Shalaine sauntered towards her house.

"That's your BM?" Justice asked.

"Yeah, but the kids don't know, so we act like we're only friends in front of them. She has baby daddy drama. Actually, she's married. She wants a divorce, but the fuck nigga won't cooperate. He's out on bond and has a case coming up for wire fraud, identity theft, and some more shit. He's acting like a bitch because she doesn't want to be with him anymore, and he beat her in front of the kids, so me and Orlando stomped that nigga out. They've been through some shit, so we're chilling right now."

"I was about to say you better be careful dealing with a married woman, but if he's a fuck nigga like that I'd taunt his ass every chance I got."

"Damn right. Shorty found out she has Lupus. He still put his hands on her. Straight beat her like a man with her kids there." Just thinking about it had me pissed all over again, and I hit the blunt in an effort to calm my nerves down. This was a joyous occasion, and I didn't want to get pissed off thinking about Cliff's lame ass.

Our grandfather came back, and I could only laugh when I saw that he'd bought a large sheet cake. "You really went all out huh old man?"

"Damn right I did. We're going to party like it's our birthday. This is a special occasion. Lord, how I wish your grandmother was here to see it."

I wished she was there too. For many reasons. Family members started to arrive, and we introduced everyone to Loyal and Justice. Everyone was in awe at how much we looked like. Orlando's father had brought a few bottles of liquor and a cooler of beer. More kids arrived for Tevin and Janay to play with. The entire situation was a vibe. I was high as a kite from the few shots of Henny I had and the weed I'd smoked. I licked my lips as I flipped the burgers on the grill and gave Shalaine the side eye.

"You gotta stop standing so close to me 'cus I'm fucked up,

and I almost keep forgetting that your kids are here. I want to rub on that booty so bad. And back up. You don't need to be around all this smoke."

Shalaine sniggered. "I swear you think you're my parole officer, daddy or something."

"You know what it is," I stated flirtatiously as my eyes roamed the length of her frame.

"The fuck?" she frowned, and I followed her gaze to see what she saw.

"This nigga," I sighed when I saw that Cliff was pulling up in her driveway with a car full of niggas. "I guess he brought back up," I chuckled.

Shalaine walked towards her house, and I watched her like a hawk. The only time I looked away was to glance over my shoulder to see where the kids were. I didn't want them to see their father acting an ass for a second time. They were busy running and playing with about seven other kids. More than thirty people were congregated in the house and the backyard, and there was a Spades game going on, so unless shit got really loud next door, I hoped the kids wouldn't hear any commotion.

"Fuck you mean you sold my jewelry?" Cliff yelled walking up in Shalaine's face.

That was my cue. "Aye, you good?" Justice appeared at my side.

"Shalaine's husband is over there acting stupid. I guess he wants ass whooping number two."

"Yo Loyal." Justice didn't hesitate to call for Loyal. He was in no position to do anything because he still wasn't fully healed. I didn't care if I had to go up against Cliff and his niggas by myself. He wasn't about to keep fucking with Shalaine and getting away with it.

"Nigga. I needed money to move with."

"Then you should have sold your shit!"

"You're not supposed to be at my house. The jewelry that I sent to your mom's house is all that was left. What was I supposed to do?"

"I don't give a fuck what you had to do. You didn't hold me down. You didn't want to stick it out with me, but you wanted the money from selling my shit."

"I'm not doing this with you, Cliff. Again, you're not supposed to be over here. Do you want to go back to jail?"

I walked over to them. "I think she asked you to leave. More than once." I spoke up.

Cliff kissed his teeth while still staring at Shalaine. His three homeboys got out of the car, and I didn't even blink. When Cliff finally looked over at me, he did a double take. I didn't have to look to know what had him in awe. He had seen Loyal and Justice.

"Everything good fam?" Orlando and Hendrix made their way over to us, and it was five against four.

"Yo homie you good?" My neighbor Tommy yelled from across the street. He had just pulled up and was making sure we didn't have to stomp some ass before he went inside.

"I'm good homie. Light work."

"Aight."

I smirked at Cliff. "Unless you want your ass beat again, I suggest you leave. Bringing them changes nothing, and if I get on yo' ass again, it's gon' take an act of God to get me off. This is my last warning."

"You coming at me over a bitch that's still legally married to me. This is my wife! This hoe has my last na——"

I ran up on Cliff, and he was trying to get away from me so fast he tripped over his own feet. I commenced to beating the brakes off him.

"Don't do it," I heard Loyal warn from behind me. All Cliff's friends could do was watch as he got his ass handed to him because my people were there waiting to make sure nothing happened.

"You done yet?" I asked out of breath before I punched Cliff in the head. "You done with this dumb shit? I'll put you in the dirt 'bout Sha Sha," I punched him again and blood spurted from his nose. "You better be glad I don't want the kids to end up seeing this shit. That's the only reason I'm leaving you conscious." I backed up, and Cliff got up off the ground. It took him a few seconds because he was dazed. Eventually, two of his friends stepped forward and pulled him up.

"I'm sorry," Shalaine looked at me with eyes full of regret.

"For what? Don't apologize for that nigga. Come on. I'm thirsty."

"Yeah, this nigga our brother for sho'," Justice laughed hyped up behind what he'd just witnessed. "He beat the Mario coins out that nigga!"

All I could do was chuckle. There were really three of us. I had just poured a shot of Hennessey and sat down in an empty chair when a sudden chill went through the muggy air. I heard someone mumble, "Oh shit," and I looked around to see what was up.

My nostrils flared as Simone, her large round belly, and her boyfriend, Monte stepped into the backyard like they'd been invited. Her gaze found me, Loyal, and Justice, and her lips parted and formed an O. The four of us engaged in a brief stare down until Simone tore her gaze away. Her eyes traveled over the sea of faces until they landed on my grandfather.

"That's how you gon' do me, daddy? I wasn't invited?" She had the nerve to look hurt.

"Simone, this isn't the time for this. I invited the boys over here, so they could get to know family. Until the day Wise sought them out and found them, you hadn't uttered their names. Why would I think you wanted to be here?"

"Or that they wanted to meet you?" I spoke up.

"Not today, Truce. I know you hate me. You don't have to let the world know."

"Fuck outta here," I waved her comment off. "The day I saw you and you told me you were having a baby, those were the most words you spoke to me in years. You don't fuck with me. The child that lived in the same house as you for three years. Why would anyone think you wanted to see the ones you sold?"

"I don't need anybody speaking for me and putting false narratives out there. I didn't *sell* my kids. There is nothing new about people paying money to adopt kids."

"Now isn't the time, Simone. Let them reach out to you on their own and if they do so, you can talk to them in private."

"Respectfully, she's their mother." Monte spoke up.

"Nigga, disrespectfully she's not shit," I spat.

"Let's go." Simone stormed off, and Monte followed her like the simp that he was.

There was a brief moment of awkward silence before Justice pulled a blunt from behind his ear. "This what we been missing having family functions? Shiiittt, we need to have some more of these."

All I could do was laugh. There were really three of us.

JUSTICE

I walked into the house that Wise owned. Truce and his crew were in the house doing the floors in the living room. Truce stopped what he was doing long enough to give me dap.

"I'm supposed to be meeting Wise here. This is a nice lil' spot," I looked around.

"Yeah, it is. It's gon' be dope as hell when I'm done with it."

It had been two days since the cookout at our grandfather's house, and the shit was cool I couldn't even front. Everyone welcomed us with open arms and was nice and inviting. Nothing felt forced, and I could tell they were really interested in getting to know us. Seeing Simone was interesting. I had gone twenty-four years without knowing what my mother looked like. I wasn't really moved by her little speech. I wasn't inclined to believe that she'd treat me any better than she'd ever treated Truce, and I was good on her. I had a mother figure for thirteen years, and that was better than nothing. I still thought about Janice often. I couldn't even be mad at her that she couldn't handle three kids but a part of me wondered how life would have been had she decided not to take any of us, so we wouldn't have to be split up. Growing up with Truce would have been dope.

Wise walked into the house with a tall dark-skinned guy behind him. The man was carrying a black tote bag. Wise walked over to me and gave me a homeboy hug. "This is my right-hand man, Jake."

I nodded at Jake, and he returned the gesture. He passed me the tote bag, and my adrenaline rushed as I grabbed it. I knew there were twenty bricks inside, and that was a whole hell of a lot of money. I had copped one brick in the past. A nigga wasn't broke, but I wasn't in the big leagues either. I made enough money to live a comfortable life, but I wasn't balling. Those twenty bricks were about to change all that. Wise had let me know that I didn't have to pay him shit for the bricks. If I sold them whole and charged around $24,000 for each brick, I would be in possession of $480,000. Wise also told me that when I wanted more bricks, he would sell them to me for $10,000 cheaper than what he charged everyone else.

I hadn't forgotten my promise to Loyal that I would get serious about investing money and try to wind down my time in the streets. If a person really twisted my arm and forced me to choose, I'd probably just own some laundromats and cleaning businesses or some shit. I wanted other people to work for me. I didn't want to have to put in work. If I hustled with Wise as my plug for a year and did things the right way especially with a $480,000 head start, I knew I would be set. Wise had also stayed true to his word and had his realtor show Loyal some buildings. Wise put an offer on the building that Loyal liked, and the offer was accepted. Bro was about to have his own tattoo shop.

"I appreciate you looking out," I told Wise and gave him dap.

"No problem. Hit me up if you need anything else and um,"

he stepped closer to me. "I know you don't know her like that, but if you happen to see Lauren, I'm still looking for her."

I cocked my head to side. "If shorty doesn't want to be found why not leave her be? You don't think she's paid off her debt to you?"

Wise smirked as if what I'd just said was funny. "She is cute. Ass is fat, and she has some okay pussy. I can see if you'd be caught up with her especially since she saved you and all, but my business with Lauren is my business, son. Don't get caught up trying to play Captain Save a Hoe."

Wise and I had a brief stare down before I nodded at him and walked off. "I'll holla at you later, Truce."

It lowkey pissed me off when Wise said that Lauren had okay pussy. It only reminded me that they'd had sex once. I wasn't even about to get into it with Wise, but he was really on some sucka shit. Migo put me and Loyal on when we were thirteen. He could have had morals and standards and turned us away, but he was a businessman, and we came at him with money. We asked to be put on. From my understanding of the history between Lauren and Wise, he offered her a place to live then forced her to move dope for him. That was some foul shit because her back was against the wall, and if she didn't want to sleep outside or sell her body for a place to stay, she had to do what Wise told her to do. The fact that he dragged shit out for as long as he did was some cruddy shit.

I was going to mind my business though. I used the word friend very loosely but aside from Loyal, the only other person that I halfway trusted was Jock. I'd known Jock for nine years, and he never came across as someone that I had to side eye. In fact, when he learned that me and Loyal lived alone, every time his mom cooked a big meal, he used to bring us plates and shit. When we weren't eating fast food we ate basic stuff like cereal, Ramen noodles, and microwavable dinners. Jock was the same age as us telling us we needed to eat vegetables and more fruit. His mom was a beast in the kitchen and anytime he brought us plates piled high with food, our mouths started watering instantly.

He told me that he wanted to cop some weight from me, and I was going to look out for him and charge him less than I would charge anyone else. "What it do playboy?" he jested as he gave me dap.

Jock used to deal with Carmen's sister. For a while, we would run into each other in passing. He would be leaving their crib and I'd be going in. They stopped dealing with each other a few months before Carmen got pregnant. He was talking to a white girl and though she was bad, I couldn't do it. I wasn't completely against dabbling in other races, but white girls were a strong hell muhfuckin' no.

"The hoes do love me," I joked back as I sat down on his couch.

Jock pulled money from his pocket, and I passed him some of the coke that I had already taken out of one of the kilos and broken down into the five ounces that he wanted to buy.

"I bet this shit is like that," Jock marveled as he looked over the package. "It's hard to get in with Wise. That nigga is selective as hell about who he serves, and he's still rich as fuck. I can only imagine what his pockets would look like if he served everybody who wanted to cop from him."

"Being greedy is how people get jammed up. It's hard to trust anybody, but being selective definitely might save a lot of trouble in the long run."

"You're right about that." Jock passed me the blunt he'd been smoking.

Aside from my brothers, he was probably the only person I'd smoke with that I didn't see roll the blunt. My phone rang, and I didn't recognize the number.

"Hello?"

"Hi. May I speak with Justice Edwards?"

My brows hiked at the professional voice that was on the other end of the phone. "Speaking," I replied as I expelled weed smoke from my lungs.

"My name is Megan Lawrence, and I work at Orange Med Hospital. Are you familiar with a Ms. Enchanted Davis?"

I drew back a bit with a frown on my face. I used to rock with Enchanted heavy for about a year. She got pissed about me and Carmen, and we had a big argument. I hadn't seen her since. "I am." I was trying to figure out where the conversation was going.

"Ms. Davis recently gave birth. Two days ago, to be exact, she had a very difficult delivery. One of those problems landed her in the ICU. While she was conscious, she gave your information and said if anything happened to her to give him to you. We're calling because Shiloh is ready to be discharged, and Ms. Davis is still in ICU on a breathing machine in a medically induced coma."

I had to be high as hell and hallucinating. I sat up straighter. "Um, I'm not sure why she gave you my information, but I didn't know anything about a baby. I haven't talked to Enchanted in about seven mo——" I stopped talking as the reality of the situation hit me. It had been seven or eight months since I saw her.

"I'm only doing what she asked me to do. I don't know the back story, but if you don't come get the child or know a way to reach her next of kin, we'll have to call social services."

I closed my eyes and tried to gather my thoughts. Any child going into the system was a trigger for me. I wanted to say the situation wasn't my problem, but even if I wasn't the father, I might be a better temporary home for the child than anybody else. A lot of foster parents didn't have good intentions and should have never been granted custody of anyone's child. I may seem mean and heartless to a lot of people, but when it came to kids, I didn't play games, and I didn't like fuck shit.

"When do I need to come get him?"

"He will be officially discharged in the morning. You can come get him around 9 AM. I'll give you until five PM before I call someone."

"Okay."

I ended the call and stared into space. "You gon' pass the blunt?" Jock asked. "Who was that?"

It took me another few seconds to acknowledge Jock. I passed him the blunt while still stuck on stupid.

"Yo, Justice who was that? Damn you look like you just got the worst news of your life."

"Enchanted had a baby, and she told those people it was mine. She's in a coma, and I have to go get the baby. How in the fuck?"

Jock's eyes bucked. "Damn. Maybe that's why she was so mad about Carmen."

I ran my hand over my frizzy braids. Weed wasn't enough. I jumped up and went into Jock's kitchen. "Please tell me you got a bottle in this muhfucka." My eyes darted around the room.

I spotted the bottle the same time as he responded. "I have a swallow of Henny."

I grabbed the bottle that appeared to have about two shots left inside. I drank straight from the bottle. I ignored the burn in my throat and chest as I thought about the fact that I had to go pick up a three-day old baby. Once the bottle was empty, I didn't feel a bit better. How was I going to trap with a damn baby? I didn't know anything about babies. I didn't have a mother or a grandmother to run to. I had just met my family, and I didn't even know half their phone numbers. Winter was a female, but she was young. Did she know anything about babies? I knew that Loyal was just as clueless as me.

I went back into the living room. "I gotta go. I need to make some moves and get some more alcohol because I can't do this shit sober," I shook my head still in shock. Two babies? I was wilding like that? I was going to take a paternity test to make sure, but I knew there was a good chance that Shiloh was mine. Me and Enchanted messed around heavy for about five months. We had sex at least five times a week. That's why she was so hurt when she found out about Carmen. Enchanted was never my girl, but we used to be together almost daily. I may have made her my girl eventually, but Carmen was bad as hell and had some good pussy. Plus, I had a few other women beating my door down. I just wasn't quite ready to take myself out of the game and be faithful. I couldn't be mad at her if she got tired of sharing and tired of waiting. But she was dead ass wrong not to tell me about the baby.

After I got in my car, it took me a minute to start the engine. I just couldn't get it together. I racked my brain, and the only person I could think to call was Lauren. She was probably the only female that would help me without having an attitude and being in her feelings about me having a kid. As shocked as I was, I didn't feel like hearing anybody's mouth or trying to coddle anybody. I said the words, 'I'm single' so much it was ridiculous. I had never gotten attached to a female because her pussy was good. There had to be way more like her personality and character. My character was A-1, but I didn't have the best personality. The way women fell in love with me over looks and dick was insane. not even treating them badly deterred them from wanting me. Therapy should be free for women with those kinds of issues.

"Hello?" Lauren's voice was deep, and sleep filled.

"Damn you still asleep?" I asked with a frown.

"Nigga, I worked last night. What do you want?"

"I don't have time for you to be rude. I need a big ass favor, and I'll compensate you for your time. You don't have to do it right now, but I need it done before the day is over."

"And what would that be?" I could hear the skepticism in her tone.

"I got a call from the hospital, and apparently, I have a kid that I didn't know about. His mom is in ICU, and I have to go get the baby in the morning. I don't know how long I'm going to have him, and I don't know anything about what he needs. Can you go shopping with me?" Lowkey my ass was panicking.

"Another one? Damn. You don't like condoms, huh?"

I kissed my teeth. "Nigga, now is not the time."

Lauren chuckled. "I can meet you at like four. I need a few more hours of sleep if I want to function properly. Where do you want to meet?"

"I don't know where I need to get baby stuff from."

Lauren groaned. "I'll meet you at Target. I'll text the location nearest me."

"Aight bet. Thank you."

"Ummhmmm."

I exhaled a sigh of relief. Now, I just had to go make some money, so I could go baby shopping.

A few hours later, I was walking towards the entrance of Target. Lauren was already there, and she had her hair slicked back in a bun with two curly coils hanging by her ear. She had three diamond studs in each ear, and she was dressed in a yellow tennis skirt, a white sports bra, and white sneakers. Each leg had gold anklets, and shorty looked good as hell. My manhood stiffened as I started at her feet, and my orbs trailed all the way up her body and to her face. Her juicy gloss covered lips had me wanting to do some things to her. She smirked, and I kissed my teeth.

"Don't start."

"You're about to have two infants. That is ghetto as hell. Anybody can get that wood, huh?"

"You can't."

"Baby, I don't want it."

"Yes, you do." We walked inside the door, and I eyed her behind as I pulled out a shopping cart. "I'm already going through it, and you're not being supportive. What am I going to do with a newborn? I have to feed it and change the diapers? I don't even know if he's mine, but if I don't go get him, he's going in the system."

Lauren's facial expression softened. "That's really nice of you. Okay. I'll stop the jokes. Come on, Justice." She said the last part in a lil' baby voice, and I narrowed my eyes and stared at her.

Lauren erupted into laughter. "Okay damn. Come on. You get sensitive when you're nervous. I'm only helping you because I feel sorry for the baby. I don't work tonight, so I can come help you if you want. I've never taken care of a baby myself, but I've been around my cousins and their kids."

"Yoooo," my shoulders slumped with relief. "You're not that ugly after all. Thank you. I'll pay you. Whatever you want."

Lauren's upper lip curled. "Ugly? Don't make me go back on my word. Asshole."

I chuckled as she led me to the section of the store that we needed to be in. I watched her hips sway with each step that she took. Lauren was the furthest thing from ugly that I'd ever seen. I hated all the impure thoughts that were running through my mind because I'd just been stressing this kid that I didn't know about. Thinking with my dick had gotten me in trouble more than a few times, but I was still a man with great vision, and I saw what I saw.

"You're definitely going to need diapers." Lauren stopped in front of various brands of diapers. "They come in different sizes according to the baby's weight. Even though he was just born, if he's on the big side, he may not even fit newborn, or he may not be in newborn long. I'd say get one of each to be on the safe side. Newborn and size one.

I bobbed my head grateful that I brought her because it was simple stuff like that, I had no clue about. Lauren grabbed some wipes and put them in the cart. "Bibs are a must. Sometimes when babies burp, they throw up a little milk. Socks, blankets, onesies," I watched as she tossed items in the cart. "Formula is necessary since mom can't breastfeed, and you'll need bottles. A car seat, somewhere for the baby to sleep. Whew, one cart might not be enough."

"This is crazy," I sighed as item after item was placed in the cart. "What if I spend all of this money, and he's not even mine. She gave my information to the people at the hospital, but she went nine whole months without telling me she was pregnant?"

"Just look at it like you're doing a good deed. The baby is innocent. Just like you want to keep him out of the system, buying him these things will ensure that he comes home with everything he needs to be comfortable and cared for properly. And you need to air your house out. The smell of marijuana isn't good for the baby."

I groaned. "This is some straight bullshit."

Lauren giggled. "He'll need a little bathtub, some soap, washcloths, awwww look at this wittle robe."

"Bro, why do babies need so much stuff?"

Lauren cut her eyes at me. "Really?"

We spent more than an hour in Target. I shelled out a little over $1,000 on baby items. There were so many bags that Lauren had to put some stuff in her car because I also had huge boxes that contained the car seat, a swing, a bassinet, and the bathtub. If Shiloh turned out not to be mine, then Enchanted got one hell of a come up by putting him off on me. All kinds of thoughts ran through my mind as I drove, like what if she died? I'd never let my son go into foster care, but most people had nine months to prepare for a kid. I didn't even have nine days. Enchanted was cruddy for keeping the baby from me, but if she died, it would be messed up. I didn't know how to get in touch with her people, and obviously they didn't know at the hospital either.

Enchanted was from New Jersey, but she moved to Diamond Cove to attend college. After she graduated, she decided to stay around, and she worked at a bank. I knew she had a mom and two sisters that she talked about often. Did they know she was pregnant? The entire situation was weird. At my house, Lauren started taking items out of her car, and she carried them up to my door. After numerous trips to the car, we finally had everything inside the house.

"I can organize everything for you and put it away. I know niggas just throw stuff anywhere."

I kissed my teeth as I pulled some money from my pocket. "Look around my house. I'm neat and clean. I do this every day. But you can put the stuff away if you want. He's going to go in the bedroom right across from mine. There's already a dresser in there, but that's it."

"Okay."

"Here." I counted out $2,000 and gave it to her.

"I would have done it for free, but I don't be turning down no money."

"You're not supposed to turn it down apple head." Lauren

balled up her fist and punched me in the arm. My eyes bulged out of my head. "Shorty, are you crazy? That's the arm I got shot in."

"I don't care," she scowled at me. "You gon' get enough of insulting me."

"Don't get in your feelings over my insults. You know you're one of the baddest things walking the streets of Diamond Cove."

"You definitely don't have to gas me."

"I can't win for losing with your super dome as——" I jumped out of the way before she could hit me again. "Aight damn." I laughed. "I need to roll up. My entire day has been blown with this shit. I'm supposed to be out making money, and I'm spending bands on a possible son that I just found out about."

"Stop your blood clot crying," Lauren spoke in a fake Jamaican accent as she walked away.

All I could do was chuckle and shake my head. Shorty was something else. I rolled the blunt and took several tokes before going into what would be Shiloh's room granted he was mine.

"Justice," Lauren whirled around to face me. "You're smoking in here? Really?"

"Chill out. He's not coming home until the morning. I'm going to open the window and spray the room down." I lowkey liked how strongly she felt about a kid that she had never even seen. Lauren and I shared some of the same kinds of trauma, and I think it affected us both in similar ways.

There were way too many predators in the world ready to prey on kids that didn't have proper love and guidance at home. Wise hadn't done shit to me, and he'd been cool so far, but he preyed on shorty, and I'd never sugarcoat that shit just because he was my pops. Lauren went back to putting things away, and I leaned against the door frame and studied her as I smoked. Shorty was sexy. And I liked the way she was making everything all neat and organized. She'd grabbed some grey baskets, and she was

organizing his lotion, creams, Vaseline, etc. in one and putting
socks, bibs, etc. in the others before placing them in the closet.

"You want to hit this?"

"Yeah." Lauren took a break from putting everything away
and walked over to me to retrieve the blunt.

I peered at her through hooded lids. "You might not want to
stand in front of me like that," I warned her with a lick of my lips.

Lauren stared into my eyes as she blew weed smoke out of her
mouth. "Why not? I know I'm not tempting you. I can't get the
dick, remember?" she smirked.

"I can make an exception for you," I stated in a low tone. I was
high as shit, and my dick was harder than steel.

"If you don't get the fuck," Lauren kissed her teeth and rolled
her eyes.

"Nah, I'm fucking with you. I'm for real though. I know I
told you the last time you came over that I wasn't going to try
anything. I'm not gon' front like I'm not attracted to you though.
I might have to go in the other room while you finish this."

There was an expression on Lauren's face that I couldn't quite
read. She cleared her throat and passed the blunt back to me. "I'm
not about to be that hoe that slept with a father and son."

I frowned. "Who said you're a hoe?"

"Really, Justice?" she chuckled. "No one would have to *call*
me a hoe. That would simply be some hoe shit."

"I'm a hoe," I shrugged passively.

Lauren glowered and turned her back to me to head back over
to the closet. I gently grabbed her arm. "Look, on some real shit,
you don't have to sleep with me. You don't have to do shit you
don't want to do, but what I'm telling you is that I'm attracted to
you. The chemistry is there whether you want to acknowledge it
or not. I already told you how I felt about the way Wise handled
you. I don't have any respect for that shit. You and him are some

old shit that never should have happened, and it's not on my mind. It shouldn't be on yours either."

Lauren didn't respond, so I cupped her chin in my hand. We had a brief stare down before I spoke again. "You got it?"

"I got it."

My dick was still hard, and she hadn't made any moves to get away from me, so I took my chances. I dipped my head and pecked her lips softly. When she didn't protest I did it a second time, but I went a step further and snaked my tongue into her mouth. I was still holding the burning blunt between my fingers as Lauren and I shared a deep tongue kiss. Finally, she pulled back.

"Whether you think I'm a hoe or not, I know you like to have sex as a past time. And that's cool, but I already had sex with your father. That's not something I can forget. I'm not going to have sex with you just because I'm here, and we're both horny."

"What you want, Lauren? You want me to tell you that I look at you as more than ass? I do. I'm not trying to be in a relationship with you at this very moment, but I let you come to my crib because I look at you as someone that I'm developing a friendship with. I asked you to help me today because I look at you in *that* way. Not just a sexual way. We don't have to have sex though. I promise it's cool."

Lauren stepped closer to me, and that was all it took. I scooped her ass up so fast, I may have given her whiplash. In my bedroom, I placed her on the floor and put the blunt in the ashtray, so I could undress.

"I hope you have condoms," she gave me a look as she unzipped her jeans.

"I do, and I have my STD records in my phone." I stuck out my tongue at her, and she giggled while shaking her head.

"Childish."

"I'm 'bout to show you that I'm all man."

The moment Lauren was on her back, I placed a trail of kisses down her stomach and to the inside of her thigh. I sucked gently on her flesh while rubbing her clit slowly. Lauren released a soft moan as I French kissed her clit. A nigga didn't eat pussy often, but I knew I hadn't lost it. When I sucked her clit into my mouth, Lauren's moans grew louder. She smelled and tasted clean as fuck, and her sticky essence had her flower coated. Those were all good signs that the pussy was good. If her shit was just okay with Wise it may have been more on him than her. Maybe he felt he was turning me off from wanting her by telling me the pussy was okay, but he hadn't stopped anything.

"Justice," she whined as she lifted her hips off the bed and bucked against my face. My ego was stroked because I hadn't even been down there for five minutes.

The moment I came up for air and made my way upwards, Lauren attacked my lips. She kissed me hungrily as she gently jacked my dick. Her hands on my tool felt so good, I couldn't wait to push up inside of her. I felt around on the bed for the condom. I broke the kiss. "Put it on," I instructed her.

Lauren peered into my eyes as she got on her knees. "I want to taste it first."

She didn't have to tell me twice. I laid on my back while she gazed at my dick while jerking on it. I hissed as Lauren pretty much swallowed my dick. She clenched my member in her hand as she devoured me. Lauren gagged a bit then pulled back and spit on my dick. Her tongue slid up and down my shaft before she circled her tongue around my tip then took me back into her mouth. Lauren cupped my balls as she sucked the tip only. While jacking my member, she moved her mouth down to my balls and sucked them into her mouth.

Grabbing a handful of her curls, I murmured her name as I fucked her face. Lauren cleaned all of her saliva off my pole before tearing open the condom wrapper and rolling it onto my penis. I got up and she laid down. After climbing in between her legs, I sucked on her neck as I pushed myself into her inch by inch. Lauren opened her legs wider and invited me in as she caressed the back of my head and released soft groans.

I nuzzled my face in the crook of her neck as she locked her legs around my waist and wound her hips. Wise had the game fucked up if he thought Lauren's pussy was simply okay. She felt so good that I had to dead the slow strokes and turn my savage up. The moment I began to pound in and out of her, Lauren locked her arm around my neck and cried out as she came.

"This pussy fye," I growled before pecking her on the lips. I needed to pull out of her for a moment, so we could change positions if I didn't want to cum. "Face down ass up," I panted.

I licked my lips as I admired Lauren's round ass and her pretty, pink, glistening, pussy. My dick stood at attention, and I spread her cheeks open as I guided myself into her. Lauren tossed her head back and moaned loudly. I smacked her ass cheek so hard that my hand stung.

"Justice," she cried out as she twerked on my pipe.

"Say that shit again," I demanded through clenched teeth.

"Justice, oh my, ummmmmmm."

"You sound sexy as fuck." I smacked her ass again before grabbing a handful of her curls. I slammed in and out of her until her body was convulsing. "Got damn, Lauren," I grunted as I came inside the condom.

She collapsed on my bed on her stomach, and I smacked her butt cheek. "You gonna have to change my sheets."

"I don't live here."

"But you messed my bed up. Matter fact never mind. Don't change them yet. I want some more of that before you leave."

LAUREN

I wasn't sure why I was nervous sitting across from Niles, but I was. We had finally decided to meet up for breakfast, and my stomach was doing somersaults to the point that I didn't even really have an appetite. I sipped my orange juice because my mouth was super dry while he eyed me with a smile on his chestnut-colored face.

"I definitely think you look like me."

"That doesn't really hold much weight because some people swore I looked like James too."

Niles scoffed at the comment. "Is he still in your life? He never told you that he wasn't your father?"

"I haven't seen James since the day he packed his belongings and left my mother. I just assumed that because they were no longer together, he didn't want anything to do with me. I didn't think it was fair, but I didn't ask any questions. My mother wasn't the kind of woman you said a lot to unless you wanted to be cursed out and called names."

"She's always been an evil bitch. That's the main reason I left her, but I think it goes deeper than her being mean. I don't know if she's bipolar or what, but she has issues. When she took up with James as fast as she did and told me you weren't mine, I was almost happy to be rid of her. But when I saw your baby picture. I knew you were mine. She was so vindictive though, she kept saying James was your father. I hate that bitch."

"You aren't the only one," I chuckled. "I often wondered why she even had me if she hated me so bad. I never did a thing to her, but that's water under the bridge," I stated sadly.

"No, it's not because I can tell that it bothers you, and I'm sorry you had to go through that. She's going to find herself a bitter, lonely, old woman because no one wants to be around her evil ass."

"Do you have any other kids?" I was tired of talking about the woman that birthed me.

"No. I never had other kids. I kind of wished I had, but I never got married, and the situation with your mother left a real bad taste in my mouth. I never got to experience any part of fatherhood. All I can do is hold my breath and hope I live long enough to have grandkids."

"Don't hold it too long," I chuckled, and he laughed.

"You're still young. You have plenty of time, and I hope I do too. I go to the gym and try to take care of myself. I hope I live a long life but hey we never know."

"No, we don't."

"I know you're here, but I still have to ask. Are you open to having a relationship with me? I know I missed a lot, but there's still so much that we can do. We still have time."

He looked so hopeful that it melted my heart. "I'd like that." I smiled. Having at least one parent that cared about me and wanted a relationship with me was better than not having either parent in my life. I wasn't going to let my mother rob me of the chance to have that. "So, tell me about yourself. I'm all ears."

Niles was going all in, and we hadn't even discussed the paternity test. He was a handsome man standing about 5'11 with a salt and pepper beard and bald head. If he wasn't harping on a paternity test, then I wasn't either. It would suck to get to know him and then find out he wasn't my father, but disappointment wasn't an emotion that I was unfamiliar with.

"There's not a lot to tell. I'm a bartender. I make pretty good money, but I don't think bartending is something that I want to retire from. I really like animals, so I've been thinking about taking classes to become a vet tech. Other than that, I live alone and have a pretty boring life." I wasn't about to tell him that from sixteen up until a few weeks ago, I had to sell dope and do whatever one of the biggest drug dealers in the city told me to do.

Niles laughed, and my brows furrowed. I hadn't said anything funny, so I was confused. When he saw my perplexed expression, he held his hands up. "I'm not laughing at you. It's just funny to me because I loved animals when I was a kid. I mean loved them to the point where my mother had to start searching me when I came in from playing to make sure I didn't have animals on me. Once I tried to sneak a baby bird in the house that had fallen out of its nest, and another time I tried to sneak in a frog."

I giggled. "I have never loved animals *that* much, but they are interesting to me. I can watch Animal Planet all day."

"Let's go to the Aquarium one day. And the zoo." The excited gleam in Niles' eyes was enough to make me want to cry. I had never in life felt wanted or loved by a parent. This man had been around me for two seconds, and he was already more invested in me than my mother ever had been. No matter how touching it was, I wasn't going to cry in front of him, however, so I sucked it up.

"Okay. We can do that," I agreed slowly. "Do you have a big family?"

"My father is one of my best friends. My mother had a stroke two years ago, and she's not quite the same, but she's fighting. My father is determined not to put her in a nursing home, so between him, me, and my mother's sister, we all take care of her. I drive trucks locally, so I don't go too far, but some days, I drive long hours. I do what I can for her though. I'd love to introduce you to my parents and my Aunt Wanda."

I shifted in my seat. I couldn't keep ignoring the obvious even though I'd tried. "You want to do all this before you take the paternity test? I know you might be confident, but what if you aren't my father? What if my mom was telling the truth, and James is my father?" The thought made a bitter taste appear in my mouth out of nowhere. Neither one of them was fit to raise dogs let alone a child.

"I see myself and my mother all in your face, but if you want to take a test to be sure, we can. In my heart, I know you're my daughter."

I smiled, and Niles and I sat and continued to converse for another thirty minutes. I really didn't want breakfast to end, but I had promised Justice that I would help him with the baby. In the car, I went from being happy about meeting my father to remembering the sex I had with Justice, and I couldn't stop smiling for a different reason. That man's dick was everything. I felt like such a whore comparing a father to a son, but my young, dumb ass had really thought that Wise's sex was all that. Justice showed up and showed out. And the fact that he didn't care that I made a mistake and slept with his father made me feel unjudged, but I would never forget it. No matter the circumstances, I had slept with father and son, and that was lowkey cringe to me. It would forever be fuck Wise though.

It may have been unfortunate that I slept with Justice's father, but the similarities that we shared made him the most relatable person I'd ever met in my life. My connection to Justice was kind of trauma based, and I knew that wasn't a good thing, but I couldn't help but look at him with stars in my eyes. I could try and fight it all I wanted, but when he stopped being an asshole and threatening me, he was charming, funny, and fine as the fuck. I felt for him when he talked about being on his own since the age of thirteen because it was hard for me at sixteen. I could have never fathomed being on my own at the age of thirteen.

It also tripped me out that we both had just found our fathers. Even though in my eyes Wise was a shitty person, Justice might have a totally different experience with Wise, and I loved that for him. He may have seen himself as this big gangsta nigga that didn't need a father, but no one deserved to be in this world without either of their parents unless they were deceased. Like my mother did me, Justice's mother did him dirty too. I wanted him to have a good relationship with Wise even if I hated the man.

I arrived at Justice's house, and my stomach did back flips as I walked to his door. I was a grown woman and shouldn't have been that nervous to come face to face with a man that I had sex with, but I was. I rang the doorbell, and a few seconds later, Justice answered the door looking like he'd swallowed a rock.

"What's wrong?" I laughed.

"Bro, that baby is so muhfuckin' little. I'm scared to even pick him up. He just started squirming. He's been asleep since we got here an hour ago. How can I take care of him if I can't hold him?" Justice looked so stressed out, I had to laugh. "I'm glad you think this is funny."

I walked past him and entered the house. "Justice, you're not going to hurt him as long as you're gentle. You just have to pick him up and hold him. You've never handled a puppy or anything small?"

"No," Justice replied with a frown as if that was the most absurd question he'd ever been asked.

I walked over to the car seat and pulled the blanket back. "Oh my God, he is so freakin' cute and perfect," I whispered at the small brown baby with the chubbiest cheeks that I'd ever seen. His hair laid on his head like black silk. I was in love. I looked over at Justice. "He is so freakin' adorable."

"Yeah. And little." Justice's eyes darted towards his son. "I'll pay you however much you want. You can't leave me with him, Lauren." Justice was real life panicking, and every time I laughed, he got mad. He kissed his teeth. "Bro."

"Okay okay. I'll stop laughing. Look, you will be fine. Let me teach you how to make his bottles. He might be waking up to eat soon." We walked into Justice's kitchen, and I still had a smile on my face. Seeing him so perplexed and frazzled was more cute than it was funny.

"You always always always have to use sterile water. I'm sure you have bottled water," I looked around the kitchen. "Don't ever make his bottle with tap water."

Justice bobbed his head and grabbed me a bottle of water from the fridge. I removed the bottle warmer that he purchased from the box and walked him through making the bottle and warming it up. I had just finished teaching him how to check the temperature of the milk to make sure it wasn't too hot when Shiloh's soft cry floated into the kitchen. Justice followed me into the living room, and I sat down on the couch and unbuckled Shiloh. I lifted him out of the car seat. He was tiny indeed. I cradled him in my arms and held him close to me as I rubbed the nipple of the bottle along his lip until he opened his mouth and latched on. I looked up at Justice.

"See, it's not hard."

Justice sat down and shook his head. "I need to smoke."

With a giggle I shook my head. "I'm sure you smoked before you picked him up."

"That shit has worn off. Bro," Justice ran his hand over his braids. "Please tell me that you're able to help me today. I mean if you have something to do, I'll figure it out, but I have moves to make. Money has been calling me for the past few hours."

"I don't have anything to do. I'll babysit for you. I go back to work tomorrow night. I can help you until tomorrow afternoon. I have to get some sleep before my shift starts."

"Damn I could kiss you right now," Justice sighed with relief.

I looked down at the baby. His eyes were open, and he was the cutest thing. "How is his mom doing?" I continued to stare at him while I spoke to Justice.

"She's still not awake. They stopped the medication that was keeping her in the coma. Now, they're waiting to see if she wakes up on her own. I took a paternity test before I left the hospital. I guess now we wait."

I turned my attention back towards Shiloh. I had no clue what kind of person his mother was, but I prayed that she loved her son, and that she would do right by him. I also prayed that she would make it, so he wouldn't have to grow up without her.

"There's food in the kitchen, but I'll text you before I come back to see if you want anything."

"Okay."

Justice leaned down, so that his face was directly in front of mine. "Thank you." His minty breath tickled my face.

"You're welcome."

He pecked my lips, and my entire body grew warm. That man did something to me. The only other man that I'd ever lusted after was Wise, but that was on some kid shit. I was a grown woman, and I knew what to look for in a man. My attraction to Justice was more than physical, and it didn't have anything to do with me being enthralled with who he was or what he had. He had a rough life and though he was somewhat guarded and reserved, once he opened up, the Justice that he truly was, was beautiful. He didn't seem like the type to commit, and he was about to have two children only months apart. I had also slept with his father, but I couldn't count him out just yet.

James was the first person to teach me that men weren't shit. But that wasn't on a romantic level. Wise didn't necessarily break my heart, but he was my first crush gone terribly wrong, and he definitely showed me that men had some mess with them. I'd never been in a relationship, and I'd never experienced true heartbreak. Life was too much of a bitch and too tricky for me to believe that Justice was my knight in shining armor. I had a feeling in my gut that if I got in too deep with him it might end bad, but I was already caught up.

I finished feeding Shiloh and burped him. "You are literally perfect," I rubbed my nose across his cheek. "And you have that baby smell," I sighed as he yawned and closed his eyes.

"I bet your mommy would love to hold you." I got teary eyed thinking about Enchanted being in a coma. I didn't have to know her to feel for her. I rocked Shiloh gently until he was knocked out, and I eased him back into his swing.

I went into the kitchen and made him some more bottles for Justice to already have for later. After opening the pantry door, my eyes scanned over all of the snacks. "This nigga is a true smoker. He has snacks for days," I mumbled before choosing an oatmeal cream pie and a bag of chips. I walked over to the fridge and opened the door. I did a little dance as I stood there deciding what I wanted to drink. Finally, I grabbed a can of Sprite and went back into the living room.

I had only been gone a few minutes, but I still glanced down at Shiloh and made sure he was good before flopping down on the couch and finding something to watch on TV. I made a mental note to change his diaper in the next fifteen or so minutes. Growing up, I always told myself that if I had kids, I would never treat them the way my mother treated me. I'd never been in a serious relationship, so I'd never been in love enough with a man to think of having his baby. I knew I wanted at least one child in the future, but I was still figuring out life, and I was still single, so babies were very far off. I'd be lying though if I said Shiloh didn't have my ovaries tingling.

Shiloh slept for more than two hours before he woke up crying for another bottle. I fed him, burped him, and was holding him and cooing since his eyes were open when Justice texted me. He told me the area that he was in, and I asked him to bring me some pasta from an Italian restaurant that he was near. With my pointer finger, I lightly rubbed Shiloh's silky hair. He passed gas causing me to giggle.

"Is that your way of telling me you need your diaper changed?" I went into his room and changed his diaper. After washing my hands, we went back downstairs, and Justice came in the house carrying a large bag of food.

"He been good?"

"Yeap. At his age, all he's really going to do is sleep. It seems like he's eating every two hours and drinking two ounces of milk each time. So when you make his bottles, only make two ounces of milk. As he gets a little older, he'll start drinking more. His eyes have been open for the past thirty minutes or so. He'll probably be asleep again soon."

"Let me see," Justice set the bag of food on the coffee table and came over to the couch. He sat down and looked over at Shiloh.

TREACHEROUS TWINS: JUSTICE

"Here. Hold him, Justice. You have to get used to it. And you have another one on the way."

Justice stared at Shiloh as he scratched his head. "Aight man," he finally sighed. I eased Shiloh into his arms, and he sat back with him.

"See? What's so hard about that?"

"It'll be a damn shame if I fuck these kids up. I don't know nothing about being a father."

"You are not going to mess them up. Stop being dramatic. Think about all the things that your mom did to make you feel good or to make you feel loved and do that. Think about all the things your parents did that made you feel like shit, and don't do that. See, simple."

"Just like that, huh?" he glanced over at me.

"Just like that."

His doorbell rang. "That's probably my brother. Can you get that for me?"

"Yeah."

I went over to the door and unlocked it. When I opened it, Loyal was standing there with fresh braids and a fresh edge up looking just like his brother or should I say brothers. "Hi," I greeted him.

Loyal nodded his head at me. "What up?" He walked into the living room and stood in front of Justice. "You in a competition with Nick Cannon?" Loyal sat down and peered down at Shiloh as I sniggered.

"Nigga, I didn't know about him until they called me from the hospital."

"You haven't been wrapping it up? You hitting all these broads raw?"

"That's what I said," I butted into the conversation as I looked through the bag for my food.

Justice kissed his teeth. "Fool don't worry about my dick. You either big forehead."

I stuck my tongue out at him and sat down with my food.

"What are you going to do when she leaves?" Loyal asked Justice.

Justice's head whipped in my direction. "She's not leaving until tomorrow evening. Right?"

"Wrong. I'll stay kind of late, but I wasn't planning on spending the night. I don't have any clothes or anything."

"Man, go buy something, or run by your crib. I'll double what I was going to pay you."

The panic in his tone made me laugh.

"How are you that afraid of being alone with your child?"

"I don't know anything about babies. I'll be done had the lil' homie screwed up. I've never been around a baby this small before. When Tonya had her baby, we were already out of her house and living on our own. As far as the baby I'm having with Carmen, I thought she'd be around to teach me how to take care of babies. I didn't expect to just get thrown to the wolves like this."

I rolled my eyes upwards as if the thought of spending the night with Justice didn't have me wet. "I guess I'll stay. You better pay attention because I have to work tomorrow night," I reminded him.

"Hopefully, his mom will wake up at any moment and be good within the next week or so. I don't have an issue with taking care of my child, but not having time to prepare kind of put a wrench in my plans. I'm sitting on mad dope and can't move like I want to in order to sell it."

"My last tattoo appointment tomorrow is at six PM. I should be done at the shop by eight. I can come help you tomorrow. I don't know a lot about babies either, but it can't be too hard to figure out."

Justice snorted. "Shit. Did you know you can't make a baby's formula with tap water?"

"No."

"See? Shit is complicated."

I finished my food then stood up to throw my trash away. "I'm going to run to Target to get some stuff. That's closer than me going all the way home."

"Here." Justice passed Shiloh to Loyal and dug around in his pocket.

"You don't have to give me any money. You paid me for helping you yesterday."

"I already told you I was going to pay you, so don't act like you don't want this money."

I kissed my teeth. "Can't even be nice to your uncivilized ass." I walked over to him, and he placed a knot in my palm.

I grabbed my keys and left the house. In my Jeep I counted the money, and it was $790. "Damn Big Money," I marveled. I had made $2,790 off Justice in twenty-four hours. I wasn't mad at that at all.

Hours later, I fed Shiloh, bathed him, got him ready for bed, and placed him in his bassinet. "About tonight," I said as I sat down beside Justice after I took a shower. "He'll probably be getting up every two hours to eat. How many of those shifts you gon' handle?"

Justice looked down at the watch on his wrist. "I need to make two plays. When I come back, I'm going to take a shower, and I'll probably be up for a lil' minute. I might go to bed around two or three."

"Okay that's cool."

Justice placed his hand on my thigh. "I really appreciate you." He was right up in my face, and I was glad I'd just brushed my teeth.

"It's not a problem."

Justice kissed me on the lips then the corner of my mouth. He moved his mouth over and started sucking. "What are you doing?" I asked as my lids fluttered closed.

"Trying to give you a reason to wait up for a nigga," he said then went back to sucking.

By the time he stopped assaulting my flesh with his tongue, my panties were moist. "The way you just teased me only to get up and leave is real lame."

Justice chuckled and licked his lips. "I'll be back soon. I gotta get this bread, but it won't take long."

Justice stayed true to his word because less than two hours later, I had my eyes closed while my toes curled, as Justice placed soft kisses down my spine. I was flat on my stomach, and he was behind me. He spread my cheeks and slid his condom covered dick into me slowly making me blow out a shaky breath.

"You had this shit marinating for a nigga," he whispered before placing a kiss on the nape of my neck.

I threw my head back as Justice massaged my breast and gently bit my earlobe. The satisfaction I was experiencing from his strokes had me trembling underneath him. Justice increased the pace of his strokes, and my vagina spasmed uncontrollably on his member.

"Fuck baby," he groaned as he sexed me harder and faster.

Justice pulled out of me. "Turn over," he demanded breathlessly, and I wasted no time complying.

He plunged back into me, and my back arched. His mouth crashed into mine, and our tongues did a sensual dance as he pinned my arms above my head and stroked me savagely.

"Justice, baby," I moaned against his lips.

"You got me 'bout to bust. Fuck," he groaned as he released into the condom.

I could feel his heart racing as he lay on top of me. We were both trying to catch our breath. After a few minutes, Justice got up and went into the bathroom. He was in there for about three minutes when Shiloh began to cry.

"I got it," he rushed from the bathroom and grabbed his boxer briefs and pajama pants from the floor.

I knew I needed to be resting because I would be getting up early with Shiloh. If a guy ever approached me and told me he had two women pregnant at the same time, I would have politely told him to have a nice life. The fact that I was up in Justice's house helping him with his newborn son that wasn't even a week old spoke volumes. It was one of the craziest things that I'd ever done, but my heart had never been more full of joy.

SHALAINE

I used my fingers to swipe tears from my face before wrapping
my arms around my knees that were to my chest. I buried my
face into my thighs and tried to comfort myself. Everything
happened for a reason. The dull cramping in my stomach was a
constant reminder of what I'd endured hours earlier. After waking
up that morning with terrible cramps and light spotting, I drove
myself to the ER. The kids were with my mom for a few days
visiting family in Virginia. I couldn't go because I didn't want to
take time off work just yet.

When I arrived at the hospital, an ultrasound was done
immediately, and the doctor informed me that he couldn't find a
heartbeat. With tears streaming down my face, I had to get a
D&C. The doctor emptied my womb, and I was no longer
pregnant. The doctor assured me that it may not have anything to
do with me having Lupus, and that a lot of pregnancies ended in
miscarriage. I knew that too, but I still felt like I was cursed.
Maybe I was being punished because I was still legally married
while sleeping with another man. How could I expect my

pregnancy to be blessed when my child was created from me committing adultery? Cliff was stressing me the hell out, and I couldn't even really enjoy being pregnant.

I was a little overwhelmed with the thought of having another baby, but when I found out he or she didn't have a heartbeat my world fell apart. A knock at the door made my heart jolt. I dragged myself off the couch and walked over to the door with legs that felt like lead. The moment Truce and I locked eyes, he rushed into the house and looked around.

"What's wrong? Why you been crying?"

I dreaded saying the words out loud. I also dreaded the questions that would follow my announcement. I opened my mouth, but no words came out. Truce's orbs fell on the hospital band that was still around my wrist.

"Shalaine." When he said my name with authority it meant I only about two seconds to get my shit together because he was getting frustrated.

"I had to go to the ER this morning. I was cramping and spotting. The baby didn't have a heartbeat, so they had to do a D&C. They basically scraped it out of my uterus." I couldn't even look him in the eyes as I broke the news to him.

I was met with silence, and I wasn't surprised. I stood there looking everywhere but at Truce's face. "Why didn't you call me?" he finally spoke. His tone was low and respectful, but I could tell he was upset.

"You were at work and," tears filled my eyes. "I was hoping it was nothing and by the time I got there everything just moved so fast and," as fast as I wiped the tears off my face fresh ones replaced them.

When Truce didn't move to comfort me, I knew he was upset. "None of that sounds like a good reason for not calling me. You didn't think I'd leave work to come be with you? Haven't I shown you that there's nothing that would keep me from being by your side if you need me?" The disappointment in his voice sliced me like a knife.

"I'm sorry." My words came out in a weak whisper. "I just I don't know. My mind was all over the place."

"That was some selfish shit, and you know it. That's why you can't look me in the face."

I looked at Truce, and the pain in his eyes made me feel worse. "I wasn't trying to purposefully hurt you or leave you out. I was scared, but I was hoping it was nothing. You do always drop whatever you have going on to run to my rescue. Time and time again. You've gotten into two different fights with Cliff. I just feel like one day you're going to get tired of having to save me. Having to be my support system while I constantly go through shit. It's got to be draining."

"Fuck outta here," he kissed his teeth. "Have you ever heard me complain? I'm not that last nigga you were with. I'm built different, and if I say I'm here for you for whatever whenever that's what I mean. You didn't get pregnant by yourself. You think I didn't deserve to know what was happening in real time?"

"Truce, I'm sorry. I take full responsibility. Maybe it was selfish. I can't take it back."

"Are you okay?" His tone was flat, and his face was void of emotion.

"Yes," I murmured.

"Do you need anything?"

"No."

"Aight. I'll catch you later. I'm about to go home."

I couldn't breathe as he turned his back on me and walked out the door. My chest was uncomfortably tight. Truce had never been mad with me before, and it wasn't a good feeling. Our first argument and it was because of something I had done. A person would have to be a bird-brained fool to fumble a man like Truce. I burst into tears and stood there sobbing like an idiot for the longest time. Finally, I locked the door and set the alarm. I just wanted to take a shower, take some medication for my cramping, and go to bed. Maybe not having a child at the moment was a blessing in disguise, but I just couldn't see the good in it at the moment. I was glad that I hadn't told the kids yet. No one knew besides Truce. In bed, I stared at the television screen waiting for sleep to take over. All I could do was pray that Truce wouldn't be upset with me for too long. It didn't feel good not having his arms around me. We still hadn't told the kids about our relationship, so anytime they weren't with me, we spent the night together. I pushed out a deep breath and closed my eyes.

My ringing cell phone woke me up. I woke up confused as I looked around the dark room. My phone was on the nightstand, and when I grabbed it, I saw that it was almost midnight. My heart rate increased when I saw Truce's name on the screen. I cleared my throat and answered. "Hello?"

"Disarm the alarm, so I can come in," Truce's gruff voice came through the phone.

"Okay."

My heart was still drumming in my chest, and that was the craziest thing to me. I wasn't afraid of Truce. He would never put his hands on me. But I was afraid of him looking at me again as if I had broken his heart. Having him look at me like that was worse than any of the blows that Cliff ever delivered to me. I scrambled out of bed and disarmed the security system. I heard Truce's feet hitting my porch steps, and I unlocked the door.

He entered the house wearing grey sweats and a white tee. Truce walked past me and went straight into the bedroom. I locked up, set the alarm, and went back into the room where he was already getting undressed.

"I couldn't sleep knowing that you were here alone, but I'm still pissed. I don't want to argue, and I don't want to talk. I'm tired. I just want to sleep."

"Okay."

I got back in bed and breathed a sigh of relief. I had upset him. Probably disappointed him and made him wonder if he still wanted to be with me. But he still didn't want me to be alone. Truce had protected and cherished me more in the time that I'd known him than Cliff had after eight years of being together. He was it for me. I never wanted to be with another man because Truce had set the bar so high, I was more than confident that no one could come behind him and top it. I had to let all of my insecurities and overthinking go before I fumbled the best thing that ever happened to me. I was a work in progress, and prayerfully, Truce would see me through my healing and growing.

The next morning, I woke up before Truce and decided to cook breakfast. I was still down about my miscarriage, but I was more bothered that he wasn't talking to me. Truce came into the kitchen as I was removing bacon from the pan.

"You want me to fix you a plate?" I turned to look at him.

Truce leaned against the wall and stared at me. "How do you feel about the miscarriage?"

"I was sad. I am sad. When the doctor told me he couldn't find a heartbeat all I could do was cry. He wanted to do the D&C right away. I know I could have called, but I just didn't. I kind of started feeling like I was being punished because our child wasn't conceived in the right way."

Truce blew out a frustrated breath. "There you go with that shit. If you go down to file the divorce papers and they serve Cliff, what's the first thing he's going to say? You haven't been separated for a year because he's a bitch. He's not going to cooperate and sign the papers. Therefore, it's not your fault that you're still married. All that technical bullshit is pissing me off. Technically you don't owe that abusive ass nigga shit."

"Okay, Truce," I mumbled. "I'm sorry I didn't call you. I wish I could take it back, but I can't."

He didn't respond, but he sat down at the kitchen table. I took that as a cue to fix his plate which I piled with bacon, scrambled eggs, two pancakes, and strawberries. "You want juice, water, lemonade?"

"I'll take some lemonade."

He still felt some kind of way, and he had every right to. But he was there. He had spent the night, and he was eating my food, so all hope wasn't lost.

"When are the kids coming back?"

"The day after tomorrow."

"You staying with me tonight?"

If my heart could have smiled, it would have. "Yes." I walked over to Truce and placed his lemonade in front of him. Then, I wrapped my arms around his neck from behind. "I apologize, and I'm going to keep apologizing. I'm so sorry."

"You don't have to keep apologizing, Shalaine. It was fucked up, but apologizing over and over isn't necessary. If you apologize to someone once and it's not enough, then fuck it."

"I could never say fuck it when it comes to you. I hate that I hurt you, disappointed you, made you mad, or whatever I did. You didn't deserve that. Your feelings matter too. There's no excuse. I'm sorry."

"Bro, don't say sorry again. Fix your plate and sit down and eat."

"Can I have a kiss?" I asked hopefully.

Truce turned his head to the side, and I leaned around and kissed him on the lips.

"How do you feel about the miscarriage?" I asked him the same question that he asked me.

"I'm disappointed, but these things happen. The pregnancy did catch both of us off guard, and I was happy, but things happen for a reason. Next time, the baby will be planned, and we'll do it the right way."

I sat down at the table. "But what if because of the Lupus, I can't have anymore kids? What if my Lupus is the reason why I miscarried?"

"What did the doctor say?"

"He said that women miscarry all the time and it probably didn't have anything to do my Lupus, but wh———"

"We're going to go with what the person with the medical degree said. I told you a hundred times about stressing yourself out over what if. We're not doing that. When the time is right, we'll have a kid."

I smiled. "Okay."

I got up to fix a plate, and my entire mood was better. Had I called Truce from the moment I noticed I was bleeding, he may have comforted me and made me feel better through the D&C. I was done being hardheaded, stubborn, and all that other shit. Truce was a wonderful man, and he deserved the same kind of energy back that he poured into me. I was going to focus on learning my body and how to watch for Lupus flare ups. I was also going to continue to eat better, take care of myself, and make sure I was as healthy as possible because when we were ready, I would give Truce as many babies as he wanted.

JUSTICE

I walked into Enchanted's hospital room, and I was relieved to see that her eyes were open, and she was no longer hooked up to a ventilator. The nurses had finally gotten in touch with her mother and her sisters, and they were on their way to North Carolina.

"Where's Shiloh?" Enchanted asked in a hoarse voice that I could barely hear. I didn't miss the panic in her eyes.

"He's with my brother's girlfriend."

Her brows furrowed. "Loyal has a girlfriend?"

"Long story. I have another brother, Truce. His girlfriend offered to watch Shiloh for a few hours."

"Oh."

I could tell that she was skeptical about who I may have left him with, but we had bigger issues than that. "Shiloh is fine. I've been taking great care of him with the help of my brothers and a friend. But can you explain to me why I didn't know anything about him?" I had gotten the results of the paternity test, and Shiloh was indeed my son which pissed me off even more.

Enchanted's throat bounced as she swallowed hard. "When I found out about Carmen, I was going to get rid of the baby. I never wanted to be a baby mama. I really thought we were going to be together. I refused to share you, and I wasn't interested in co-parenting."

"So, your selfish ass didn't want the baby if you couldn't have me. But you ended up keeping the baby. You still haven't told me why I didn't know about him. That Carmen excuse is some BS. You knew about Carmen when you gave the nurse my information."

"Because I thought I was going to die and if my son couldn't be with me, I wanted him with his father."

"How fucking sweet."

"Justice, I almost died. I started hemorrhaging, and I lost a lot of blo——"

"And if you would have died, I would have pulled up at your funeral, looked you in your dead ass face, and told you how wrong you were." Enchanted gasped, but I didn't care. "You don't just spring that kind of news on somebody. What if I was a lesser man, and I refused to come get him? He'd be in foster care right now with strangers. Why didn't you give them your mom's information?"

"Maybe you thought I was playing when I said I almost died. I barely gave them your name and number before I passed out. My mom didn't even know I was pregnant. I told you I wasn't going to keep him and by the time I decided to do so, I was ashamed to tell anyone. I came here to go to college not to get knocked up and become a single mother."

"Boo fucking hoo, Enchanted. Shit happens. You're single, and you're a mother, but you damn sure aren't doing it alone. I've spent damn near $2,000 so far on everything he needs. He has a room at my crib, and I got him until you come home.

Once you get home, we can work something out as far as me giving you money on a monthly basis, and me coming to pick him up."

"Thank you, Justice. I really appreciate you for stepping up."

"Yeah whatever. You better be glad your ass didn't die. I should kill you though," I frowned and turned towards the door. "Let me know when they're going to discharge you. I'll bring Shiloh to your crib even if you're not up to keeping him. I'm not bringing him to this germ-infested hospital." I didn't even wait for her to respond before I walked out the door.

I went and made some money then headed home. Shalaine was watching Shiloh at my house because if my son was in her custody, and her husband showed up on that rah rah, I would end up in prison for sure. I had already seen that she had a real live fuck boy on her hands. When I got home, she was feeding him. "All his ass does is eat," I watched Shiloh suck the nipple like he hadn't eaten in days. His eyes were closed, but he was drinking milk like a starved baby.

Shalaine giggled. "Say I'm a growing boy, daddy."

Taking care of Shiloh for the past few days had been crazy. I was really somebody's father. I had no clue how Simone was a female, and she gave her kids away for a measly three racks because whether I felt I was ready to be a father or not, the moment I saw in black and white that Shiloh was mine, my daddy mode turned up real quick. I'd lay anybody down about my son. Maybe she didn't want three kids while she was pregnant, but how could she lay eyes on us and still not want us? That shit was cold. Especially when her parents were willing to help her. She just didn't want to be bothered with us, and no one could convince me otherwise. Fifteen is young to have three kids, but she was old enough to fuck and make three kids she could have raised us with her parents' help.

135

But that shit was water under the bridge. I pulled money from my pocket and handed Shalaine $200. "Thank you."

"I only babysat him for three hours. You sure you want to give me this much?" she asked with raised brows.

"I know how long you were here, shorty. It's cool."

"Thank you." She burped Shiloh, changed his diaper, and put him in his swing.

Truce told me that she miscarried, so I was hesitant to ask her to babysit, but he said she was cool. If being around Shiloh bothered her, she didn't let on. I had made a few thousand dollars for the day, and I was in for the rest of the evening. Having kids changed the hell out of a person's life. The doorbell rang, and I walked towards the door with a scowl on my face because no one had gotten permission to come to my crib. It had better be one of my brothers, or somebody was getting cursed out. When I looked out of the peephole and saw Carmen, I kissed my teeth and my grimace deepened. I hadn't spoken to her since she threw a tantrum, and I knew that she knew better than to pop up at my house.

"Your phone broke?" I asked after I opened the door.

"Huh?" she asked with confusion etched onto her face. Carmen's nose had spread, and her lips were bigger. It almost looked like she'd gotten lip fillers or had an allergic reaction. Seeing the changes that pregnancy was taking her through was interesting as hell, but I was still perturbed.

"Why are you here if you didn't call first?"

"Justice, I'm pre——" her words were halted when Shiloh began to cry.

Carmen pushed past me, and it took a lot of effort on my part not to snatch her ass back. Rolling up in my crib uninvited was bold, and my reflexes had my fingers twitching, but I'd never grab a pregnant person.

"Are you another sister?" Carmen asked Shalaine with a shaky voice. She was on the verge of nutting up. She was trying her best to be calm, but I could hear it in her tone that she thought Shalaine was my girl or something, and she was about to go in.

"I——"

I used my finger to do a slicing motion across my neck. "You don't have to explain shit to her," I told Shalaine, and her mouth clamped closed. "He good?"

"Yeah, he may have a little bit of gas," she was rubbing his tummy in a circular motion.

After I made sure Shiloh was good, I turned to Carmen who had tears in her eyes, and I pinched the bridge of my nose. I wasn't in the mood for dumb shit. "Yo, I don't owe you any explanations especially when I didn't even invite you in my crib, but this is Truce's girl. She's helping me with my son that I didn't know anything about until a few days ago."

Her eyes bucked. "You have a son?! By who?"

"That's what I just said. His mother had a complicated childbirth and ended up in ICU. I have him until she's better. Now, why are you here?" I ignored her last question because who I had a child with was none of her business.

"Wow." Carmen just stared at Shiloh and Shalaine with tears sliding down her cheeks.

I was trying so hard not to be annoyed, but I was teetering on the edge of dragging Carmen to the door by the collar of her shirt and tossing her outside. The amount of times that I had to remind her that we weren't in a relationship was becoming irritating. If she didn't like having to share me, she should have taken a page out of Enchanted's book and got missing. Enchanted was wrong for not telling me about my son, but she wasn't wrong for leaving me alone if she didn't like what I was doing.

I never treated either of them bad, and that was the problem.

You could tell a female that you didn't want a relationship a million times, but if you hung out with them, gave them a few dollars, and treated them like a human being, your words meant nothing, and they would really make the situation way bigger than it was. Me taking a female to the movies didn't mean I wanted to wife her. It meant that I wanted to see a movie, and I didn't want to go alone. Moving forward, I would have to remember to just stick dick to broads and act as if they didn't exist otherwise. Except when it came to Lauren. I wasn't trying to be in a relationship with her, but I wasn't trying to leave her alone either.

Shiloh passed gas, and Shalaine giggled. "Yeah, it was just a lil' gas. I have to get going. You want me to put him in his swing?"

"Nah. I'll take him." I walked over to the couch and sat down. Shalaine put Shiloh in my arms, and I looked up as Carmen wiped tears from her face. "You can follow Shalaine to the door. I'm about to bond with my son. Is the baby good?" I checked.

"You haven't been asking that question," Carmen snapped.

I chuckled. "Can't even be nice to you. Get the fuck out. If it's not about my child, don't call me or come by. Thank you, Shalaine."

"No problem."

Carmen was glaring at me like she wanted to jump on me and slap the taste out of my mouth, but she knew better. We had a stare off and even though she was pissed, she wasn't stupid. She eventually pivoted and stormed out of the house.

"Crazy ass broad." I mumbled looking down into Shiloh's face. "One of the first things I'm going to teach you when you're old enough to understand is to stay away from psychotic females."

The sound of my cell phone ringing woke me up out of my sleep. I was confused as shit until I felt Shiloh on my chest. We dosed off on the couch after I ate, took a shower, fed him, and bathed him. Looking at my phone, I saw that we'd been asleep for about two hours. That was some good ass sleep. I was exhausted from running the streets and taking care of Shiloh. Lauren's name was on my phone screen, so I swiped to accept the call and put her on speaker. I stood up carefully, and walked towards Shiloh's room to put him in his bassinet. I knew he'd be eating soon, but I needed to smoke a blunt.

"Yo."

"Oh, you were asleep. My bad. I just got off work and wanted to check on Shiloh."

"Nah, this is my sexy voice," I joked. "I wasn't asleep. And damn you knew me first. You only called to check on Shiloh?"

"I knew you first, but I like him best."

"That was real rude." I eased Shiloh into his bassinet and watched him for a few seconds before leaving the room.

"How are you doing, Justice?"

"Don't be fake now. Shiloh is asleep. I'm about to turn this baby monitor on and sit on the porch and smoke. I know he'll be up in a minute for his bottle. We were just knocked out for some hours."

"I knew yo' ass was asleep. Okay. I just wanted to make sure my homie wasn't over there taking you through it."

"So, you can't come see me if I got things under control?" my dick stirred at just the thought of seeing Lauren's face. "I had a power nap, so I'm up now. I might need you to put me back to sleep."

There was a slight pause. "Let me run home and take a shower. I worked for seven hours, and those people had my ass running."

"I understand if that cat is a lil' musty."

"Ha!" Lauren shouted loudly. "My shit doesn't get musty on a bad day. You tried it. I just like feeling fresh and washing germs off me when I leave crowded public places like bars and airports. You might not know anything about cleanliness, but it's how some people like to live."

I chuckled. "You done swallowed this dick before. You know my shit is as clean and fresh as they come."

"And you've devoured this cochie before, so you know the same thing."

I licked my lips. "Clean and fresh it is. Juicy and sweet too. Damn hurry up," I sat down in one of the chairs that sat on my back porch and fished a lighter from my pocket.

"I'll be there in about an hour. I'm just getting home."

"Bet."

I smoked and stared into the darkness while thinking about how crazy life had been over the past few weeks. After twenty-four years of not knowing either one of my birth parents, I met them both. My father had put enough bricks in my hands to really change the game. I could go from being comfortable to being borderline wealthy if I kept hustling for a minute. I literally became a father overnight and taking care of Shiloh had changed my perspective on a lot of things. It went from Loyal being the only blood relative that I knew to me meeting my other brother, a sister, and a slew of family members including a grandfather. A nigga's head was spinning from all of the changes that had taken place.

Lauren was also a nice addition to my life. In the group home, I heard a lot of sad stories. There were crack babies that had been sold by their mothers. Some of the stories were grimy as hell and made my situation with Simone look like it was nothing in comparison. But actually, bonding with Lauren and being able to relate when it came to so many things was refreshing. Neither of us got to experience high school like a normal teenager. I didn't go at all and even though she went, she didn't attend prom or have curfews like most kids. Her mother wasn't at parent teacher conferences, and Wise signed her report cards. Lauren went to school by day and lived like an adult on her own by night. From trafficking drugs to cooking her own meals and doing her own laundry, we both had to pretty much raise ourselves.

Wise made sure she was good in many ways, and that's something that Loyal and I didn't have, but he still didn't deserve to be praised. Not with the things he had her doing. She had survived though, and she was good people. When I was done with the blunt, I went inside and washed my hands. I removed my clothes and put on a fresh pair of pajamas that didn't smell like za. I checked on Shiloh and went to the kitchen to get something to drink for my cotton mouth. The weed had me so zoned out that I almost forgot Lauren was coming over until the doorbell rang.

With a bottle of water in hand, I opened the door and took in her sexy ass standing there dressed in a black sundress that hugged her body. Her hair was wet, and it smelled like mangos. It was slicked up into a high ponytail, and she didn't have on any makeup. A light floral scent followed her inside, and the French tips on her toes had my dick hard. No makeup, no long weave, no fancy clothes, and shorty had me ready to take her straight to the bedroom and handle that.

"You smell good," I pulled her into my body and inhaled the scent of her hair before nuzzling my face into the crook of her neck and sniffing.

Lauren giggled. "Why are you sniffing me like a dog."

"I just told you, you smell good." My eyes felt super heavy, but I held them open enough to peer into her pretty face. "Shit got my dick hard," I mumbled before snaking my tongue into her mouth.

I was in a zone and went in for the kill. I sucked her bottom lip, bit her shit, and tongued her down so nasty and sloppy that she moaned into my mouth. Then boom, Shiloh's cries came through the baby monitor, and I groaned. "I know the fuck..."

Lauren giggled and eased out of my embrace. "I'll go get my friend."

I watched her walk away with a frown on my face. Kids were certified cock blockers. I stood in place waiting for my erection to go down before walking into the living room and sitting down on the couch. I was guzzling down my water when Lauren sauntered into the room with Shiloh cradled in her arms. I almost told Lauren that she looked good carrying my baby, but I held it in. I didn't need any more kids any time soon. Having ghetto twins was already ghetto enough. I didn't need kids of the same ages by different mothers spread out everywhere. Maybe one day, I'd like to have one more with a woman that I was actually with and could be there from day one. I went to the kitchen to warm a bottle then went back in the living room and passed it to her.

"How did the visit with his mom go?"

"I didn't stay long. I told her that what she did was messed up, but I assured her that he's good with me until she gets better and even after that. She texted me earlier and told me that they were going to discharge her in two days. Her mom and sisters are here now and are going to help her with the baby. I'm going to take him to her when she gets home, but we're going to work out a visitation schedule. I'm going to keep him a few days a week."

"I'm glad she's doing good. I was worried for a minute. Growing up without a mother is hard."

"Yeah it is," I mumbled. "Work was cool?"

"I wouldn't describe it as cool. Those people got on my nerves real bad, but the tips were good," she chuckled.

Carmen sent me a long text message that I didn't feel like

reading, so I scrolled Tik Tok while Lauren fed Shiloh, then burped and changed him. He was fast asleep, and she still had him cradled in her arms staring down into his face.

"You want one of those?" I asked.

Lauren looked at me with raised brows. "One of what? A baby? Hell no," she laughed. "Not right now. I like to love on them then give them back."

"Well, he's asleep, so I need you to come love on me."

"So jealous."

Lauren put Shiloh in his bassinet and came back into the living room. With a devilish smirk on her face, she straddled me and wrapped her arms around my neck. I palmed her ass and snaked my tongue into her mouth. I was about to fuck the shit out of shorty.

Shiloh was still young, so I was skeptical about taking him to the cookout at Wise's house, but eventually, I decided to take him. I would just make everyone wash their hands before they held him, and I better not catch anybody breathing directly on him or kissing on him. I didn't know any of them like that. Not even Wise. But I was going to give his family the same chance that I had given Simone's. I talked to Truce and my grandfather every day. He had even met Shiloh, and he was stoked at the fact that he had a great grandson. Seeing him hold Shiloh felt surreal to me. I finally had family. A lot of family.

"Shit," I breathed as I pulled up in Wise's long circular driveway.

His house had a four-car-garage, and there were six luxury cars parked in the driveway. I wasn't sure which ones if any belonged to Wise, but there was a burnt orange Range Rover, a blue Audi, gold Maserati, black Bentley, and a brown BMW. Forget the cars, my jaw dropped at the sight of the house. I knew Wise had money, but he lived in a real-life mansion. The brown brick and black shutters gave the home a castle-like appearance. I wasn't sure who lived in the house with Wise but even with me having two children, I couldn't see myself living in something that big. I for sure wanted an upgrade though. If my next crib was a fraction of what Wise had, I'd be content.

For years Loyal and I lived in a roach infested project apartment, so the three-bedroom two-bathroom home that I lived in felt like a mansion to me. But when I moved again, my next crib would have at least four bedrooms and a mancave was necessary. I parked behind the Bentley and got Shiloh's carrier out of the backseat. I rang the bell while taking in the huge, black double doors. They appeared to be glass, but I couldn't see inside of the house. Wise had to have dropped a few million on his home. I had to keep myself from cursing out loud when a bad ass broad opened the door. She didn't look old at all, but she looked too old to be one of my sisters.

Shorty had a bronzed skin tone. It looked as if she'd been kissed by the sun numerous times. I didn't know if her curly hair was a wig, a sew-in with a leave out or what, but the jet-black curls looked like they were coming from her scalp. Her hair cascaded down her back, and I knew it wasn't all hers, but it looked natural. She had on light makeup and a brown bodysuit. The body on ole girl would have had my dick hard in normal circumstances, but I didn't know who she was and if she was related to me, so I refused to ogle her, but I saw enough to know that she had a coke bottle figure out of this world. During my quick inspection of her, I saw a rock on her ring finger that could freeze hell. That diamond probably cost as much as one of the cars out front.

She smiled wide. "Hi, I'm Alana, Wise's fiancée. It's so nice to meet you," she gushed.

Damn Wise was doing it like that? "What's up?"

She stepped back, so I could enter the house. The foyer smelled like cinnamon, and the floors were so shiny and clean it looked like a person could eat off them. I heard voices and laughter coming from the room on the left.

"Everyone is in the living room. The chef is in the kitchen, and Wise's brother, Chicago is on the grill. The food should be ready in about ten minutes."

"Cool." I bobbed my head and followed her into the living room while trying to keep my eyes off her behind.

The living room in Wise's house was huge. The room could comfortably fit at least thirty people with no furniture in it. There was a chocolate leather sectional and a matching recliner. A huge portrait of Wise and Alana hung on one wall while a huge television was mounted on the opposite wall. The room was decorated like something out of a magazine.

"Hi, Justice," Winter jumped up off the couch and rushed towards me. She took the carrier from my hand. "Oh, he's so cute. I love babies."

"It better be a long time before you love them enough to have one of your own," Wise warned from the couch while holding a glass with brown liquid in it in his hand. "What's up, son?"

"What's up. Winter, do me a favor and wash your hands if you want to hold him. He's fresh out of the oven. Only a week old."

"Okay."

"This is Fatima, your other sister." Wise jerked his head towards a pretty light-skinned girl with green eyes and curly dark brown hair. She looked nothing like Wise, so I assumed she was the spitting image of her mother. I was quickly learning that my

145

father dealt with some bad ass women. Shit, I wondered what Winter's mother looked like.

"I'm Imani," a miniature, female version of Wise spoke up.

"What's up?" I smiled down at her. "My name is Justice."

"Hi, Justice," she smiled bashfully while I nodded my head at Fatima.

Winter was clad in black leggings, a black sports bra, and Louis Vuitton sandals. Fatima had on white shorts, a red Gucci shirt, and red and white J's. Imani was decked out in denim shorts and an Amiri shirt. I could tell that my sisters were spoiled as hell, but Wise was their father, so I expected nothing less.

"You want a drink?" Wise asked. "I have a fully stocked bar over there. Make yourself at home."

"I don't mind if I do."

There were so many oddly shaped bottles and expensive looking liquor that I'd never heard of before. I was sure that everything was top dollar, and I couldn't go wrong with any of it. I grabbed a clear silver bottle that was square shaped but slanted on each side.

"Great choice," Wise spoke up. "My plug actually gifted that to me last year. "That's Hennessey in a Baccarat crystal bottle. That cognac cost almost $8,000."

I wasn't easily impressed, but my eyes bulged out of my head at hearing that someone paid almost $8,000 for something they would drink and piss out. If Wise could afford to give me twenty bricks, there was no doubt in my mind that he was well off, so his plug had to be rich rich. The most I'd ever splurged was $6,000 on a chain. I looked down at the bottle of alcohol that cost more than my most expensive piece of jewelry. Well, the Patek that I wore was the most expensive piece of jewelry that I had, but I didn't buy that. I stole it.

I poured the equivalent of a double shot of Henny in my glass and took a sip. It was definitely smooth but for $8,000 it should have tasted like rainbows and glitter and shit. I could have been tripping, but by the third sip, I felt a lil' something. Man, I couldn't wait until the day that I could afford to spend $8,000 on alcohol. Even if I didn't do it, I wanted to be able to have the means to do so if I wanted to.

The doorbell rang, and Wise got up to answer the door while I took a seat at the end of the large sectional. Winter, Fatima, and Imani were on the floor fawning over Shiloh. Wise came back to the room followed by Loyal.

"Dang y'all look just alike," Fatima's head whipped back and forth between me and Loyal.

"They're triplets, duh," Winter stated. "There are three of them."

"That's crazy. I can't imagine being pregnant with three babies."

"You don't need to imagine being pregnant with any babies for at least ten more years" Wise gave Fatima a warning glare, and she rolled her eyes upwards.

By the time Loyal and I reached that teenage rebellious stage, we were on our own. We did what we wanted to do, and that was the reason I had an issue with authority. I had the mindset that no one could tell me anything. I wondered how it would have felt to have a father figure in my life. The years that I had Janice, she was cool. I never really challenged her or gave her a hard time. Once she died and the reality of my situation set in, it made me hard. I thought I didn't have any family that wanted to be bothered with me. I felt no one wanted us, and that Loyal and I were just discarded like trash. Life would have been way different had we grown up in a house like the one Wise lived in.

That was the past, however, and water under the bridge. Wise introduced Loyal to everyone, and he came over to me last and gave me dap. "What you drinking?" he asked.

"Some $8,000 Henny and that shit is like that."

His brows lifted. "Henny that cost how much?"

"Eight bands."

The doorbell rang again and, that time, Fatima went to answer it. She came back with Truce, and Alana alerted us that the food was ready. I thought Wise's living room was huge until I saw his kitchen. The kitchen was bigger than some living rooms that I'd been in. I was far from a groupie, but Wise's home had me in awe. There were two people in the kitchen preparing food and on the long marble topped island, was a plethora of dishes. Shiloh started whining, and I grabbed a bottle from his bag and asked Wise if I could use his microwave.

"Of course. Jamisha, you mind feeding my grandson, so we can eat?"

"Not at all, sir." One of the chefs smiled at Wise, and I sipped my drink with an appreciative nod. Wise was that nigga.

She walked over and took Shiloh from Winter. When his bottle was ready, I passed it to Jamisha, and she took him into another room. I finished off the Henny in my glass and had a nice buzz going on. Was it worth $8,000? No. But it was way better than regular Henny. I was faded off two shots, and that never happened with regular alcohol.

I needed two plates, and I piled them both high with crab cakes, grilled shrimp, fried oysters, grilled chicken, steak, a hamburger, a hot dog, deviled eggs, pasta salad, macaroni and cheese, corn on the cob, and potato salad. The first few minutes after Alana said grace, all that could be heard was smacking and chewing.

"For Christmas, I'm thinking Aspen. Tell your mothers when you go home that we're doing five days in Aspen for Christmas."

Wise's eyes swept from my face to Loyal and Truce's. "I want you all to come of course. I will pay for everything, and we can fly using my private jet. Invite whoever you want. Just let me know, so I can make sure we have enough room to accommodate everyone."

"You just reminded me to email you my Christmas list," Fatima said after taking a large bite of her hot dog.

Five days in Aspen paid for. So, this was what it was like to have family? For some reason, Lauren entered my mind. If I ever decided that I wanted a girlfriend, she would be a candidate for sure, but how could I bring her around Wise given their history? As far as I knew, he was still looking for her, and I didn't even know what he planned to do to her if he found her. I was trying to stay in my own lane because the business they had was before me, but I couldn't see myself letting Wise fuck with Lauren. Not over that old stale ass debt he claimed she owed him.

The food was phenomenal, and I was stuffed. After we ate, the men went into Wise's mancave, and we smoked some premium weed, and I drank some more $8,000 Henny. Maybe it was because I was inebriated but kicking it with my brothers and my pops felt good. In all honesty, it felt damn good, and I was grateful.

LAUREN

One of the bartenders, Kendall used her hip to playfully bump me. "I'm ready to get up out of this hell hole," she sang making me laugh.

"Girl, these folks are different. I've been a bartender for years, so I don't know why my feet always hurt when I leave here. Maybe it's these floors, or the worrisome customers," I sighed.

The tips were pretty good, but I worked for them. There was hardly ever a dull or slow moment in the lounge. It was usually so packed that my shifts flew by because I stayed busy the entire time, and that was a plus.

"Tell me about it," Kendall rolled her eyes. "You're lucky. What you got left?"

"Thirty minutes," I smiled and ran my tongue over my teeth. "I can't wait."

I was so ready to go home, take a shower, and unwind. I had the next two days off, and I was going to enjoy them. Thanks to the good tips I made and the money that Justice had given me for helping with Shiloh, I was going to enjoy my days off rather than picking up extra shifts. For the first time, I was paying all of my own bills, and I loved it. Being free from Wise was priceless. Even if it took the bulk of my money.

"Hey, what can I get for you?" I asked a guy that approached the end of the bar.

"Let me get a double shot of Azul. Damn you sexy, what's your name?"

Even if a customer didn't have a chance in hell with me, I was never rude because men that liked you and wanted to impress you for real were great tippers. The guy in front of me wasn't ugly, but I wasn't looking. Justice wasn't my man, and I was sure he hadn't cut off any of his women for me, but I was content dealing with just him. I probably should have kept my options open, but it would be okay. I really didn't want to deal with anyone that frequented the lounge because it would be too hard to duck them if I decided that I didn't like them.

"Lauren," I smiled at him before I walked off to fix his drink.

I poured his double shot of Azul and took it to him. "Lauren, you single?" he wasn't letting up.

I thought about it quickly and tried to determine if I wanted to lie or tell the truth. "I have a boyfriend," I lied. Most times, that didn't work, but men would be extra pushy if they felt you were single versus just a little pushy if you were taken.

"I bet that nigga can't love you like me."

I laughed. Dead in his face. "You don't even know my man, so how can you say that?" I asked with an amused smile.

"Because I know it. That nigga isn't me. I'm one of a kind. My name is Jock, and I promise if you give me a chance, you won't regret it."

I still had a smile on my face because I was just that amused, but before I could part my lips to politely turn him down, Justice appeared out of nowhere and gave the man dap.

"What up, homie?"

The way my kitty purred when I saw Justice's handsome face should have been illegal. That man and everything about him had me in a trance. I was all set to ask him what he wanted to drink when he gave me a pointed look. "Damn you fuck friends too?"

I drew back because I had to have heard him wrong. I had just met that man and told him I had a boyfriend, but he thought because I did my job and was polite, that Jock had a chance in hell of having sex with me? Not to mention, his comment was super rude. He was the main one saying he didn't care that I slept with Wise, but the disrespectful comment that he made said something totally different. My face burned with shame, and I walked away from him with a racing heart. I couldn't believe that Justice had played in my face like that.

I was so pissed that I didn't know what to do. While I tried to steady my breathing, I cleaned up behind the bar and got ready for the end of my shift. Kendall and another bartender, Jamison were going to finish up the night. Jamison came over to me. "That fine ass nigga at the end of the bar with the braids wants to be served by you."

I already knew that he was referring to Justice. I looked down at my watch. "Fuck that nigga. My shift is over."

I walked from behind the bar with flaring nostrils. "Lauren, why you ignoring me?"

Justice grabbed my arm, and I whirled around and slapped him so hard, my hand stung. Justice's eyes widened. He was shocked, but I didn't care. His surprise didn't outweigh my anger. "Fuck you," I spat with tears in my eyes. "You will never disrespect me and then act like shit is sweet. I fuck friends too?" I looked him up and down. "I don't even know that man. I was doing my job, but thanks for letting me know what you really think of me. Fuck you and your daddy." I turned my back on him and stormed off.

I was embarrassed and hurt. Of course, I knew Justice could be an asshole, but it had been a while since I'd seen that side of him. Maybe he said what he had to say and acted how he had to act in order to get me to sleep with him. I grabbed my things and left the lounge as fast as I could. The entire way home, I blinked back tears. I refused to let any of them fall. Justice wasn't worth my tears. He was just like his hoe ass daddy.

When I reached my apartment, I was at my door about to stick the key in when I saw someone coming up the steps in my peripheral vision. I pushed my key in the lock and turned it as fast as I could. I wasn't even going to look at the person, I was just going to get in my apartment as quickly as I could.

"Damn you're a hard one to find." That voice made the hairs on the back of my neck stand up.

I didn't even want to look. I wanted to cry. I didn't have to look in his face to know that Wise had finally found me. My heart fell into my ass. He was up on me in no time. "Open the door," he spoke into my ear in a low gruff voice.

All of the times that I transported his dope, he stressed to me the importance of looking in my rearview mirror and paying attention to my surroundings to make sure I wasn't being followed. I knew more than likely that Wise was still looking for me, but I was so caught up with Justice's hurtful words, I wasn't paying attention like I should have been. I pushed the door open with a sense of dread gripping my body. What if he killed me?

Inside the apartment, Wise took it upon himself to close my door and lock it. "What have I been telling you for years?" he asked with a menacing glare. I assumed it was a rhetorical question, and he didn't really want an answer. "Didn't I tell you that I wasn't going to be done with you until I said I was done with you?"

"Wise, I just wanted to be on my own," I stated in a low tone. "I don't want to keep risking my freedom. I don't want to sell dope. I don't want to risk my life drugging people. I just want to be done with this." I wanted to come off as confident and sure, but my nerves were getting the best of me.

"I don't give a fuck what you want," he gritted. "You should have thought about that all of the years that you let me keep a roof over your head. You thought what? I was a nice nigga. That I cared about your orphaned ass?"

I wanted to curse Wise out. I wanted to smack him the same way I smacked his smug son, but I wasn't all the way crazy. I wasn't going to talk to Wise crazy or put my hands on him. "You think I'm dumb?" he asked. "You all of a sudden wanted to get away from me after I told you to drug my son. You want to fuck that nigga?" That was the closest I'd ever seen Wise come to jealousy.

"No," I lied.

"Yeah, 'cus this was my pussy first, and that's what it's always going to be." Wise invaded my personal space and wrapped one of his hands around my neck. "It's been a long time, but I'm going to get what's mine."

I opened my mouth, but no words came out because he was restricting my air flow. Wise stared directly into my eyes as he tugged at my shorts. The thought of him penetrating me made me panic worse than the fact that I couldn't breathe. My head felt like it was going to explode right along with my heart as it hammered violently in my chest. If I tried to get away from Wise and I failed, he would make me suffer. I was sure of it, but I had to try. With everything I had in me, I kneed him in the groin. His eyes bucked out of his head, and I kneed him again, and he dropped to his knees. I used that opportunity to run into my bedroom. What I needed was on my bed. Foolishly, I hadn't taken my gun with me to work that night, but it was out in the open and within arms' reach when I needed it. I always slept with my gun by my side because if I needed it in the middle of the night, having to go get it from a hiding place would take too long and could be the deciding factor in my life or death.

I was trying to gulp in as much air as possible as I cocked my gun back. "Bitch," I heard Wise behind me, and I whirled around with my gun pointed at him.

Wise's eyes darted towards the weapon in my hand, and I could tell by the anger flashing in his orbs and the way he ran his tongue over his bottom lip that he was plotting. I backed up, and a devilish grin tugged at the corners of his lips. Wise didn't even take a full step forward before I sent a bullet slamming into his arm. Once again, his eyes widened at my audacity. If Wise thought he was going to show up and punk me, I was more than happy to disappoint him. I wasn't the same naïve, weak, scared sixteen-year-old that he caught trying to steal his dope. I was a grown woman, and I was fed up.

Wise was a tough bastard, or he had a death wish because he took another step in my direction, and I shot him again but that time in the leg. "The next shot will be a head shot," I warned him as he groaned loudly.

"Fuck!" He roared. He ate the first bullet, but the second one was making beads of sweat form on Wise's head. "The biggest mistake you made here tonight was not delivering a head shot first." Wise backed out of my room while staring a hole into me. I could see the threat in his eyes and knew that I had indeed messed up by letting him live.

Two days later, I was beyond stressed as I sat on my cousin's couch. Shooting Wise not once but twice and letting him walk or hobble out of my apartment rather was the dumbest thing I'd ever done. I was sure I'd signed my own death certificate. Even if I could claim self-defense, I didn't want Wise's blood on my hands. It wasn't safe for me to stay in my apartment, so when Wise left that night, I cleaned up the trail of blood that leaked to my front door, packed a bag, and got the hell out of Diamond Cove. I had a few thousand dollars left in my bank account after moving, but I needed to be working and not trying to survive off that.

I couldn't run forever. I didn't know what to do. My cousin lived four hours away from me in Virginia. She was a nurse and worked overnight at a hospital. She slept during the day. I didn't want to burden her or interrupt her routine, so I spent most of my day on her couch watching TV, reading a book, or going for a walk all while trying not to stress myself into a heart attack. My phone had been off since I arrived in Virginia, and I was sure that Loso, Sade, and anyone else that I talked to on a regular basis was going crazy. The only person I called since I shot Wise was my boss at the lounge. I lied and told him that I had a family emergency, and I had to go to Georgia for a few days. I wasn't going to tell him that I was in Virginia even if I didn't mention the city. The good thing about being a bartender was there were so many places in Diamond Cove or surrounding cities that I could apply to work at. If I was ever able to peacefully walk the streets of Diamond Cove again.

"I should have just left," I mumbled. Trying to escape Wise but not moving out of the city was stupid. Nervously, I bit my bottom lip as I powered my phone on. I waited patiently as it came to life.

Not even a full minute after I powered it on, notifications started coming in like crazy. One after another they were sounding off in rapid succession. Sure enough, I had more than fifteen text messages and more than five voicemail messages. I swallowed hard when I saw that three of them were from Justice.

I listened to the message. "Yo, I don't know what went on, but you need to call me, ASAP. I need to make sure you're good."

The second message came in an hour after the first. "Yo, Lauren, I'm trying to be patient, ma. I fucked up. I'm sorry. I get that. But put that to the side and let me know you're okay."

The third message simply said. "Fuck it."

I pushed out a deep breath. It wasn't time to be petty. I was in trouble, but even if I could overlook the disrespectful comment that Justice made to me, how could I be comfortable talking to him, and it was his father that I shot?! Whether he'd known Wise his entire life or not, I wasn't sure I was willing to take that chance. He was getting to know the man going to dinners at his house and meeting his siblings. If it came down to it at the end of the day, why would he choose me over Wise?

I decided to call Loso back first. "Where are you at, Lauren? You know how many times I've called you. I even went by your apartment."

"I'm in Virginia."

"Virginia? Why?"

"Wise followed me home from the lounge the other night. He came in the apartment, and he choked me, and I think he was going to rape me. I was able to get to my gun, and I shot him twice. Once in the arm and once in the leg. He pretty much told me that I messed up by not killing him."

I was met with silence, and I knew Loso was pissed. Loso was strong, muscular, and I'd seen him knock people out with one punch. When it came to fighting, he could hold his own, and he had a license to carry. Loso wasn't a punk, but he wasn't street either. He worked legit jobs, and he didn't sell drugs, guns, or anything else illegal. I would never put my friend in the position to go up against a man like Wise but as a man and my friend, I knew he was fighting the urge to get at Wise.

"It'll be okay," I told him in a soft tone even though I didn't even believe that myself.

"I wish there was something I could do. Let me think on it an——"

"Loso, it's not your problem to fix. I appreciate you. I really do, but no one needs to get caught up with Wise because of my mess. He has a hundred grown ass men ready to crash out and do anything he tells them to. I don't want you beefing with Wise on my behalf. It will be okay," I repeated slowly.

"How long are you staying in Virginia? Do you need some money?"

Hell yes, I needed some money, but I refused to make my problems anyone else's burdens. I got myself caught up with Wise, and I had to deal with the consequences. "I'm not sure yet. I still have like eleven months on my lease. I can't afford to pay to live there and somewhere else, and I damn sure don't need an eviction on my credit. I'm still trying to figure it out."

"Call me if you need anything even though I know your stubborn ass won't."

"You know me well," I smiled. "Bye, Loso. I love you." I never told him I loved him, so I was sure I sounded cryptic.

"Yeah big head you too," Loso mumbled and ended the call.

My friend was worried, and I hated that I had him and other people stressed. I was about to return Sade's call when I got a notification from Cash App. All I could do was shake my head when I opened it and saw that Loso had sent me $500. I texted him thank you and called Sade.

We talked for thirty minutes and when I got off the phone with her, I didn't feel any better. There wasn't anything I could do except run forever or go back to Diamond Cove and risk running into Wise. I knew without a shadow of a doubt that the next time that man saw me, he was going to kill me. A small part of me wanted to call Justice just to see what he had to say and try to gauge where Wise's head was at but fuck him too. If I never saw Wise or his disrespectful son again, it wouldn't be too soon.

JUSTICE

I was sitting across from Wise in his living room. I had sold the twenty bricks he'd originally given me, and I stopped by his house to purchase some more bricks. To my surprise, he wouldn't take the money. "You're good on this shipment too. You can start paying me next time."

"Why?" I asked curiously.

Wise shrugged. "I bought both of your sisters cars, and all of the girls have trust funds. I never thought I'd meet any of my sons, so I don't have trust funds for you, but you all deserve as much as I've given your sisters over the years. I'm paying for Winter's college out of pocket. We don't do that student loan bullshit. I also bought her a BMW when she turned sixteen. Twenty bricks were cool, but it wasn't enough. I got your brother a building for his tattoo shop, and I'm going to buy the house that Truce is selling for $100,000 more than his asking price."

I bobbed my head. If Wise wanted to give me more bricks, I damn sure wasn't turning them down. He wanted to play daddy, and I was going to let him. I started getting it out of the mud at thirteen. Forget pride. I knew I didn't *need* anyone, but if he wanted to keep offering, I was going to accept it.

"I appreciate it. You gon' tell me what happened with you and Lauren, or you just going to leave it at she shot you?"

Wise's jaw muscle flexed at the mention of Lauren's name. The day after she slapped the taste out of my mouth, Winter texted me and asked if I knew that Wise got shot. I immediately called to check on him, and he said he was fine, that he only got hit in the arm and the leg. He also said that he ran into Lauren, and she did it. Someone came in the room, and he said he'd talk to me later. I needed to re-up anyway, so here I was.

"I finally found that bitch. I got word that she was working at a lounge, and I followed her home. Made my way inside of her apartment. She managed to get away from me, and she went and grabbed a gun." Wise chuckled angrily. "I told that bitch she should have killed me."

"She managed to get away from you? So you were what, roughing her up?" I asked with a frown. Wise was about to piss me off. I had said some out-of-pocket shit to Lauren because I was drunk and jealous. I'd never in my life been jealous of any female talking to another man. Jock was my homie, and the thought of Lauren flirting with him sent my ignorance into overdrive. She had no way of knowing that he was my friend, so I was just petty and childish for saying what I did to her.

"You damn right I was roughing that bitch up," Wise boasted proudly with a grimace on his face. "I asked the bitch if she wanted to fuck you, and she said no. I've been taking care of Lauren since she was sixteen, and I only had sex with her once. I could have been slutting her out. I could have been making money off her pussy, but I let her live, and she spit in my face? I was about to take that shit, but the hoe shot me."

"You were about to take that shit?" I drew back. "Yo," I paused for a moment to compose myself. I had to have heard him wrong. There was no way he was sitting in front of me bragging about the fact that he was about to rape Lauren.

Wise had more money than he could spend and some of the baddest chicks in the city, and he was going to resort to rape to get his point across? I would never and could never respect that.

"Is that a problem son? I know she saved your life and all, but you act like you have some kind of attachment to that bitch."

"I do," I stated adamantly daring him to say the wrong thing. "And I don't understand why you keep fucking with her," my nostrils flared.

Wise laughed. A good hearty laugh that lasted about a minute and the longer he laughed, the more it pissed me off. "Oh shit," he clutched his stomach. "You serious, Justice? You bucking at me over a hoe I already fucked? I don't mind you hitting her behind me. But please don't tell me you fell in love with a pass around."

"You preyed on that girl when she was sixteen. You knew what you were doing. What homeless kid is going to turn down a place to live if it's offered to them? You didn't tell her she'd be selling dope or anything else you had her to doing for years of her life. Threatening to kill her. All of that was lame as hell."

"Lame?" Wise sat up and glared at me. "I know you don't know me like that, but you're real emotional right now, and I'd suggest you calm down," warning flickered in Wise's eyes, but I was unmoved.

"I know you don't know me like that, but I'm a grown ass muhfuckin' man," I stared right back at him. "I might have had it rough for a bit, but the woman that raised me for thirteen years instilled some kind of morals in me and beating women and raping them is some sucka ass shit. It's lame and cowardly, and I don't respect it. It has nothing to do with me fucking Lauren. She had sex with you 'cus you played with her head, and she thought she had a crush on you. She had sex with me as a grown woman that simply wanted to, so we aren't the same."

Wise laughed again. "You are really dead serious right now. I know I have some making up to do, but don't you ever in your life get it fucked up, Justice. Ever. My business is mine, and it would be smart for you not to insert yourself in it. I suggest you get over whatever attachment you have to Lauren because she's as good as dead if I ever see her again."

I stood up and spoke to Wise with more seriousness than I'd ever spoken with in my life. "You can keep the bricks. I won't be needing them. And if you kill Lauren, you better kill me too, 'cus if not, all the kids that you spoiled and raised from day one are going to be crying over your grave."

I turned and left that sucka ass nigga's house mad enough to spit nails.

Two hours later, I was still pissed. Loyal's building wasn't ready yet, so he was still doing tattoos out of the old spot. I sat in a chair in his room bouncing my leg up and down as he finished up a tattoo. Truce had joined us and was alternating between looking through his phone and watching me. I wasn't going to talk in front of Loyal's customer, so I hadn't had a chance to vent. Pissed was an understatement. I was shocked there wasn't actual steam coming out of my ears.

"Yo my nigga roll a blunt or something," Loyal sprayed the tattoo he'd just completed and wiped the excess ink off his client's skin with a paper towel. "You making my nerves bad with all that bouncing and moving over there."

I texted both of them and told them I had gotten into it with Wise. I would never try to turn them against him. If they wanted to continue a relationship with him, they could, but I wasn't fucking with the nigga. I would take the money I made off the twenty bricks he gave me, and I'd reup with the same plug I had before I found out Wise was my father. I was street through and through, but I always tried to respect Loyal. Most of his clients were chill and didn't mind smoking, drinking, loud music, etc. but I never came into his place of business with ghetto antics. He didn't have to tell me twice to roll up though.

By the time I was done rolling the blunt, Loyal's client was gone. "What's good?" he asked.

"I found out why Lauren shot Wise. He admitted that he followed her home, and he was going to rape her. She got away from him and got to her gun."

A deep scowl covered Loyal's face. "Ain't no way he said no shit like that."

I directed my attention back to the weed that I was rolling because I wasn't lying. Loyal already knew if I said it, it happened.

"What did you say?" Truce asked.

"I told him what he was doing to her was lame as hell. He told me to stay out of his business, and he said if he sees Lauren again, he's going to kill her. I told him he might as well kill me too because if he didn't, I was gon' have his daughters crying over his grave."

"The fuck?" Loyal asked with wide eyes. "You've known the man for less than a month, and you're threatening to kill him?"

I stared at my brother. "Tell me Wise isn't foul."

Loyal ran a hand down his face. "He is but damn."

"You can keep rocking with him," I scoured the room for a lighter because mine was in the car. "You're your own man with your own brain. You don't have to be on the outs with him just because I am." I spotted a lighter across the room and stood up to go get it.

Loyal kissed his teeth. "You out your mind and talking stupid. If you have beef with him, then there is no rocking with him on my part. It's me and you until the world blows. Goofy nigga."

I lit the blunt and took a long deep pull. "I definitely can't get behind a man sexually assaulting a woman. You have a good reason to be going against him. I hope it doesn't come to you killing him, but I'm definitely on your side," Truce spoke up.

It made me feel better that my brothers didn't think I was tweaking but with or without them taking my side, I still wouldn't be fucking with Wise.

"This man gonna say I'm attached to a hoe. It was never my business to tell, and I don't care about it for real, but she slept with him one time years ago. Because of that, I'm supposed to be okay with him putting his hands on her and attempting to rape her. Wise is a sucka," I hit the blunt feverishly.

"Wise has too many yes men around him. No one probably has the balls to call him out on his BS. So him getting checked by you was foreign to him. You didn't say anything wrong, and if he can't respect that, then fuck him. He has no reason to kill that girl. He went to her crib bothering her and is mad because she defended herself," Loyal chimed in as I hit the blunt.

"I left the bricks right there at his crib. I don't want anything from him. I'll get it how I was getting it before I ever knew he was my father. You're still getting that tattoo shop though," I stared at Loyal for a few seconds before my gaze shifted in Truce's direction. "And let him buy your house. Don't mess up what he was going to do for y'all on my account."

Loyal kissed his teeth. "I'll accept the building as long as he doesn't make any wrong moves against you. You already know how I get down, so don't act like you don't."

"I feel the same way," Truce spoke up. "This isn't a regular

165

disagreement. You threatened to kill the man. If the beef gets real, I got your back."

Three men sitting in one room that looked exactly alike would always be miraculous to me. Truce and I were both wearing black hoodies. People that had known us for years wouldn't even have been able to walk in that room and tell us apart.

"Where is Lauren?" Loyal asked.

"I haven't seen her or talked to her. We kinda got into it the same night that she shot Wise. I've been calling her, but she won't answer the phone." The weed had kicked in full throttle, and my lids were heavy. I passed the blunt to Loyal though I'd smoked almost half of it.

"She's probably trying to figure out if she can even trust you for real. Even if you and Wise did just meet, you're still his son. Maybe that makes you the opp by default," Truce offered.

"She must not have been paying attention to anything that I said to her because I told her that I think Wise was foul. He was in his thirties when he let her live in his crib at the age of sixteen. The moment she turned eighteen, he slept with her. Sick ass predator ass nigga," I spat.

"Remember when you started sleeping with Janine when you were sixteen?" Loyal asked with a shake of his head. "Anytime you wanted her to go to the ABC store for us, you had sex with her."

"Do I remember when I had sex with her?" I asked incredulously. "If I recall you had sex with her one time too."

"But only because I pretended to be you. You wanted some Henny, but you wanted to chill with Miranda, so you had me having sex with that old ass lady."

I snorted. "She was only twenty-nine at the time. Dry pussy ass," I mumbled as he passed the blunt to Truce.

"The amount of adults that will prey on teenagers is crazy," I stated with disgust. Back then, I thought I was cool because a woman that was almost thirty was throwing herself at me. That shit was sick.

I got an idea. I licked my lips and peered at Loyal. "Text Lauren from your phone and tell her that it's very important that I speak with her."

"She got you blocked?"

"I don't think so, but she's not responding to my text messages or phone calls. Just do it."

"That's not how you ask someone to do a favor for you," he retorted as he picked his phone up off the table behind him.

I ran my hand down my face. I wasn't in the mood to be annoyed by Loyal. After a few minutes of silence, he spoke up. The message isn't saying delivered, so she must have her phone off. She doesn't have my number to block me."

I was beyond annoyed. Loyal's phone rang, and my head snapped up.

"It's Wise," he announced, and I scoffed. "Hello."

I stared at the floor while Loyal listened to whatever it was that Wise was saying. I couldn't care less about anything he had to say. My mind was on Lauren. Why didn't she just kill him? She had known him longer than I had. She had to know that letting him live would be a mistake. Lauren couldn't have expected anything less from Wise.

Loyal ended the call, and I looked over at him. "He said he knows who shot you. It was Rico. He also said either he can handle it, or you can handle it."

My upper lip curled into a snarl. "I don't need Wise to handle anything for me. If he thinks I'm joking about the situation with Lauren, he's in for a rude surprise. I can handle Rico myself."

LAUREN

Six days after I shot Wise, I drove back to Diamond Cove and crept into my apartment at five in the morning. My apartment was on the second floor, so there was no way anyone could break in unless they picked the lock somehow or kicked in the door, and the door was intact. I still checked every inch of the apartment from closets to underneath the bed. Once I was assured that I was alone, I took a shower with my gun in the bathroom on the sink. I put a scarf on my head, brushed my teeth, and crawled into bed. Even though I was stressed in Virginia, I'd gotten some good sleep because I knew Wise didn't know where to find me. I doubted I'd be able to sleep peacefully at home.

Something had to give, however, because I needed to make money. I couldn't stay out of work forever. Even if I kept getting jobs at different bars, as long as I was in the city or near it, Wise would eventually find me. What was the point of working and paying bills, if he was going to find me and kill me anyway? I received Loyal's text message that Justice wanted to talk to me, but I still hadn't reached out to him. I closed my eyes and when sleep didn't find me after about twenty minutes, I let out a frustrated groan and snatched my phone up. All of the saliva in my mouth dried up as the line trilled, and I waited on Justice to answer.

"Yo."

"I'm returning your calls."

"Where are you at?"

"I was out of town. I just got home about an hour and a half ago."

The call ended, and I looked at the screen in confusion. I assumed he was coming over, but he could have at least said something. Rude ass. Literal disgust crept through my core when I realized that my lady parts were throbbing from the anticipation of seeing Justice. After what he said to me that night, I would be a real idiot to sleep with him. Someone that swore they didn't have an issue with me sleeping with Wise because it was long ago, and I was young, and a victim. Wise was the one in the wrong and should have been ashamed of himself. Yet, the first time he got in his feelings he didn't hesitate to insinuate that I was a hoe. Perfect example of men will tell you what you want to hear, so they can climb in between your thighs.

I didn't care how my body was betraying me. I was going to stand my ground and not sleep with Justice. I only finally called him because he'd been blowing me up for a week. It would also help a little to see where Wise's head was at. Ten minutes after he hung up on me, Justice was at my door. At least I assumed it was him. Sitting up, I tossed back the cover and walked to the front door.

Damn! A week may as well have been a lifetime because I had forgotten just how fine Justice was. He had obviously just taken his braids out because his hair was wild and crinkly. The style made him look extra rugged. He walked into my apartment, and the intensity that he stared at me with made my breath catch in my throat. Justice gripped my chin in his hand, and heat coursed through my body.

"You know how scared I've been?" The worry in his eyes melted my heart. "You thought ignoring me was cool?" his brows furrowed, and he looked genuinely hurt.

"Why wouldn't I ignore you after what you said? You think that was cool?" He wasn't the only one that was hurt. Shit, I was slightly embarrassed too.

Justice released my chin and shoved his hands in his pockets. "I was wrong for that. I was drunk and jealous. I've never in my life been jealous over a female. I guess in my case, jealousy is like anger. It makes me reckless and ignorant. The way you were smiling at that nigga made my blood boil, but I was trying to keep it cool."

"I had literally just told him I had a boyfriend. You think I get tips by frowning and cursing people out? There's a difference between being polite and flirting. How don't you know that at your big age?"

"I said I messed up. You already slapped the taste out of my mouth."

"Once wasn't enough," I frowned.

He stepped into my personal space, and I swallowed hard. "If you feel like you need to do it again, that's what it is."

Slapping him was tempting, but I didn't want to. "I'm good, Justice. So, what did you come by for? If it was because you were worried, as you can see, I'm good."

"I came to tell you that I miss you. I'm sorry. And I told Wise that if he touches a hair on your head, he's dead."

My jaw slacked. "You did what? Why would you tell him that?"

Justice drew back. "What you mean why would I tell him that? Why did you shoot him?"

My heart sank, and I looked away. I didn't want to say it, but something told me that he already knew. "He was choking me, and he was..." I paused for a moment. "He was asking me if I wanted to have sex with you, and I said no. He was going to rape me. So, I kneed him in the groin and ran to my room where my gun was. Letting him live was a mistake, but I don't want anybody's blood on my hands."

"And that's why I told him what I did. You gon' run from him forever? Let him control you? He's going to leave you alone, or whatever happens, happens."

"That's your father, Justice."

"What does that mean?" his scowl was intense. "The nigga was going to rape you. That's not a problem? I don't even know that nigga like that."

"And you don't know me like that. Not to go against your father."

Justice ran one hand down his face, and I could tell he was frustrated. "Why do you keep harping on the fact that I came from Wise's nut sack? That man didn't raise me. And even if he had, what does that mean? I'll never condone someone raping a woman. You shot him in self-defense. The shit should be over." Justice's nostrils expanded with each breath that he took. He was pissed. The way he was standing up for me was one of the sexiest things I'd ever seen. No one had ever attempted to protect me the way Justice was.

"My father and I are going on a family vacation to Mexico in a few weeks. I'll be gone for a week. I'm hoping this shit will die down," I stated lamely. I knew like Justice did that Wise wasn't just going to let the situation go.

"You really believe that?"

"No, Justice!" I threw my hands up in exasperation. "But what am I supposed to do?"

"Let me handle it!"

I didn't have a response. Mentally, I was drained. Wise had been consuming my mind for the past week. He was the last person I thought about when I went to bed and the first person that crossed my mind each morning. He wasn't shit, but I still didn't want Justice beefing with his father on my account.

"If that nigga would have raped you, he'd be dead anyway." I could tell by the anger that flashed in Justice's eyes that he was telling the truth. "You forgive me?"

I rolled my eyes upwards. "You had stopped talking to me crazy. Mad or not, jealous or not, don't start it back up," I warned.

"Got it."

Justice and I had a brief stare down before he placed his hand around my neck and squeezed lightly. He continued to stare into my eyes as he inched his face closer to mine. He tongued me down and had me forgetting all of my troubles. His tongue probing my mouth had me dizzy with desire. This man was ready to go to war with his daddy behind me. That alone had my pussy wet. Justice broke the kiss, and with his hand still wrapped around my neck, he walked me all the way to my bedroom.

We had barely gotten out of our clothes before he was softly sucking on my nub. "Justice," I panted as my back arched. "Oh my God," I grabbed a handful of his hair as his tongue swirled over my clit.

Justice licked and slurped on my pussy hungrily. My eyes rolled back in my head as my vagina began to contract violently. My stomach caved in, and my body jerked as he moaned into my peach and lapped up every drop of honey that flowed from my center. Justice came up for air and stared into my eyes as he pushed his member into my opening.

"If you get pregnant, Wise won't kill you, and I won't have to kill him."

My mouth fell open from the pleasure that his dick was giving me, but his words had me in shock as well. "Say what?" I had to have heard him wrong.

"Have my baby." He didn't even give me a chance to respond before he snaked his tongue into my mouth and began to pump in and out of me.

So many thoughts were swirling through my head. He already had a newborn and another child on the way. When he finally removed his tongue from my mouth, I was able to find my words. "You want three kids under the age of two, Justice?"

"What's the problem? I was a triplet. Had my mother not given me away, she would have had three babies all the same age. I don't see the big deal. I can take care of my kids."

"Justice," I half whined half moaned. "I can't think straight with you fucking me and talking about something serious."

"Don't talk then." He began sucking on my neck. My lids fluttered closed, and I bit my bottom lip.

He was talking crazy, but I didn't want to die. I didn't want him to kill Wise either. I didn't give a damn about Wise. If he dropped dead any other way, I might rejoice, but I didn't want Justice to have his father's blood on his hands on my account. I had seen first hand that he was a good father, so I wouldn't have to worry about that. I would be the third baby mama added to the list. Justice let my neck go and placed soft kisses on my breasts.

"You better tell me something before I cum all in this pussy," he moaned.

"This is crazy," I whispered.

Justice latched onto one of my nipples, and orgasm number two ripped through my core and had me moaning loudly.

"Shit, Lauren. You got me bustin' quick as hell," he grunted as he released his load into my womb.

"You know when you ovulate?" he pecked me on the lips before pulling out of me.

"I have an app on my phone. Justice, this is crazy. The only way for Wise not to kill me is if I get pregnant with your third child?"

"Why you so focused on how many kids I got?" he asked with furrowed brows. "I'm going to take care of all my kids."

"While I'm just your baby mama."

"What you want to be, Lauren?"

"Nothing, Justice." I grabbed my phone off the nightstand. Crazier things had been done.

"Listen," Justice pulled me into his embrace. "I'm willing to go against my blood father for you. That has to tell you that I fuck with you the long way. If you get pregnant, I'll be here every step of the way. And not just on some baby mama baby daddy type shit. Okay?"

"I still think it's crazy, but I don't want you having to kill Wise on my behalf. I also don't want Wise to kill my ass, but he's not exactly a sentimental person. How do you know that a baby would save me?"

Justice kissed his teeth. "That nigga doesn't want to beef with me, but he's just adamant about not looking like he backed down. If you were pregnant with my child, I know Wise would let that shit go. I don't want to have to kill that nigga. Just work with me. You were good as hell with Shiloh. I know you'd be a good mom."

"Speaking of Shiloh, how is he?"

"He's good. Enchanted's mom and sisters have to go back to Jersey. I'm going to pick him up tomorrow after they leave and keep him for a few days. She's a lot better, but she's still getting her strength back. I told her I don't mind getting him for two or three days, so she can get some rest."

"I'd love to see him."

"I got you. Now, when do you ovulate?"

I went to the app on my phone not believing that I was even considering getting pregnant by Justice. "How do you know about these apps?" I gave him the side eye.

"Because both my baby mamas used to keep up with their periods. It never dawned on me until after they got pregnant that they could see when they ovulated too. Both of those hoes trapped me."

I chuckled as I opened the app and looked at the dates on the calendar. Before I could even process what it said, Justice took the phone from my hand. "Excuse you," I hit him on the arm.

"Damn you ovulate in three days. I guess that means I gotta spend the next three days in that pussy."

Two days later, I walked as normal as possible to my door to open it. Justice stayed true to his word and had practically been living inside my vagina. His dick wasn't small at all and when he was drunk, that man could last almost an hour. My vagina was sore as hell. I didn't want to see penis again for at least two days. The way he'd been ejaculating inside of me, if I didn't get pregnant when I ovulated then it truly wasn't meant to be. Every time I thought about the fact that I had actually let Justice unload all that sperm in me so close to me ovulating, I broke out into a sweat. Was I really trying on purpose to get pregnant by a man that I hadn't known for that long all so his father wouldn't kill me? That shit sounded strange as hell.

I opened my door and took in the sight of my friend looking stressed. "Hi," I said slowly. Loso looked terrible, but I wasn't going to tell him that.

He was long overdue for a shave. His eyes were red as apples, and he had bags underneath his eyes from lack of sleep. He had told me the night before that he went through Arielle's phone and found out she cheated on him. They got into a terrible argument at three in the morning, and it got so loud that someone called the police.

I felt bad for Loso. He had finally settled down and stopped being a hoe. I could tell that he really loved Arielle because not only was he faithful, but he cashed out on her. Loso did good for himself, but he wasn't a dope boy. Any time Arielle wanted pricy purses, jewelry, or expensive trips, Loso would work overtime for weeks to save up enough money to get her what she wanted. I truly felt bad for him.

"What's up?" he mumbled and walked over to the couch.

I hadn't ovulated yet and even after I did, it would be about two weeks before I would know if I was pregnant. Until then, Justice wanted me to lay low. I couldn't go to work. He didn't even want me to go to the grocery store. And he'd given me $5,000 to pay my bills. He was out making money and told me he would come by later with Shiloh.

"You want something to drink? I have tequila and vodka."

"Yeah, let me get some tequila."

I walked into the kitchen to fix Loso's drink while wondering if I could have a shot or two. Technically, I hadn't ovulated yet if the app I followed was accurate. I was sure one or two shots wouldn't stop Justice's sperm from doing what it needed to do and that's if it was meant for me to get pregnant. There were plenty of people that wanted kids that didn't get pregnant the first, second, or even third time they tried, and it had nothing to do with fertility issues. It was all in God's timing.

"You want chaser?" I yelled into the living room.

"Nah, I'll take it straight."

After passing Loso his drink, I sat down on the couch and sipped mine. "Have you talked to Arielle today?"

Loso kissed his teeth. "I don't have anything to say to her. There won't be any long drawn out conversations or sex one last time. Fuck that bitch. If I see her again, I might put my hands on her. She really had the nerve to stand in my face and cry and say she didn't mean it. This broad was conversing with several niggas, and she even went out of town with one. The birthday trip her sister supposedly took her on, she was with a nigga. And this was after I spent more than $4,000 on the surprise dinner and her gifts."

"Damn."

"I have $3,500 left to pay on my student loan. I could have paid off my debt. I could have paid off a credit card. I could have spent that money on myself or just let it sit in my savings. But I busted my ass barely getting any sleep for two months working sixty plus hours a week for her birthday."

Loso was pissed and rightfully so. Arielle was foul. If she wanted to be free to date other men, she should have broken up with him before he cashed out for her birthday. That was messed up. Loso downed his drink and went into the kitchen for a refill. I decided I was good with my one drink and when I was done, I placed my cup on the floor. When he came back to the living room, I still hadn't found the right words to say. What did I say? I'm sorry? Loso didn't waste any time drinking the alcohol he'd refilled his cup with.

"This break up is her loss. I saw how good you were to her. I know you're pissed. Anyone would be. And you have every right to be hurt. Just be glad you found out now before you spent any more time with her or any more money."

"Proposing to that bitch had actually crossed my mind a time or two," Loso chuckled angrily. "I'm glad I didn't spend my money on a ring. Knowing her money hungry ass, it would have taken me another year or so to save up for a ring anyway. If I would have proposed to her with a little diamond, it would have been no out the gate."

"I just assumed she liked nice things, and there's nothing wrong with that, but she's money hungry like that?"

Loso snorted. "Two of the niggas she was texting were flexing about what they could do for her. Shopping sprees and trips out of the country. I don't know if they're dope boys, scammers, or what, but I worked hard to make Arielle happy because I loved her. We wouldn't have worked out anyway because I wasn't going to keep busting my ass just to buy her expensive things. Working like crazy to save up for a house, an engagement ring, a wedding. Those are things I can lose sleep for. But working myself to the point of exhaustion for a purse? Yeah, I was stupid as hell," Loso swallowed all of the contents in the cup.

"I'd rather have a man that treats me well and really loves me than a man that just buys me things, but she'll realize that one day."

"I doubt it," Loso laughed. "Men that work nine to fives have to compete with the scammers, dope boys, rappers, and athletes. We take a broad out on two dates, and she starts asking for Chanel bags. A hundred dollars for braids, those days are over. Braids are $300 and up."

"Not all women are like that, Loso. There are some regular women out here that like regular dates, that wear their real hair, and appreciate a hard-working man."

"Like you?" Loso looked over at me. "All you had to do was give me a chance. You wouldn't fuck with me because you said I was a hoe, but I changed for Arielle. Had you given me a chance, we could be happy right now. I never would have started dating her."

My brows lifted. "Are you drunk? You tried to talk to me and every other girl that worked at the club, Loso. No, I didn't take you serious, but it worked out because we're great friends. You ended up with who you were supposed to be with at the time."

"Friends turn into lovers all the time."

"Really, Loso?" I was perplexed. "You really think that little of me to try and use me for a rebound. You're over here sad about Arielle cheating. We're going to what? Confess our love for each other and have sex, and you haven't even been single for twenty-four hours. You know we're better than that."

"But you're fucking that nigga Justice who has a newborn and a baby on the way."

"You're really doing this, Loso?" I drew back. "I don't know if you had anything to drink before you got here, but let's not do this." I was trying to be patient with him, but he was pissing me off. Loso had never disrespected me or our friendship. I wasn't sure why he thought anything would change just because he broke up with Arielle. I never talked down on her even when all she seemed to do was run his pockets. The fact that he was judging Justice for having two kids had lowkey pissed me off.

Before he could respond, the doorbell rang, and I figured it was Justice. It had been my plans to try and comfort Loso, but I really didn't care if he left. He needed to sober up or get out of his feelings. I looked out of the peephole, and sure enough, Justice was standing at my door with a carrier in his hand.

I gave him a small smile. "Hi."

"Hey, Sexy." Justice kissed me on the lips and entered the apartment. I saw his left brow hike when he noticed Loso sitting on the couch.

"This is my best friend, Loso. Loso, this is Justice."

They both nodded and greeted each other. Loso stood up. "I'll get out of here. I'll holla at you later, Lauren."

"Okay. Drive safe." I closed and locked the door and when I turned around, Justice was sitting on the couch looking at me.

"Why did I never know you had a male best friend?"

I really hoped he wasn't about to start because Loso had already given me a slight headache.

"And you in here drinking? I thought you were trying to get pregnant?"

"Okay first of all, Justice, you don't know any of my friends. Friends never came up. I wasn't hiding that I have a male best friend. And second, according to the app, I haven't even ovulated yet. You think your sperm are going to get drunk and forget how to get to the egg?"

"How long have you and him been friends?"

"A few years now. He used to be a bouncer at the club I worked at. At first, he thought that me and Wise were like that because Wise got me the job. Once he realized that me and Wise weren't sleeping together, he tried to talk to me but by then, I'd seen how much of a hoe he was, and I wanted no parts. So, we just became really good friends. He was in a relationship, and he just found out last night that she cheated on him. They broke up."

"And he came over here, so you could give him a shoulder to cry on, and he could try to give you a dick to ride on?"

"What?" I asked with a frown even though that's really what Loso had tried to do.

"That man doesn't just want to be your friend. He settled for that role because you wouldn't give him any play. Don't be naïve. Now, he's playing the heart broken good guy. I know you're not falling for that shit," Justice gave me the side eye.

"First of all, I've had sex with you so much that my vagina feels like it's been ripped in two. If you think I was go——"

"That's not what I said," he cut me off. "I don't put it past him to try. I didn't say you would do it."

Shiloh began to cry. "Perfect timing because I'm not trying to have this conversation," I mumbled.

"I bet you aren't."

"So, me having a male friend is an issue, Justice? You really need to stop being so jealous."

"You need to stop giving me reasons to be jealous."

"What?" I chucked. "I'm not doing this with you."

"You don't have to."

He took Shiloh out of the carrier and grabbed a blanket from his diaper bag. After spreading it out on the couch, he laid Shiloh down and removed a diaper and wipes from the bag. I was hoping that Loso was just in his feelings and drunk when he came at me how he did. I wanted him to sober up and hit me up the next day apologizing for making things weird. If he did that, we could go back to being cool, and I would act like the situation never happened. I hated that Justice was right about Loso. Maybe he knew because all men were the same. This entire time, I'd been thinking that Loso was just a really good friend, and he no longer looked at me in that way.

Justice's jealousy was annoying, but in a very small way, it was kind of cute. Both of us were stubborn, so there was no talking while he changed Shiloh's diaper. When he went to put the diaper in the trash can, I picked Shiloh up.

"Hey lil' homie. Your daddy is an idiot," I whispered. Shiloh smiled, and that made me giggle. "You agree?"

"Agree with what?"

"I told him you were an idiot, and he started smiling."

Justice kissed his teeth. "Fuck you."

"Justice," I warned.

He pushed out a frustrated sigh. "Look, I'm trying. Give me some credit."

"Try harder. Every time you see me around or talking to a guy, you don't have to feel some type of way. Especially not about me and Loso. I don't look at him like that. I never have. He ran through about every female employee in the club. Even the ones in relationships. I'm good on that."

"I hear you," Justice mumbled.

I played with Shiloh for about twenty minutes before he spoke again. "He good with you for about an hour? I need to go handle something."

"Sure. Where you going?" I knew that Justice sold drugs and normally, I would just assume that's where he was going. But something made me ask him where he was headed. He had been acting off since he arrived, and I doubted it was all because of Loso. I knew he was coming over with Shiloh, so if it was anything like that with me and Loso, I wouldn't have had him at my apartment, and I hoped Justice knew that. He was willing to go against his own father for me, so I wanted him to know that I was as loyal to him as he was to me. In more ways than one.

"I just said to handle something."

"It's a secret?" I asked with hiked brows.

He ran his hand over his braids. "Lauren."

"Justice."

"You get on my nerves, bro. I'm going to handle the nigga that shot me." I didn't respond, and he looked at me with shock on his face. "You don't have anything to say?"

"What am I supposed to say? You're going to do what you want to do anyway."

"See this is why I didn't want to say anything," he sighed.

"Justice, I literally didn't say anything."

"It's the way you're looking at me. And the way you aren't saying anything."

I didn't respond. Instead, I stroked the top of Shiloh's head and looked down at him. Of course I was worried. Justice was about to go do something illegal and dangerous. There were too many ways that things could go wrong, but I had quickly learned that Justice did what Justice wanted to do. I just prayed that nothing would happen to him because he had children and family that loved him and needed him. I wasn't so sure I was quite in love with him, but my world would damn sure be turned upside down if something happened to him.

"I'm coming back, Lauren. I'm gon' always come back to you shawty. And my kids. I'm good. Just stop looking at me like you're disappointed in me man."

There was no way I could smile and pretend that I was happy about what he was going to do, but I lifted my head and rolled my eyes. "Ain't nobody disappointed in you," I smiled.

Justice grabbed my chin and pulled my face towards his. After a sloppy tongue kiss, he followed up with three quick pecks to my lips and then he was gone. I looked down at Shiloh. "That nigga better come back because I don't have any way to get in touch with your mother if he doesn't."

Shiloh smiled like he could comprehend my words and I'd told the funniest joke in the world. "Silly just like your daddy," I giggled.

My nerves instantly made my giggles dissipate. The reality of what Justice left to do had my chest tight. It was crazy to me how Justice was so much like Wise, and I hated Wise's guts. But Justice, I pushed out a small sigh. That man had me right in the palm of his hands, and I hated it. I could see myself really ready to crash out and wild out behind his ass. I'm talking beating chicks up, holding his gun, giving him head until I got lock jaw. That type of love and infatuation was always dangerous in my book, but Justice's lil' treacherous ass had me doing things I'd never done before. He had me thinking about doing things I'd never done before. He was like Wise 2.0 because he was better than his father in every way in my opinion. I just had to hope that our plan worked and that Wise would fall back off me because if not, Justice wouldn't think twice about killing him, and I didn't want that. As much as I hated Wise, I liked Justice way more, and I didn't want him having to live with that.

"Cross your fingers and toes for me that your grandfather has a change of heart about killing me," I mumbled softly as Shiloh drifted into a peaceful sleep.

TRUCE

I stood back while Wise walked around the house. I had completed work at his first property and though he'd only seen two rooms in the house so far, I could tell by the expression on his face that he was impressed. He had already paid me for the job, and I delivered in a professional and timely manner. After he went to each room of the house, Wise came back out to the living room and gave me an appreciative nod.

"You for sure did your thing. I'm very pleased with the house. I don't want to overwork you, so don't think you have to rush, but when can you start on the next property?"

I lifted one shoulder into a passive shrug. "This is what I do. I don't have an issue with overworking. Too much time in between jobs means less money. I can start on the next house on Monday."

"I'll meet you there Monday morning, and I'll have the payment for you. I'm sure you heard about what happened with me and your brother. I was almost thinking you'd tell me you didn't want to do any more work for me."

I placed my hands in my pockets and leaned against the wall.

"I have bills to pay. I'm not going to turn down a good paying job because you and Justice exchanged words. I haven't known each one of you long but just to be clear, if those words turn into more than words, I'm riding with my brother." There was no threat in my tone whatsoever, but I knew Wise could tell that I was as serious as a heart attack.

"I'd rather my sons go against me than each other. I would never want to bring harm to Justice, but I don't think he understands that threatening another man's life is serious business. Business that he might have to stand on."

"I don't doubt that he would. But you'd rather beef with your son than let the shit with Lauren go?"

Wise chuckled and flicked the tip of his nose. "My business with Lauren started long before Justice knew her. I didn't have the pleasure of raising him, but my blood still runs through his veins. I can't believe he's that open that fast off that broad."

I shook my head at Wise. "I don't think you understand it's not about him being *open*. She shot you because you were about to rape her. What was she supposed to do? Just lay there and let you take it? If you kill her, you're foul as fuck. Nothing she did could warrant you feeling like you're supposed to have a hold over her life to where she can't get away from you. You're almost acting like she's the one that has you open."

Wise laughed. "Got damn boy. I missed the rebellious teenage years, so I guess this is my payback. I have some business to handle. I'll meet you Monday morning at the house off Slaughter Street. If you need the address again text me. I'll pay you the same amount I paid you for this one. Cool?"

"That's cool."

Wise bobbed his head. "Later."

"I guess I better get all the money out his ass that I can before Justice kills his ass," I mumbled. I couldn't understand why Wise wouldn't just let the situation with Lauren go. He couldn't be that stubborn. I didn't want anybody to die but if it came down to it, Wise wouldn't live long anyway if he harmed Justice. I already knew that Loyal would take him out with a smile on his face, and I'd be right there with him.

I finished up at the house and locked up. I was done for the day. Thanks to Wise's investment, I had a new work truck, and I had some new equipment. Hendrix was also helping me on a regular basis, and Orlando helped out some. I had small landscaping jobs lined up that they could handle for the next three weeks. Every day someone was reaching out to me about work. My business was growing, and I was proud. With all of the properties that I was working on for Wise, the money that I made from that would set me up nicely. My savings was growing, and I was still selling weed for the moment. Financially, I was in a good space.

I had my plug come through while I was working and bring me a pound of weed. I had to go home and bag it up, and I was going to spend a few hours getting money before going home for the night. Once the weed was gone, I was done selling. Shalaine and I were still waiting to tell the kids about us, so I still didn't spend the night if they were home. That was cool though. It gave us time to miss each other. Some nights, we were like teenagers falling asleep on the phone.

Orlando had gotten paid from the post office, and I already knew he wanted an ounce of weed. I sat in the truck and checked my phone to see how many other people were waiting on me to get off. After I called everybody back and gave them a time frame, I started the truck and backed out of the driveway. I hated the fact that Shalaine had a miscarriage, but I knew it wasn't really the time for her to have a baby. I wanted to buy my house, and I wanted her kids to know about us. I could be more supportive during her pregnancy if I didn't have to hide how I felt about her from her kids. Even though we knew the truth about how foul Cliff was, we didn't want the kids thinking that she was with their father one day and with another man a few months later.

I was getting to know her and the kids, and we were trying to take things slow even though we ended up moving kind of fast. I was ten minutes away from home when I saw blue lights in my rearview. I knew I hadn't done anything wrong. I for sure wasn't speeding, and my tags weren't expired. I didn't need this shit today. As I tried to figure out what I'd done to get pulled over, I also tried to remain calm. I didn't want the police to take my weed, and I didn't want to get arrested, but I wouldn't get life in prison for having a pound of weed. There was no need to panic. I was more frustrated than anything.

"Good evening, sir," the police officer nodded his head at me after he approached my window. "You have your license and registration on you?"

"I do, but can you tell me why you pulled me over?"

"You didn't use your turn signal back there before you turned right."

I chuckled. "You're serious? You pulled me over because I didn't use my turn signal."

"Yes sir. Do you have your license and registration?"

I chuckled again as I opened the glove compartment. Either he had a serious quota to meet, or something else was up. If he pulled me for that, he was super petty. "Thank you." He took the items and went back to his car. I really hoped he would just give me a ticket and let me go. I didn't have any warrants. I didn't even have a record. I kissed my teeth three minutes later, when he still wasn't back. I had been working all day, and I was tired. Having to be inconvenienced for not using a turn signal in the turning lane was crazy. I was in the fuckin' turning lane that meant I was going turn.

"Here you go Mr. Trent." The officer finally came back to the car. "Do you mind if I search your car?"

Here came the bullshit. "Search my car for what? You search everybody's car that you pull over for traffic violations?"

"I do if I have probable cause."

"And what probable cause do you have?"

"I smell marijuana."

"Bullshit." The weed that I had was vacuum sealed in plastic, and I didn't smoke in my work truck. He didn't smell weed, but he knew I had it. Someone had been running their mouth. I kissed my teeth as the revelation entered my mind.

"You don't have to give me permission. But if I call for the K-9 an——"

"Whatever yo," I spat cutting him off.

My black ass was going to jail.

Three hours later, I was walking out of the county jail with Shalaine by my side. I had called her to come bail me out. She got a bail bondsman, so I'd only have to pay ten percent of the bond that they gave me. My first court date was in three weeks. I was pissed. I just had to come up off a few thousand dollars on top of losing my weed. I was agitated. I looked over at Shalaine.

"I didn't want to call Wise, because I made it this far in life without him bailing me out and saving the day, but he has connections. If he can find out who may have snitched on me and if it was Cliff, I'm not giving that nigga any more passes," I warned.

Every city had haters, but I'd been moving weed for years problem free. Most of my customers were regulars. I sold weed to dope boys, jack boys, schoolteachers, lawyers, nurses, stay at home moms, etc. if anyone snitched on me, I doubted it was anyone that I sold weed to. I had beat Cliff's ass twice, and I was fucking his wife. He hated my guts, and I was sure he wanted me out the way. It only made sense if he called and snitched on me. Most people snitched anonymously, however. I knew he wouldn't be dumb enough to leave his name.

Shalaine sighed and shook her head. "I really hate Cliff's ass. I want him to go back to jail so bad." She turned to me with tears in her eyes. "I'm sorry I keep getting you caught up in my mess. I know this isn't what you signed up for. What if you get jail time?" The fear in her eyes was real.

"I told you to stop apologizing to me for stuff he did." My jaw muscles flexed. I wasn't for sure that it was him, but who else would it be? I had already beat him twice, and he still wouldn't stop poking the bear.

I could call my plug and get some more weed, or I could leave it alone. Maybe that was my sign to just leave things alone. I gave Wise the same price that I would give anyone else, but he paid me a little more than I asked for. I had several more jobs to do for him, and he'd already invested in my business. Not to mention, he was going to buy the house that I was renovating. I would just hold my L from losing the weed and stop being greedy. I would get where I needed to be the legal way. I would be playing with fire to get caught with more weed while I was out on bond.

I told Shalaine where my truck was parked, and she dropped me off. "You about to go home?" She looked stressed, and I didn't even want her worrying because I knew stress could make her Lupus flare up.

"I'm going to stop by my grandfather's house and check on him. I gotta holla at Orlando too. I'll call you after I take a shower and get settled." I leaned over the arm rest and gave Shalaine a kiss before getting out of the car.

If I would have run into Cliff in that moment, I would have taken his life with my bare hands. I drove home furious. "Great," I gritted my teeth together when I arrived at my grandfather's house and saw Simone's car.

I definitely wasn't in the mood for her cruddy ass. I didn't realize that she was sitting in her car until I got out of the truck, and she got out of her car. My grandfather told me when she had her baby, and I didn't give a damn. I wasn't sure where the little girl was, and I didn't care. I didn't even know her name. It wasn't her fault that Simone was her mother, but if I had to go through Simone, I wouldn't have a relationship with my sister until she was an adult.

"Truce, I need to talk to you and your brothers."

"You don't need to talk to me about anything," I stared straight ahead as I kept walking.

"You don't have to listen to me, but at least let them decide if they want to hear what I have to say. Can you give me their phone numbers please?" I had never heard Simone sound desperate before, but I still wasn't moved.

I stepped up onto the porch, and she rushed up behind me. Simone pulled my shirt, and I whirled around so fast that she jumped back and almost fell down the steps. Her eyes were wide with fear while I simply glared at her. "Please don't touch me."

"I'm already the bad guy in everyone's story, so I may as well tell you the last piece of the puzzle and make you hate me even more. I don't know if Wise is your father. It's either him or his brother, Chicago.

JUSTICE

I had no clue why Truce wanted to talk to me, Loyal, Wise, and Chicago. He had to pretty much beg to get me to meet him at his place knowing that Wise would be there. Lauren had ovulated, and we'd had plenty of sex, but it was too early for us to test and see if she was pregnant. I had already made up my mind that I would tell Wise she was even if she wasn't. If he still attempted to take her life after I told him she was carrying my child, I really wouldn't feel bad about putting him in the dirt.

I was sitting on the couch beside Loyal, and Chicago was beside him. Wise and Truce sat on the love seat, and Truce looked stressed as hell. We'd all been seated for about a minute. "You gon' tell us why we're here?" I questioned. I knew he didn't know me well, but I prayed he wasn't going to try and be the mediator and get me and Wise talking 'cus fuck that nigga.

"Simone came to see me yesterday. She said she wanted to talk to all three of us, but I made it clear that I didn't want to hear anything she had to say. She asked me for your numbers, and I ignored her. I'm not trying to start any beef or drag any skeletons out of the closet, but what she told me can't be ignored. She doesn't know if Wise is our father or Chicago."

The room was so quiet, you could hear a mouse piss on cotton. Wise sat up with his gaze trained on his brother. I looked over at Chicago with a slack jaw, and his eyes were wide with shock. "She said what?"

"She said one night, Wise told her to come over to the house, but he stood her up. He was out with another girl, and Chicago was comforting her, then he came on to her. She was pissed with Wise, so she did it even though she had just slept with Wise a few days before. After that, she never slept with either one of you again, and she found out she was pregnant a few weeks later."

"You knew that all these years, and you never thought to say anything?" Wise asked with his elbows resting on his knees.

"Man," Chicago drawled. "You know long ago that was and how drunk and high I used to be? I barely remember that shit. By the time you told me she was pregnant, she was a few months along, and I for sure didn't think the kids were mine."

"She claims she never expected for us to all meet, so she didn't think she'd ever have to come clean. Apparently, she now has a conscious, and she wanted us to know."

"This is 'bout some ghetto shit," Loyal chuckled.

"I won't even act like I won't be pissed if you're not mine, but you'd still be my nephews, so I can't be too upset. Even if you're my nephews, everything I've ever said still stands." Wise's grimy ass really looked disappointed that we might not be his kids.

"Shit," Chicago sighed. "I don't even know what to say. I don't have kids. Never thought I could make them. I've been with my ole lady for five years, and she's never gotten pregnant."

"If everybody is free tomorrow, we need to all meet and get the DNA tests done," Wise suggested.

I stood up. "Just let me know when." I had no desire to kumbaya with Wise.

"Justice, let me holla at you." He wasn't going to let me get away that easily.

I leaned up against Truce's door and waited for Wise to approach me. "You still hung up on protecting Lauren?"

"I am. She's pregnant with my child, so you have to know what it is if you touch her. And I put that on everything holy."

Wise chuckled and ran his hand over his silky waves. "Pregnant? You rocking with that broad like that?"

"What is your issue with her?" I frowned. "A grown ass man was trying to fuck her when she was sixteen. She needed a place to stay, and he would only help her if she gave up the ass. She didn't want to sleep with him, so she attempted to rob him. You know how many niggas I robbed and how much dirt I did just to have a place to stay and food to eat? We couldn't help the hand that life dealt us. She made that one mistake, and you've had it out for her since then?" I asked incredulously.

Wise flicked the tip of his nose, but I wasn't done.

"Unless she lied, she has done everything you ever asked her to. Moved your dope, cooked your dope, the whole nine. She doesn't owe you shit else. Her debt is paid. If you want smoke with me behind that, that's what it is."

Wise eyed me with an intense gaze. I wasn't sure if he respected my stance or if he was contemplating pulling out his gun, but it didn't matter one way or the other to me. Finally, after a brief stare down, Wise used the back of his hand to tap my chest.

"I'm gonna let you have this one, Justice. All is forgiven. I won't kill Lauren." He nodded his head at me, and I moved out of his way, so he could leave.

I hadn't expected it to be so easy, and I hoped he was telling the truth. If a hair on her head was harmed, I was going to assume that he did it and handle him accordingly. It didn't even bother me that I might possibly have three kids together close in age. If telling Wise that Lauren was pregnant got him to change his mind about killing her, then I would never be upset if she was pregnant.

Chicago nodded his head at me before leaving the house. "Yo mama's a hoe," I shouted at Truce, and Loyal, and they started laughing.

"She yo mama too nigga," Truce spoke up.

"I don't know her like that." I shook my head. "This is wild. Ghetto as hell and wild. I have some moves to make though, so I'll see y'all later."

"You gon' dip without telling us what you and Wise talked about?" Truce inquired.

"I told him that Lauren was pregnant, so she's off limits. He didn't like the shit, but he said he won't bother her. Now, if she's not really pregnant, then I have to get her pregnant."

"How many kids are you trying to have?" Loyal asked with a frown.

"As many as I want," I matched his frown with one of my own. "What does it matter?"

"What does it matter? You want three kids all under the age of two? So, if you get locked up th——"

"Here we go," I threw my hands up in the air and kissed my teeth. "I get real tired of this same song and dance my G."

"I don't care! You started hustling because I suggested it. I got you in this shit, and I feel responsible for getting you out."

"You can't get me out!" I yelled. "I have to want to get myself out. Stop trying to save me nigga. I'm not a hoe. I don't need you to ride in on a white horse and save my life. I'm kind of tired of repeating myself."

"You selfish as hell," Loyal looked me up and down. "Don't

worry though. If you get killed or locked up you have two brothers and a father that will pick up your slack."

"Nigga, fuck you," I spat.

"Fuck you back. Pussy." Loyal pushed past me and left the house.

Truce was standing there with raised brows. "I'm out man." I left the apartment and walked out to my car with a scowl on my face. Loyal was the one that suggested we start hustling, but we didn't have any other options. For the past however many years, I had been hustling by choice. He didn't have to feel responsible for the fact that I sold drugs. I was a grown man with my own mind. I had taken Shiloh back to Enchanted that morning, so I made money for a few hours then went home to take a shower. I decided to tell Lauren in person that Wise thought she was pregnant, and he agreed to fall back. I rang her bell and waited for her to answer. When she opened the door, I could tell that she'd been asleep.

"You sleep already? It's not even ten yet."

"I'm tired. I fell asleep watching TV."

"That ass is pregnant," I grinned and palmed her booty.

"We'll see."

I kissed her on the forehead. "Have you eaten?"

"Yeah, I had some shrimp lo Mein and egg rolls." She yawned as we walked to her bedroom where she'd been watching TV. I took my shoes off as she climbed back into bed.

"I saw Wise earlier." I noticed her body stiffen. "I told him you're pregnant. He doesn't like it, but he said that he'll fall back."

"You believe him?"

"Yeah."

"And what if I'm not pregnant?"

"Then we get you pregnant, or we say you had a miscarriage. Wise needs to go ahead and get this notion of killing you out of his head. He can't chase you forever. Baby or not, he should just leave it alone."

"You don't know Wise like I do. He's stubborn, and he hates losing. He wants to always feel like he came out on top."

"He'll be aight. You really might need to get pregnant though because if he finds out that he's not my father, he just might go back on his word." I got in bed with Lauren.

She looked over at me with knitted brows. "Why would he find out he's not your father? He was pretty sure before, right? I mean, the four of y'all look just alike."

"My mom was something like a hoe. She had sex with my uncle Chicago too. She's not sure who our father is. She confessed it to Truce."

Lauren's eyes widened, and her jaw dropped. "Are you serious? Your uncle might be your father?"

"According to Simone."

"Damn. Was Wise pissed?"

"He took it well. I don't think he was upset. I get the feeling that maybe him and Chicago passed women around before. Shit, Winter and Fatima's mother are half-sisters. He knows about keeping it in the family himself. He also said he won't be mad about all the things he's done for us because even if we're his nephews, we're still his blood."

"Maybe Wise has changed because the Wise I knew might not have been mad at Chicago, but he definitely would have done Simone dirty. He's been so geeked thinking he might have triplets, and that might not even be the case."

"We may as well go on Maury. That way if neither one of them are the father, she can do that dramatic run off with the camera man following her."

Lauren laughed. "Do you take anything seriously?"

I pulled her into my arms. "You."

We fell asleep watching TV. Next thing I knew, the sun was shining through the blinds, and Lauren's phone was vibrating like crazy. I could feel it, and I realized that it must be in the bed with us. I pulled the covers back and grabbed her phone. My intention was to put it on the nightstand, but I noticed that she had mad text messages from Loso. That was supposed to be her best friend, but I wanted to know why he was blowing her line up at eight in the morning. She had given me the passcode to her phone before when I was setting up her Ring Doorbell, and the phone would lock sometimes. Damn right I was going to look at her messages.

I frowned as I read a long message from Loso apologizing for coming at her wrong the last time he saw her. He admitted that he was in his feelings about his breakup, but he was serious when he said they would be happy together. I chuckled and kissed my teeth. Lauren had really tried to make it seem like I was tripping when I said Loso was playing a part. Maybe men and women could be friends in some cases but for the most part, niggas weren't shit. They played that friend role to get in good and make a woman let her guard down. I was pissed. Lauren rolled over, and her eyes slowly opened. She saw me with her phone in my hand, but she didn't panic or try to take it from me.

"What's wrong? What time is it?"

"Too early for this lame ass Loso nigga to be texting you love letters and shit."

"Huh?" her face crumpled.

I dropped her phone on the bed and got up to get dressed. Lauren picked her phone up, and her eyes darted back and forth across the words on the screen. "You and him are just friends, right?" I asked as I zipped my jeans. "I need to stop being jealous, right?"

Lauren swallowed hard and sat up. "Justice, I swear, me and Loso have been friends for a while, and he's never come on to me.

We are really just platonic friends. We've never kissed or come close to being intimate. I chalked what he said that day up to him being drunk and heartbroken. I didn't think he was serious, and I didn't want you to be uncomfortable with our friendship."

"All I just heard you say was that you looked me in my face, and you lied. And I would think that this nigga is sober now, and he's still trying you. I guess I just look like a sucka, huh? It's play in Justice's face day, right? That nigga saw me walk in here with my son. He knows you rock with me, and he's still sending you heart felt text messages? Bet," I flicked the tip of my nose and nodded my head. "If I see that nigga again, I should make him swallow my gun."

"Justice, that's not what I was doing." Lauren's voice was all small and weak.

"Nah, talk shit wit' yo' chest like you normally do. Don't try to act innocent now. You weren't acting innocent when you looked me in the face and lied. You tried to play me like I was being jealous for no reason, and that I was tripping."

"Justice, I didn't expect it to go past that night. Loso loves Arielle. He's not in love with me. I knew that was just some rebound shit. He was talking out of pain."

"He straight up disrespected me then, and he disrespected me today when he sent that message. I'm not tripping though. I'm cool. You can have your best friend. Where was he when you needed saving from Wise?"

"Don't do that shit," Lauren jumped up. "Don't do something for me and then throw it back in my face. I told you I didn't want you beefing with your father. You could have stayed out of it. Didn't I tell you that?!"

I snatched my keys off her dresser. "I'm out."

I was pissed. Lauren knew that if she admitted to me that Loso was trying to get at her that day, my feelings would have been validated. She wanted to remain friends with him so bad that she lied to me and made it seem like he was heartbroken over his girl and not thinking about her. She lied, and the shit was sneaky. Carmen was pissed that I wouldn't make her my girl, and she wasn't the only one. Lauren was the first person that I ever considered wifing. I overlooked the fact that she had sex with my father, and I was willing to lay my own father down behind her, and she lied to me? Fuck her and her lame ass homeboy. Maybe they could be together now. I wouldn't cry about it.

I went home, ate some cereal, took a shower, and got dressed for the day. I had to meet my brothers, Wise, and Chicago at Lab Corp. I wondered if Wise was really my father. Even though I was mad at Lauren, I would still always stand ten toes down behind the fact that Wise was foul for how he carried her. That aside, I didn't have any issues with him. The entire situation was weird and ghetto as hell. Simone was only fifteen busting it open for brothers. Now, if neither one of them was our father, she would have some explaining to do for real.

"You still acting like a hoe?" I asked Loyal as I sat down beside him. He was the first one there.

He looked over at me with a frown on his face. "Watch your mouth."

"Yeah you're still mad because you're acting all serious. Keep being mad about nothing Loyal, and you can hit me up when you're ready to talk." Between his attitude and my argument with Lauren, I wasn't in the mood for anything extra.

Truce walked in and gave me and Loyal dap. I looked at my watch. Just when I thought Wise and Chicago were late, I saw a Bentley and a Jaguar pulling into parking spaces. After Wise and Chicago checked in, we were called to the back, and the situation was explained to the lab tech.

"We will be able to tell which one of you is the father, but we may have to do some extra testing, so I'm glad you told me this. By you being brothers, you will share many of the same DNA markers, but not one hundred percent. We will have to take extra care to identify each of those markers against the DNA of the triplets, and we will get accurate results."

"How long will it take to get the results?" Chicago asked.

"Normally, it takes about four to five days. Since we'll be doing extra testing, I'd be looking for results after seven to eight days. We will send the results to your email, or you can have them mailed to your home."

"Email is fine."

We all took turns getting our blood drawn and our cheeks swabbed. I guess Wise wanted to be extra sure. I wasn't in the mood for socializing, so as soon as I was done, I got in my car and headed to make money. That shit wouldn't piss me off.

SHALAINE

Alison waved her hand in front of my face. "Helloooo," she sang. "Earth to Shalaine. I've been talking a mile a minute, and you aren't listening to a word I've said."

"I'm sorry, friend. Truce told me that Wise's connect at the police station got ahold of the recorded phone call from Crime Stoppers. He let Wise listen to it, and Wise recorded it. Truce played it for me, and it was indeed Cliff. He must have found out somehow that Truce sold weed, and he really snitched on him."

"Wow. What a low-down dirty dog," Alison scoffed. "When is his next court date? He needs to go back to jail expeditiously."

"Tell me about it," I rolled my eyes. "He's determined to ruin my life. Truce was going to get his own lawyer, but Wise insisted that he use his. Truce isn't worried about jail time for what he had on him. But Wise said his lawyer could make the charge completely go away so it won't be on Truce's record at all. He won't have to be on probation or anything, but we'll see."

"Damn it must be nice to be that powerful. People with money have it made. All they have to do is throw a few dollars around, and there aren't too many problems that can't get solved. Since it's looking like your man won't get jail time, why are you sitting over there looking all sad?"

"Because what if he had more weed on him than that? He always tells me not to apologize for what Cliff did, but I can't help but feel like it's my fault. I shouldn't have started dating until my divorce was final or until Cliff got sentenced."

Alison waved my comment off. "Stop acting like your life is in shambles because you're still married to that snake. God probably doesn't even much like that nigga. You're not being punished for anything. Especially with the way he puts his hands on you. He doesn't deserve you. And you aren't wrong for not letting a good man pass you by. Don't let Cliff win like that. He wants to ruin your life, but he can't succeed."

"You're right. Truce said he was about to stop selling weed anyway. This just took him out of the game a little sooner. If Wise's lawyer can truly get everything thrown out, then maybe it's not the worst thing that happened after all. I don't care how much time they give Cliff, but I would be devastated if Truce gets jail time." Just the thought made me sad, but I was trying to be positive. It was just weed, and it wasn't a huge amount.

"If Big Daddy Wise said he's not getting jail time, then he's not getting jail time."

"Girl," I drawled wondering if I should spill the tea. I picked up my glass of wine and took a few sips.

"Don't girl me and stop talking. What's tea?"

"I'm not sure if I should be telling my man's business, but I don't really think he cares. Anyway, why did Simone tell him that she also slept with Wise's brother, Chicago, and she doesn't know for sure who their father is."

Alison's mouth fell open. "You're lying!"

"Nope. They took the DNA tests this morning."

"Baby, they should have gone on Jerry Springer or Maury. Not brothers. Didn't she have them when she was like fifteen?"

"Yeap. I wasn't getting it in like that at the age of fifteen, but I knew plenty of girls that were. I went to school with some hoes that were giving it up in seventh grade."

Alison frowned. "I was scared to go near penis in middle school and some of high school too. I'm scared to have children. If my fifteen-year-old daughter came home pregnant with triplets and didn't know for sure who the father was I'd die."

"That might be why she gave them up even though her parents didn't want her to. That's just crazy to me how Wise was so excited to meet them, and he was really warming up to the idea of being their father, then he gets hit with a curve ball."

"This is most definitely a hood soap opera. I hope they get the results that they want. I'm assuming they want Wise to be their father."

"Truce hasn't really said one way or another. He said that Wise said if he isn't their father he won't be too upset because they'll still be family. I think that's a good way to look at it." I finished off my wine.

"Yeah, that is. He's more mature than me, 'cus I'd put my foot in Simone's behind. It's because of her that a lot of secrets and BS was hidden. You know how cool it has to be to be a triplet, and she denied her sons the chance of all growing up together."

"I think that really bothers, Truce," I admitted. "I mean, they have each other now, and they're pretty tight already, but I know that he would have loved to grow up with them. Can't cry over spilled milk though."

"When are you and Truce going to quit hiding and tell the kids about your relationship? They like him, don't they?"

I smiled. "They love Truce. I just still feel like it's too soon, but we'll see."

Alison and I finished up our meal and paid the check. I got home ten minutes before the kids' bus pulled up. When I got them off the bus, Janay was talking a mile a minute, but Tevin was unusually quiet. As soon as we got in the house, she had to use the bathroom, so I directed my attention towards Tevin.

"Hey. Why are you looking so down? Did something happen in school?"

"Why isn't my dad coming to see us? Is he still mad at you? Can you just tell him that you're sorry?"

Every single time my children were hurt by Cliff's selfish inconsiderate ways, it ripped my heart from my chest. And I was always left to take the slack. I had to make excuses for him while trying to spare my children's feelings, and it wasn't fair.

"Baby, I haven't done anything to your father. I don't have anything to say I'm sorry for. Sometimes, people just make wrong decisions. I'm not keeping your father from coming to see you. I'm sorry that he's not. Maybe daddy just has a lot on his mind. I hope he'll start coming around soon for you and Janay."

"Daddy said he wasn't coming around because you had a boyfriend. You can't have a boyfriend if you and daddy are still married. Who is your boyfriend?"

"I don't have a boyfriend, Tevin," I lied. "Your father as I said is going through some things. He's upset that I don't want to be married to him anymore. That's a grownup issue, and it doesn't have anything to do with you. Cliff can still be a father to you and Janay whether I'm married to him or not."

"But why don't you want to be married to him anymore?"

Tevin having questions was fair. I couldn't be upset that my son wanted answers, but I was getting kind of frustrated. I would of course seem like the bad guy because I didn't want to be with Cliff anymore, and no matter how much I hated him, I didn't want to run him in the dirt to his son. "Sometimes people just grow apart, Tevin. It doesn't have to be anybody's fault." I really wanted to give him an answer that would make him end the conversation.

Tevin had parted his lips to speak when my phone rang. I was beyond annoyed when I saw that it was Cliff's sister calling, but I was going to answer. Hopefully, she would tell me that Cliff wanted to see his kids. There was no reason for him to ignore them because he wanted to hurt me. He was doing me a favor by not showing his face, but he was hurting his kids, and I hated him even more for that.

"Hello?" I was met with silence, and I almost said hello again, but I heard Wilena speak. She was crying.

"Shalaine, Cliff was leaving out of the corner store, and he got hit by a car. He's dead, Shalaine. He didn't make it." As soon as she spoke the last word, Wilena erupted into tears, and it felt as if my heart stopped beating.

My eyes darted over to my son who was looking at me curiously. I had to look my son in the face and tell him that his father was dead. Life just kept getting more messed up by the minute.

LAUREN

Despite the circumstances between me and Justice, I had fun in Cancun with my father. His girlfriend and two of my cousins on his side went. It was a nice distraction. The only bad thing was that I couldn't drink. I was hoping that no one noticed, and they didn't. I didn't know any of them that well, so they didn't know if I was a drinker or not. I hadn't taken a pregnancy test, but I didn't need to. I had only thrown up once, but every morning I woke up feeling nauseous. I had to start sleeping with crackers on my nightstand. I would wake up and eat four or five of them then wait about ten minutes before I got up. Despite being sick on the stomach and certain smells making me nauseous, I had a great time in Mexico. When I got back home, I stopped by Sade's mother's house for her sixtieth birthday party. I was jet lagged out of this world, but I decided to show my face for at least an hour and a half. The moment I walked in and saw my mother's face, I regretted coming.

I said hello to everyone but her, and she wasn't going to ignore it. "You don't see me sitting here? I heard you were just out of town with Niles. You letting him make you act brand new?" The way she was sitting in front of other people playing the victim made my stomach knot up.

"Brand new?" I frowned. "I don't deal with you, and you don't deal with me. There's nothing new about that."

My mother looked at me with a slack jaw. It was very rare that I ever challenged her or talked back to her, but I was an adult. I was no longer the timid child that was afraid of her. I didn't have to respect anyone that never respected me. I didn't care if she was my mother or not.

"You just gon' stand there and disrespect me?"

"Not today. Why are you doing all of that in here?" Sade's mom spoke up.

I shook my head. "It's cool. I'm about to leave. I truly hope you have a great birthday, and I will bring you your gift next week. Bye everybody." I tossed everyone a tense smile and left the house. I wasn't even mad that I didn't have to stay long. All I wanted was my bed anyway. I was so used to my mother being a bitch, that her antics didn't even bother me. On the way home, I thought about Justice per usual. He had been consuming my thoughts way too much. I had been fighting like hell to just let it go, but I felt bad, so when I got home, I called him. My heart raced the entire time that the line trilled. When he didn't answer, I felt stupid.

He got me pregnant, so Wise wouldn't kill me, but he was also supposed to be there and help me. I had no desire to be a single mother, but Justice hadn't even called me to confirm whether or not I was pregnant. Loso had called me once, and I didn't answer. It wasn't his fault that I lied to Justice, but I wasn't in the mood to talk to him. Trying to give him the benefit of the doubt and save our friendship had Justice looking at me sideways. There were times that I wished I wasn't pregnant by him. But I was. Me not taking a test and confirming it didn't make it any less real.

At home, I took a shower and got in my bed. I was always tired. I wondered if I would feel extreme fatigue the entire nine months. I wondered if it was a boy or a girl and if Justice would ever come around. Being pregnant had saved my life but sometimes, I wondered if my life was worth saving. I spent so many years miserable that I had to wonder if being put out of that misery would really be that bad. My mom felt some kind of way because Niles came around, and he was interested in getting to know me. I would never in life treat my child anything close to the way she treated me.

It was cool. At least that's what I tried to tell myself. I would be everything to my child that my mother wasn't to me. I would love my child unconditionally whether me and Justice were together or not. I was also about to see if I could start back working at the lounge. If not, I'd apply at some other places but seeing as how Justice and I weren't even speaking, I wasn't going to rely on him to pay my bills. Maybe Wise would keep his word and leave me alone and if so, that would mean that I could work freely.

I was wrong for lying to Justice. I tried to apologize, and I had tried to communicate with him. For a man that got me pregnant on purpose, he wasn't even interested in knowing if I was pregnant or not. But it was what it was. I liked Justice a lot. I made a mistake. If he couldn't forgive me for that mistake, then we just weren't meant to be, and I would have to learn to be okay with that.

"You good?" Loyal asked me the next night.

My boss didn't waste any time responding to me, and he told me that I could come back to work ASAP. Loyal just so happened to be working too. When I got to work, I was fine but after three hours of standing on my feet, I was so hot and flushed that my forehead broke out into a sweat. I felt nauseous, and I just wanted to sit down, but I was trying to push through.

"Yeah, I'm good. It's just hot in here."

"You pregnant?" he asked with a hiked brow.

He was Justice's brother, so I was sure that Justice put him up on game. However, Justice didn't deserve to know shit about me that he didn't ask me for himself. I didn't want Loyal breaking the news to him that I was pregnant.

"I'm not sure. I haven't taken a test."

"Justice is a stubborn fuck. Me and him are barely talking at the moment. It can be frustrating dealing with him, but if you are pregnant, I can assure you that he'll be a great father."

"I know," I gave Loyal a small smile. "I've seen him firsthand with Shiloh. I messed up, and he's mad with me. I won't say he doesn't have a right to be upset, but I'm not begging for forgiveness. It can be whatever," I shrugged passively.

"You look like you're about to pass out. Get off your feet for a few minutes. I got the bar."

"Thank you."

At least somebody had some sense. Yes, I was wrong for lying about Loso trying to holla at me, but if Justice couldn't get past it, I wasn't going to beg. I went to the back and sat down. I just needed ten minutes to regroup. It would have been dope if I could stay at home while I was pregnant and be taken care of, but I didn't mind working. I hoped my nausea and fatigue didn't last past the first trimester. Sitting down felt so good that it was a challenge getting up after ten minutes and going back to the bar, but I did.

The lounge was busy as usual, and the next two hours flew by. Next thing I knew it was time for me to get off, and I wasn't mad.

I also left with $412 in tips, and that wasn't bad either. I wanted Justice to help take care of his child, but he didn't have to do anything for me. I was two minutes away from home when he called my phone. I sucked my teeth while ignoring the call. I was willing to bet money that Loyal and Justice had talked. I hadn't confirmed my pregnancy with Loyal, but I was sure that he was speculating, and he had obviously shared his concerns with Justice.

We were both stubborn, and maybe we were both petty. But I didn't want Justice only reaching out to me because he talked to Loyal. I had called him on my own, and he chose not to answer or return my call. For the moment, it was fuck Justice. It hurt, but it was life. At home, I ate some watermelon then took a shower and climbed into my bed. It didn't take long for sleep to come, and that's how I knew for sure that I was pregnant. I could sleep for hours, wake up and still be tired. I knew I needed to make a doctor's appointment and get some iron pills and prenatal vitamins ASAP. I could get them over the counter, but I needed to go to the doctor anyway.

I was halfway asleep when my cell phone rang. I only opened one eye, and when I saw that Justice was calling again, I put my phone on vibrate and closed my eye. Fuck Justice.

The next day, it was noon before I dragged myself out of bed. I hated not having any energy, and I prayed that it would soon pass. I had to work that night, but I didn't have any plans to do anything else that day. I was going to call the doctor and make an appointment, but that didn't cause me to have to leave the house. I never knew that loss of appetite could be a pregnancy symptom, but I didn't have an appetite. I would try and force myself to eat fruit, salad, or soup, but if I didn't make myself eat, I could go a full day without a morsel of food and be okay.

When my doorbell rang, I kissed my teeth because my gut told me that it was Justice. I wasn't really ready to see him, but I knew we needed to have a conversation. When I opened the door and saw him holding a black, brown, and white Bully puppy, I had to stop myself from gasping. I was trying so hard to remain tough and to appear unfazed, but the puppy was the cutest thing I'd ever seen.

"My homeboy is selling Bully puppies, so I bought one. I remember you saying that you love animals and that you always wanted a dog."

I loved animals indeed, but Justice wasn't just going to pop up like nothing happened between us. I wanted the dog so bad, but I had to stand on business. "I called you, and you ignored me. So what it is that I'm supposed to do? Let you in and act like you walked on water because you got me a puppy?"

"Lauren, you can't see where you were wrong with that Loso shit?"

"And I apologized! But that wasn't good enough for you. I'm not interested in playing games."

"Me either. I can't tell you how to act when I hurt you, and you can't tell me how to act when you hurt me. You had me feeling like a real sucka, Lauren. It took me some time to get over that. But it doesn't change how I feel about you."

I blinked back tears. "And how do you feel about me? Because you got me pregnant on purpose to save my life. And even though being pregnant benefits me, I was never supposed to do this alone. But have you been here?" my voice cracked.

"Baby," Justice's tone softened. "I was pissed. I'm sorry. But you haven't even been pregnant for that long. I'm a work in progress. I was trying to get over feeling played. I still think you were wrong for lying to me, but unless you want to be with Loso, it's not worth us breaking up."

The ice around my heart melted, and I hated that it was accomplished so easily. "I told you more than once that I don't want to be with Loso."

"Okay and I told you, I've never really been in a relationship before. All of this is new to me. I was so mad I told myself that I could forget your ass and keep it moving like I never knew you. I don't know what kind of hold you have on me, but I can't shake you. You've been consuming my every thought since the last time I saw you."

I shifted my weight from one leg to the other. We had both messed up. The easiest thing to do would be to put our feelings aside and just forgive one another, but that stubborn trait that I possessed was strong. I didn't respond, and Justice stepped closer to me.

"I know you might be tired of the I'm sorry's, but can we give this one more chance, please. You can be friends with Loso. I just don't want him disrespecting me."

The ice around my heart was officially gone. "I will never allow Loso to disrespect you again. I'm sorry for not being truthful."

Justice walked inside my apartment and passed me the puppy. "It's a girl?" I asked.

"Yeah."

"Thank you." I pecked him on the lips.

Justice leaned against the wall and eyed me. "We gon' get this shit right, or are we gonna have to deal with this making up shit all the time?"

"I can't be the only one to answer that. If we're both willing to try, then we'll get it right eventually. But no relationship is perfect. Disagreements and arguments shouldn't be excessive, but there will be times that I hate you. Making up is one of the best parts though," I gave him a coy smile.

"It's damn sure going to be fun for me, because I still haven't fully forgotten. My favorite way to punish you is with this dick." There was a devilish gleam in Justice's eyes. His threat caused a subtle ache in between my thighs. "Let me go and get her stuff out of the car."

I walked over to the couch with the puppy in my arms. "What am I going to name you?"

Justice came back minutes later with a dog kennel, bed, some toys, and training pads. "She's almost housebroken, but she will have accidents sometimes. I've had her for two days. If you didn't let me in today, I was just going to keep her for myself."

"You ever thought about the fact that everything we pretty much have in common is some kind of traumatic experience? You did have a mother, but neither one of us have a relationship with our biological mothers. We both just met our fathers, and as kids, we were on our own taking care of ourselves on some real live orphan shit."

"Even though we handle what we've been through in different ways, I know at the end of the day, besides my brother, you fully understand what I've been through. If no one else gets it, I know you will. You don't get offended when a nigga just wants to sit in silence and not talk. You get my smart mouth and my lil' stubborn ways."

"So, we trauma bonded."

"I don't know the technical definition of trauma bond, but so what if we did? Our trauma made us who we are, and we rock with each other. I don't care about the terms and definitions. We got a cool lil' vibe. I fucks with you."

"I have to fuck with you too if I willingly agreed to be baby mama number three," I giggled.

Justice kissed his teeth. "You willingly agreed to be my baby mama, so I wouldn't have to kill Wise. If that wasn't the case, you probably would have told me to go to hell."

"And would have," I laughed louder.

Justice stood up. "Put that puppy in her kennel, so you can come show me how much you missed me."

JUSTICE

Truce was leaning forward with his elbows resting on his knees looking stressed. "Something in my gut is telling me that Wise had something to do with that shit," he stated in a low tone.

We were at Lab Corp, and we were the first two to arrive. We had all gotten phone calls asking us to come in which was strange because we were supposed to get the results by email. I was lowkey stressing myself because what did they have to tell us in person, that they couldn't put in an email? Truce was stressing for a different reason though.

"Even if he did, that nigga was a thorn in your side, right? He abused Shalaine, he was doing his kids dirty, and he snitched on you."

"Yeah but," Truce shook his head. "The kids are messed up. Tevin is taking it extremely hard. I hated the nigga, but I didn't want the kids hurt like this. The police ruled it an accident. Witnesses said that a car was coming down the road speeding, and Cliff was walking across the parking lot to his car. The car whipped up in the parking lot and he didn't even have time to get out of the way. Being that he was in a public place, it seems like an accident, right? But nah, if I know Wise, he had somebody following the nigga or something. That man is ruthless."

"Speak of the devil." Wise pulled into the parking lot in his Audi. Before he could get out of the car, Loyal pulled up. We spoke every day, but I could still tell that Loyal felt some kind of way, and he'd just have to get over it.

I didn't plan on being in the game forever, but he couldn't rush me out of it. I appreciated the fact that he loved me, and he wanted the best for me, but Loyal didn't pay my bills. Maybe me being in the game and not starting a legit business was lazy of me. Maybe it didn't make sense to them, but there was no business that I could think of to start that would land $24,000 in my hands from one single transaction unless I sold cars or some shit. I was brainstorming on business ventures, but it would have to make sense to me. I wasn't rushing it just because Loyal wanted me to stop selling drugs.

As Wise and Loyal walked in, Chicago pulled into the parking lot. Chicago was cool. I'd only been around him a few times, but he was chill and welcomed me and my brothers with open arms. When we all thought he was our uncle, it was cool, but knowing he might be our father, had me wondering if the dynamic would change. Wise and I had bumped heads once, but aside from that, he wasn't a bad father. If Chicago had to step into the role of father, it might not be a smooth transition. Only time would tell.

Wise went straight to the check-in desk because he wanted to know why we had to come back. There wasn't going to be any waiting on his part, and there wasn't. We were called straight to the back, and the lab tech gave us all tense smiles.

"I asked you all to come in because this is a very unique situation that would be better explained in person versus email.

So," she picked up an envelope and pulled out a paper. "In the case of Loyal and Truce, Mr. Jacobs, or um, Chicago, you are the father."

Wise's jaw slacked. He was shocked. That nigga really wanted to be our father. "And in the case of Justice, Wise, you are the father."

"The fuck?" he frowned as I drew back.

"You said what?"

"In this case, Truce and Loyal are identical twins. Meaning, their mother released one egg, and it split to make two embryos. One egg and one sperm. When she ovulated, she released two eggs. One spilt and the other was penetrated by different sperm. The sperm could have been inside of her body when the eggs were released, and it just so happened that sperm from each man made it to an egg. This is very rare, but it does happen, and it has happened before. Twins and in this case, triplets can have different fathers. Truce and Loyal are identical twins, and Justice is fraternal."

I was stumped. Truce and Loyal came from the same egg, and my ass was an egg all by myself. Those niggas were in the same sac and all. It might sound strange, but that shit made me lowkey jealous. I would have thought Loyal and I were identical, but it didn't really matter.

"This is the craziest shit I've ever heard," Wise scowled, and Chicago looked like he'd swallowed a rock. "You're telling me that Justice is my son, and Loyal and Truce are Chicago's sons?"

"Yes sir. Here's the results of the tests." She handed Wise some papers, but I didn't have to look at them.

She was the expert. If she said that was what it was, then that was what it was. Triplets with different fathers. Only hoe ass Simone could pull something off like that. We thanked the lab tech and stepped outside. Wise was pacing while Chicago stood with his hands in his pockets.

"I swear I never thought that Simone's kids might be mine. That night once we were done, she didn't really cross my mind again. I really didn't expect this."

Loyal shrugged passively. "I mean, we've gone this long without knowing who our father was. It's not like you have to worry about paying child support and shit. Your life shouldn't change too much."

"Nah, the point is, I saw how geeked my brother was thinking he found his kids, and I'm sorry I took that from him. The situation is crazy as hell, but I'm still gon' step up and build a relationship with all of you. Not just my sons. Who the father is and who the uncle is really shouldn't matter because at the end of the day, we're all family."

Wise chuckled and peered at me. "That's why you're so much like me. Got damn. Mom and pop aren't going to believe this shit." He shook his head. "Since I have you all here, I'll go ahead and ask you. Alana has started planning our wedding, and I'd like for you all to be my groomsmen. This backstabbing muhfucka is going to be my best man," Wise jerked his head in Chicago's direction.

"Don't act like you've never hit any of my hoes."

"I didn't get them pregnant. I don't think."

My phone rang, and I saw that Carmen was calling. I hadn't heard from her in a few weeks, so I didn't hesitate to answer. "Yeah just let me know what's up. I gotta run." I gave everyone a head nod and walked towards my car. As long as Wise left Lauren alone, I didn't have an issue with him, and I didn't mind being in his wedding. "Hello?"

"I'm in labor at Diamond Cove Memorial. I'm already six

centimeters dilated, so it shouldn't be too long before she gets here. Maybe a few hours if that."

"Aight. I'm on the way."

Two hours later, my daughter was born. I had Shiloh, and I had Sky. It didn't matter to me if Lauren had a boy or a girl. At the moment, I had one of each, and I was content. Thinking about what we'd gone through with Wise and Chicago, it was on the tip of my tongue to ask Carmen for a paternity test. I didn't want to offend her, but I needed to be sure. I had no way of knowing what she did with her pussy when she wasn't with me. I was thinking of how to ask her without setting her off when she spoke up.

"I'm thinking about moving to Charlotte. My cousin and her boyfriend broke up, and he moved out. She can't really afford the rent by herself, and she doesn't want to move. My lease will be up next month, and I think Charlotte would be a good move for me."

"If that's what you want to do."

Carmen's eyes widened, and it was almost funny. I didn't doubt that she wanted to go to Charlotte, but I knew Carmen. She wanted me to throw a fit and demand that she stay, and I wasn't going to do that. Charlotte was only a few hours away. I could drive and visit my daughter. Carmen wasn't my girl. She never had been. Even if she had my child, I wasn't going to dictate where she went or what she did. As long as my daughter was good, I was good.

"Wow, you really don't give a damn about me," she chuckled.

"Carmen don't start with the bullshit man. You're a grown woman. As long as my daughter is taken care of, you can go where you want, do what you want, live where you want. I'm not your nigga or your daddy. You deserve to be happy. If being in Charlotte will make you happy, that's what it is. Stop trying to turn everything into an argument."

She gave a curt nod. "It just hurts when the person you love doesn't love you back, but thank you for being mature. I appreciate it."

"It's not a problem."

I stayed at the hospital for three hours with Carmen and Sky. When all of her family started piling in the room deep as hell that was my cue to leave. In the car, I called Enchanted to check on Shiloh and see if he needed anything. I really had two kids out here with one more on the way. Me and my brothers were triplets but had different fathers. My life felt like a hood movie. If I wasn't living it, I wouldn't believe it.

TRUCE

I pulled up into my grandfather's yard wondering what he was about to tell me. He had called and told me that he needed me to come by, and it was urgent. With the way things had been going lately, I was almost afraid to pull up and see what he wanted. I still couldn't get over the fact that Chicago was my father and not Wise. I also couldn't get over the fact that Justice had a different father than me and Loyal. Leave it to Simone. When I walked in my grandfather's house, I saw him sitting on the couch feeding a baby.

"Who is that?" I asked with furrowed brows wondering who would leave my grandfather alone with a newborn. His health wasn't terrible, but it wasn't the best either.

"Your little sister, Serenity."

"Don't tell me Simone left you with another kid to raise."

My grandfather shook his head and when he looked up at me, he had tears in his eyes. "A social worker brought her to me. Monte beat Simone. He beat her almost to death. A neighbor called 9-1-1, and when they got there, Simone wasn't conscious, he was gone, and Serenity was screaming her head off. She's in ICU fighting for her life. I can't go up there because I have the baby. Your uncle is there with her."

I swallowed down a lump. "You can go see about her. I'll watch the baby."

"You will?" my grandfather looked shocked.

I chuckled. "Yes, I will. I know a thing or two about babies now thanks to being around Shiloh." I didn't give a damn about Simone, but she was still my grandfather's daughter. I knew he was worried about her and wanted to be there with her. No matter how I felt about Simone, Serenity was innocent, and she was my blood.

I walked over to my grandfather and took her from his arms. "Thank you, Truce."

"You're welcome. I'll take her home with me too. I know you can't be getting up at night with a baby."

His jaw slacked, and he touched my forehead with his hand. "You okay, son? Are you running a fever?"

"Stop being dramatic old man," I laughed. "I don't have too many nice things to say to Simone, but you raised me to be a good guy. This is my sister. I got her."

My grandfather simply nodded and gripped my shoulder. Simone wasn't my favorite person but for Serenity and my grandfather's sake, I hoped she didn't die. My grandfather lost two of his grandsons for twenty-four years, and he lost his wife. When my grandmother died, my grandfather didn't eat for almost four days. Even when he didn't cry in front of me, every time I saw him his eyes were bloodshot. For a whole month after she passed, he had huge bags underneath his eyes from not getting any sleep. I was worried about him even at my young age, but he pulled through and got past it. When my grandfather left, I looked down into Serenity's face.

"I'm getting siblings and fathers out the ass. I wonder what other surprises life has for me?"

I looked at my watch. Shalaine had been off for an hour at that point, so I stood up with Serenity in my arms and walked over to Shalaine's house.

"Hey. Is that Shiloh?" she peered at the baby.

"Nope. It's Serenity."

"Don't tell me Justice has another baby. Wait, don't tell me you have a baby."

I laughed. "You tweaking shawty. This is my little sister. It seems that my mom's boyfriend beat her bad enough for her to end up in ICU. A social worker brought the baby to my grandfather."

Shalaine gasped and covered her mouth with her hand. "Oh my God. I'm so sorry to hear that. How is your grandfather doing?"

"Probably scared out of his mind. I'm going to keep her for him tonight. How are the kids?"

Shalaine pushed out a breath. "Tevin is just," she shook her head. "He's taking it very hard. Looking at my baby cry makes me cry. Janay is sad too, but Tevin is taking it real hard. I almost don't want him to go to the funeral, but I don't want him to grow up and resent me for it. I don't know what to do, but Cliff's mother is on her way over to get them. I don't want to have to slap her ass if she sees you here. I'll come by later. She wants to keep the kids for a few days."

"Okay."

I stood up and gave her a quick kiss before leaving. I didn't even want to mention to her that I felt like Wise had something to do with Cliff's death. I didn't have proof, and I really didn't even want to know. I could have simply asked Wise, but I didn't want knowing on my conscience. Cliff was giving her hell, but she loved her kids more than she hated him, and I knew she wouldn't want him dead. I didn't tell Wise to do anything to the nigga, but that didn't mean she might not look at me different if she found out Wise had something to do with it.

I called Loyal and told him what was up with Simone and that I had Serenity. "Boy when the shit hit the fan, it really hit the fan. Stuff keeps happening left and right. When I leave the tattoo shop, I'll come by and kick it with you and help you. You and Justice keep more babies on your hips than a baby mama."

"My grandma used to always say laughing is catching."

"I'm not worried about catching shit because I wrap my dick up."

"This isn't my baby fool. It's our sister. Unless Simone's ass carried one of us and someone else carried the other two."

Loyal laughed loudly. "You not shit for that. Our mom is fighting for her life, and you're making jokes."

I shrugged. "If I don't feel anything for her, there's a reason. I do hope she pulls through though. Honest to God I do. I don't wish death on anybody. Not even bitch ass Cliff. He wasn't shit, but his kids loved him, and they're hurting bad right now."

"You think it was really an accident?"

"I doubt it, but I don't know for sure, and I don't want to know."

"I feel you. Give me like two hours, and I'll stop by your crib."

"Okay."

Serenity started whining, and I glanced over my shoulder into the backseat. "Hold tight lil' mama. We're almost at the crib. Just five more minutes."

Loyal and Justice didn't grow up around a lot of family, but I did. My mother was the only person in my family that I didn't really rock with but over the past few months, my family had grown tremendously, and I loved it. Life with Shalaine was good,

225

and I was happy that I got along with my brothers. They were receptive of me from day one as was Wise even though he turned out not to be my father. Something told me that I wouldn't have too many more dull moments because between all my new family, shit was turned up.

LAUREN

I sat Indian style on the couch with Serenity on my chest. I was rubbing my hand in a circular motion over her back. Justice was beside me with his head on my shoulder, and Truce was sprawled out on the couch with his head in Shalaine's lap. Loyal was laid back in the recliner. We were all at Justice's house watching movies. Truce kept Serentiy for one night, and then Justice and I volunteered to keep her for two nights. Simone had regained consciousness. But she had a nasty concussion and some slight swelling on her brain, so she'd be in the hospital for a minute.

I loved the way that Justice, Loyal, and Truce were bonding. I had a doctor's appointment the next day. Wise had assured Justice more than once that he wasn't going to bother me, but Justice still didn't want me working in a bar while I was pregnant. I decided to enroll in school to take some vet tech courses. I wasn't completely comfortable depending on a man, but he gave me $15,000 as cushion. I was going to make sure that I had my own income coming in sooner rather than later. After my doctor's appointment I was going to meet my dad for lunch and introduce him to Justice. Our relationship was still very new, but I had a good feeling that we were in it for the long haul.

My mom and I might never get over our past and have a relationship, and I was okay with that. Everything wasn't always meant to be resolved. She was the adult, and I'd never done her wrong. If she didn't care to change and try to make things right with me, then that's how they would stay. Since she ended up in the hospital, Justice had decided that he wanted to talk to Simone and hear her side of the story. He didn't want her to die one day and take everything she knew to the grave. He was going to give her some time to heal and get better, and then him and Loyal were going to visit her. Truce didn't want to hear the story, but I told Justice that he would come around in due time.

Wise was planning his wedding, and Justice felt some type of way that I wouldn't be able to be his date, but I didn't mind. I had no desire to be in the same room as Wise. Justice sat up. "Loyal, you're the only one not clapping any cheeks tonight. You should be on overnight duty with lil' sis," he joked.

"Fuck outta here," Loyal waved his comment off. "Who said I wasn't clapping any cheeks? Just because y'all are boo'ed up and loved out doesn't mean, I don't clap cheeks. I just haven't gotten caught up."

"Being caught up isn't so bad," Truce chimed in.

"I'm good. I promise."

"Somebody will come along and manage to wrap you around their finger," I let him know. "She's out there. You just gotta find her."

"I won't hold my breath."

I knew Justice wasn't looking for love when we met. I wasn't either, but life had a funny way of doing its' own thing. Loyal was a good guy, and I knew the right woman was out there for him.

He would just have to find her first. Hopefully, it would be sooner rather than later.

The end…. For now.

Loyal's story is up next. I didn't end this book on a cliffhanger but any unresolved issues such as Simone's version of what happened will be in Loyal's book.

NATISHA'S CATALOG

Carried Away

Treacherous Twins: Justice

The Millionaire Boys Club: Koda

The Millionaire Boys Club: Beau

Royal: At His Command

Meurtre Mafia

Athlete Status

Pleasure and Payne

How the Baptiste Boys Took Over North Carolina

The Baptiste Boys Ultimate Boxset Experience

A Gangsta and His Shawty: Heirs to the Baptiste Throne

The Return of the Baptiste Boys

The Villain: Have you ever made love to a thug?

Billionaire Status

Kasanova and Dessi: A Winter Crest Valentine's

Tales of a Gangsta

Aviana and West: A Gangsta's Wife

Uri's Interlude: The Cezar Cartel Vol. 1

Ballad of a Gangsta's Girl: The Cezar Cartel Vol. 2.

Isa's Verse: The Cezar Cartel Vol. 3

The Outro: The Cezar Cartel Vol. 4

Tales of a Menace

Savage

Noelle and Star: A Shotta's Wife

Let it Burn

From the Trenches with Love

Tarai & Jahan: Stronger than Pride

Kisses from a Savage

Cuffed by a Southern King

Islam and Azzure: Lovin' the Plug

Azaan & Jayda: Fallin' for a Haitian Hitta

Addicted to a Heartless Hitta

Cuffed by a Southern King

Gang Over Love

Diary of a Mafia Princess 1-3

Married to a Haitian Mob Boss

Southern Thugs Do it Better

Shawty Got a Thang for Them Country Boys

The Allure of a Thug

For the Love of You

Money

Power

Respect

Rihana

From the Cartel with Love

Torn Between a Haitian Boss and a Jamaican Savage

She's got the Plug in his Feelings

Trap Wives of Charlotte 1-2

Tales of a Heaux

Caught up with a Mafia Boss 1-2

To Love a King

Tammi, Meek, and Cam: A Scandalous Love Affair 1-2

The Plug's Girl 1-2

A Bisset Cartel Love Story 1-2

Her Man Has My Heart

What You Know About Love

Cherished by a Thug

Enchanted: A Hood Love

A Savage Changed my Life

Bully and Envy: Love wasn't meant for a thug

Southern Bosses of North Carolina (Akai and Azalea)

Southern Bosses of Miami (Asa and Drew)

In Love with a Haitian Boss 1-2

Addicted to Mayhem: Loving the Plug

The Bugatti Boys

A Winter Crest Christmas: Indiana and Ransom

Summer Vibes in Paradise Bay: Azul and Zada

Made in the USA
Columbia, SC
15 November 2024

46614178R00130